A Bitter Pill

BY M J ELLIOTT

Copyright

Disclaimer

ISBN 978-1-5272-9870-5

Printed in the U.K.

Dedication

We are all controlled in some way or another, sometimes by people, sometimes by circumstance, and sometimes by our own conditions of worth and our own desires too often, to be someone we are not. It's often hard to be just who you are, but it's just as difficult at times to admit who you are not.

This book is dedicated to all those people who have realised who they are and who have found the strength to be their true self and also, in equal measure, to all those who are still controlled by whoever and whatever controls them.

To be our true self, no matter what the circumstances, is often the most difficult thing to achieve in life.

Remember, no one gets out alive. Be yourself, whoever that may be.

chapter one

2016 – Carlisle, Cumbria

I'd never laughed quite as much in my life. Simon made me laugh every time we met. He was funny, charming, and thoughtful. Simon was the man of my dreams. The man I had always dreamt of meeting, marrying, having children with, going to the woods for a Sunday stroll, going on holiday and growing old together. He was perfect. He was my ideal man. Simon let me be who I wanted to be. To have an opinion and listen to my ideas. He encouraged me to excel. He supported me in whatever I wanted to do. Whatever I wanted to be. He was everything I wanted from a relationship; except he wasn't real. He was only a dream, a fantasy, a wish upon a star, a longing in my conscious mind. I wanted Simon. I wanted that man. I wanted that life. To be loved, to be thought of, to be considered, and to be who I wanted to be. The trouble was I didn't have Simon. I never would. I had Jonathan. He was nothing like the man in my fantasy. He never considered me, never thought of me, never encouraged me, or cared about any of the things I wanted in a relationship.

Jonathan has controlled me ever since we first met at university. That was eleven years ago, and since that fateful day, I'd devoted my life to this man. I hadn't noticed what was happening at first. Initially, he'd been charming and attentive. I adored him. I fell head over heels for him, but then it started. He'd put me down, tell me I wasn't good enough, tell me that I needed to support him, to support his career and that I should be at home. He then started to tell me who I should be friends with, who I could see, what I should wear. I should have seen it coming, but I didn't. I allowed it to happen. It was subtle, you see. It happened over time. Once I began to realise, it was too late. I soon had no job, no money of my own, no friends, and no life outside of Jonathan. Everything we did, he controlled. I knew what I'd become, but the problem was I still loved him. Still do. I sometimes wonder why I stay with him. I know why I do. For love and he is my life.

I'm afraid to leave. I have no life of my own, no connection with who I was in my youth. I am still called Anna, I still have blonde hair, I am still a comfortable size 12, but that's where any resemblance to Anna Fox from 2005 stops. Oh, and I forgot about my guitar. I still play the guitar. Jonathan allows me to do that when we have guests around. I had to stop playing the violin, though, soon after we moved in together. He disapproved of that. He thought it would distract me from my duties as a good housewife if I played two instruments. Being a good housewife is important to Jonathan. He thinks a man should have a devoted housewife on his arm—none of the modern independent woman crap for him.

Anyway, I digress. 2005, that's when we met. It seems a lifetime ago, probably because it was another life. I was a different person back then. I was bubbly, energetic, outgoing with lots of friends. I was popular. People wanted to be me. Nothing fazed me. I was quite happy to take on the world. I liked to party. I wanted to be noticed, to be the centre of attention. I was a good girl, though, nothing too raunchy, no drugs or anything. I was merely having a good time.

I'd always been an extrovert growing up. Right from a young age, I'd enjoyed the limelight. I always got the best part in the school play. I was always on the front row, in the school choir. I had the most friends out of anyone I knew. Everyone wanted to be my friend. I enjoyed being with people. My mother always thought I'd end up on the stage, be an actress or something. She'd always dreamed that I'd become famous, making it in the movie business or even in the music industry.

I was naturally good at music as a child. I could play any instrument. I found it easy, although my two loves were the guitar and the violin. I loved the guitar because it could be played soft and romantic or hard and loud. I loved the violin because it sounded so classical and romantic. I would often think of the band on the Titanic playing right up to the end. Even when death was all around them, they played. Classical and romantic.

I never pursued those routes, though. I went to university to study corporate hospitality. Being a people person, I wanted to excel within the hospitality world. I wanted to put on big events, be at the centre of it all and one day have my own company organising the best events across the globe. I had big dreams, big ambitions. I was going to take on the world. Then I met Jonathan, not Simon, but Jonathan, and my life was never the same again.

There are two things about my life before Jonathan, about which he knows nothing. The first one is that I had a fling with another woman. I'd only ever been with men before that happened, but one night, not long before Jonathan swept me off my feet, I had a fling with a person of the same sex. It was only once, but throughout that time in my life, I experienced feelings I had never been able to repeat. Feelings I can't describe, nor could I replicate with Jonathan. Sometimes if I see an attractive woman, I get those feelings again. Momentarily, but I get them. I never act on them, though. It was only a fling, nothing more. The second thing is that to supplement my way through university, I took a job as a pole dancer. I loved it. People noticed me, they loved me, and of course, it paid well. I could never tell Jonathan either of these things. He would not approve. He would make me feel dirty.

I still have dreams, two main dreams. The first dream is of Simon or the man I have in my head that I call Simon and the second dream is of freedom. Oh, how I dream of freedom. The thing is, though, I now know how I'm going to get it. I can see the light at the end of the tunnel. I can be free. I will be free. It is only the beginning.

Carlisle train station
March 2016

'How can I help you?'

I snap out of my trance and look up at the lady behind the counter. She's heavily made-up but pretty all the same.

'Er, two tickets please, one way to Manchester. I'm not sure when we'll be coming back, if ever.'

The lady behind the counter smiles. A smile that says she knows what was behind my remark. Maybe she does, maybe she doesn't, but I'm on my way. I grab the tickets from her and make my way to Platform One to join Sally, who's waiting for me.

'Thank you,' I say as I bend down and pick up my suitcase full of money. Carlisle railway station is busy, which is surprising as it's a Monday afternoon. I walk out of the ticket office and head towards where I was to meet Sally. She should be waiting for me.

chapter two

Nearly three months earlier
January 2016 – Brampton, near Carlisle, Cumbria

It's Jonathan's first day back at work today after the Christmas break. I have to be up early today. Half an hour earlier than usual. I was concerned that I might have forgotten the routine. It has been over two weeks since I had to get his clothes ready for work. I need to have them all laid out on the bed, ready for when he comes out of the shower. If they aren't all neatly laid out for him, I will be in trouble. I don't want trouble. I like things to be perfect for him. That way, I'm safe. He's happy, I'm happy. Just the way I like it.

Jonathan's a solicitor, you see. A solicitor who specialises in helping vulnerable women, battered wives, and women who fear for their safety. Women who are running from their controlling partners. You get the irony, I'm sure. I've inwardly laughed so many times when I think of what he does for a living. I've nearly laughed out loud when we've been at a dinner party or some corporate function or other. In fact, I did once, only once. I suffered bruised ribs and a cigarette burn on my breasts for that one, so never again. I learned my lesson. I'm a quick learner. Cigarette burns do that to you. They make you submit, be submissive, apologise for your misdemeanour.

Jonathan is excellent at inflicting pain and punishment discreetly so that the signs are not visible. No one would ever know. People love Jonathan. They love the work he does. They tell me I am so lucky to have such a wonderful man who cares so much about women. Someone who is there for women when at their most vulnerable. Someone who they can turn to when they are at their most desperate place. I smile and agree. I join in the plaudits. I numb the pain when needed. I hide the bruises. I hide the emotional scars. I do it for me, but most importantly, I do it for Jonathan. I do it to show the world what a great guy he is. I hold his hand. I link his arm. I put my head on his shoulder. I do all the things a good wife would do when out in public.

I ask myself how I feel when I do this. I feel used. I also feel safe, though, when I do as he pleases. Being safe is all that matters. I play the game, and I play it well. I've played it for so long now that it is no longer a game. It's normality. I must be happy, I tell myself. Why would I be here otherwise? I am not chained up. I am not under lock and key, yet I am scared to go against anything that Jonathan says. I want to please him. I love him. As strange as that may sound, I still love him. If I displease him, it must be my fault. It must be because Jonathan says it is. I go to the shop when he tells me. I see friends when he says I can. I drink a glass of wine when he tells me it's ok. I weigh myself every morning because he tells me I have to. I am not allowed to vary my weight by more than five pounds either way. I have to remain between 9st 4lbs and 9st 9lbs. He stands over me when I weigh myself. I must be happy. I'm still here.

I finish giving his shoes a last quick polish and place

them at the foot of our bed. I hear the shower switch off. I often listen to the shower running and know that could be my chance to go. Jonathan wouldn't know. I don't go, of course. I wait like the good housewife I am. I stand up and survey the clothes and the shoes. They look perfect. His toiletries are lined up on his bedside table, deodorant, aftershave, and so on, all neatly ready for him. I've done it. Now I have to stand here while he gets ready in case he needs me.

'Nice shower, darling?' I ask as he comes out of the ensuite. He smiles at me.

'It was great, sweetheart. Perfect. The right temperature.' He surveys the clothes and shoes. 'Did you iron my shirt again, like I asked?' He says without turning to look at me. I tense up. I did iron it again, though. He knows I did.

'Yes, darling, of course. Is it ok?'

'Mmm,' he says in a somewhat disapproving way. 'It's still a little creased on the left arm. Here come and see.' I walk over, still tense. I cannot relax until he has walked out of the door and gone to work. I stand next to him and look at the sleeve. It seems fine to me. Maybe he is a little wound up this morning with it being the first day back at work. I hope it's nothing else. He puts his hand behind my neck and strokes my hair. I am still tense. 'Can you see, Anna. There look, a slight crease down that arm. Can you see it?'

If I say I cannot see it, I will be treating him with disrespect, but if I say I can see it, he will want to know why I have laid it out for him to wear. He will assume that I must have wanted him to look a fool at work, to look shabby and unprofessional. He will think I want people to believe that he cannot ensure that his good wife is able to iron his clothes properly. I plump for being disrespectful.

'No darling, I cannot see it. It looks fine to me. I took extra care this morning, seeing as it's your first day back. It looks perfect.'

'So, I'm seeing things, am I? He asks. 'Making things up now, am I? You know how I would never make things up, Anna don't you?' He squeezes my neck a little harder. I brace myself.

'Yes, of course, darling, but I think it looks fine.'

He bends down and picks the shirt up. 'Open your mouth,' he tells me. I open my mouth. He stuffs the shirt into my mouth as much as he can. I struggle to breathe. I'm choking and gagging. He pushes my face back hard, and I fall into the glass door of the built-in wardrobe. I cough and splutter as I pull the shirt out of my mouth.

'Why do you do these things to me, Anna? We've had a lovely Christmas break, and the first day back at work, you do this to me. You expect me to go into the office looking like a tramp. What would people think, eh? They'd think I have a wife not capable of ironing a shirt. They'd be talking about you. They'd think you were useless. I'm only doing this for you. I must look immaculate. That way, people will see what a good housewife you are.' He picks me up and cups my face in his hands. 'I couldn't bear it if people were talking like that about you. Now iron me another shirt. Properly this time. Make me proud, eh?'

I nod. 'I'm sorry,' I say. 'I should have checked it again, before I laid it out for you.'

'Your standards are slipping, Anna. Too much Christmas cheer I suspect. No harm done though, eh?'

His tone changes. 'You have five minutes.'

I select another crisp white shirt out of his wardrobe

and run downstairs to iron it for the third time.

Thirty-five minutes later, after I've successfully ironed the shirt and cooked Jonathan two perfect poached eggs on two slices of brown toast, we go into the downstairs bathroom for me to weigh myself. I am always nervous. Even though I know I have not eaten anything that would make me put on any extra weight; I am still nervous. Jonathan sits on the side of the jacuzzi bath and watches as I slip off my dressing gown and step onto the scales in my nightdress. I stand with my arms by my sides and look straight ahead. I have no idea what I weigh. Jonathan walks over and looks at the scales. He kisses my neck and puts his hands on my shoulders. I now know that I am ok. I look down. 9st 5lb. I inwardly sigh with relief.

'Good girl,' Jonathan says as he runs his fingers down my spine. He then walks away and, regular as clockwork, starts to put his shoes on in the hallway. I put on my dressing gown and grab his briefcase for him.

'Have a lovely day, darling.' I say as I hand him the case.

'And you too,' he says with a certain affection. He does mean it. He wants me to have a good day. He pecks me on the cheek, and like every other day, when he goes out of the door, he shouts. 'What is it for tea tonight?'

'Fillet steak.' I shout back as he gets to the car. He stops and looks up.

'Wow, fillet steak, that sounds great.' He shuts the door, opens his driver's window and stares at me. 'I must be the luckiest man in the world, really I must.' He blows me a kiss and drives away.

I love him when he's like that. I see a glimpse of the Jonathan I first fell in love with, and I momentarily think how lucky I am to have him. I know deep down, that had I been 9st 7lb this morning, I would not be having that good day he wished upon me only a minute or two earlier, but I was 9st 5lb, which meant he went off to work happy. He was wearing a crisp white well-ironed shirt, newly polished shoes that I'd cleaned while he was eating his two perfect poached eggs on toast. He had every reason to be happy and as I stood in that doorway and waved him off, so did I. Today was going to be a good day.

I often try to piece together why Jonathan behaves the way he does. In the early days, I did ask him. I always regretted it. A hard backhander with the customary, 'there is nothing wrong with how I behave,' would always come my way. 'It's everyone else whose standards have dropped,' he would say. Followed by 'standards are what make us,' and that today's world was nothing like the world in which his parents had grown up. I had concluded over time that his parents, his mother especially, were to blame for his abusive and cruel behaviour. His mother was a matriarch, someone who ruled the roost. His father was weak and submissive, someone who would cower whenever his mother would ridicule him. She did physically abuse him, too. I have come to understand from bits Jonathan told me in our early time together, that Jonathan idolised Agnus, his mother. She was the one who would say to him that weak people are there to be ridiculed. Every woman on their street was afraid of Agnus. She would repeatedly tell Jonathan that only those with power over others were worthy. His mother, I've concluded, is the reason Jonathan is like he is. He had a real need to please Agnus. She was his world. I think deep down, he wanted to be like her.

I had my daily shower, got myself dressed, and then sat down to eat my breakfast alone. I wasn't allowed to eat with Jonathan as he needed to eat breakfast in peace, to prepare for his busy and stressful day, but I preferred it this way anyway. I had one poached egg and one slice of toast. The same as Jonathan but a smaller portion. He always insisted that I ate the same as he did but on a smaller scale. Jonathan always maintained a healthy diet and insisted that I ate likewise. That way, he could regulate his weight and mine. I've not strayed out of the buffer zone on my weight for nearly a year now. That was when I went up to the colossal weight of 9st 9Ib. Jonathan went crazy. He accused me of being obese, called me a fat slag, and ensured that I only had vegetable and fruit smoothies for five days. I wasn't allowed anything solid during that whole time. He even took five days off work to ensure I didn't go out and embarrass him. He said he didn't want a fat whale like me walking the streets of Brampton as people would know that he had an obese wife. I was confined to the house until the sixth day when I was 9st 3Ib. I then got a split lip for going under 9st 4Ib. Since then, I've made sure I've kept within his weight limits.

Being starved and physically beaten does that to you. It was like the cigarette burns I mentioned earlier. I'm a quick learner. It's my fault, I know. I was eating between meals during the day. I knew I was doing it, but I couldn't stop. Jonathan has not always put these weight restrictions on me. It was something he decided on a little over three years ago. I was a comfortable 9st 6Ib back then. I was ok right from the off. I went over once, and he beat me. He didn't starve me; he just hit me. Then I went 18 months without going over or under until that incident over a year ago. He says it's for my own good, to keep me healthy and balanced. He says I'm too silly and weak to manage my weight and that I'd balloon until I was disgustingly fat. If we ever see an obese person when we are out, he points them out and says, *'that would be you if it wasn't for me.'* His weight never alters more than two pounds, so he must be right.

I finish my breakfast, wash up, and then go into the lounge to see the list of chores that he's left me today. He leaves me with daily tasks to make sure that I have a productive day. That's my job, you see, to keep the home looking nice. We are having two of his work colleagues round on Saturday night with their wives. This week is full-on. Everything must be perfect. Today I have to trim the laurel hedge, jet wash the path from the driveway to the door and wipe all the skirting boards in the house. I also have to go to the butchers in Brampton for two fillet steaks. Jonathan's must be twice as big as mine, or mine must be half the size of his, whichever way you want to look at it. The lady in the butchers knows me well enough to know what I want. As soon as she sees me, she will weigh them out for me. I need to buy everything organic, spinach, an onion, cucumber, tomatoes, and feta cheese. Jonathan likes a salad with his steak and, for some reason, feta cheese. I also need to get some freshly made bread. I will have some salad and one slice of bread for my lunch. The rest is for our tea. Oh, and I also have my best friend Sally coming round for a cup of tea this afternoon. I do not have any friends of my own, only those whom Jonathan chooses for me.

All of my friends, including Sally, are wives of Jonathan's circle of friends. Wives of his business partners, clients, golfing, and gym buddies. Wives only Jonathan approves. Sally, though, is different. Sally's life is similar to mine. Her husband, Terry, is a bastard too. He controls everything she does, telling her what she can and can't do. The only thing good about Terry and Jonathan is that they love it when Sally and I get together. We get together every day. She comes to me, or I go to her. Sally was like me in the past, bubbly, outgoing, energetic. She grew up in Newcastle but came to Carlisle when she was around ten years old. She went to college and learnt to be a secretary. Sally had wanted a career, but, like me, she met a charming young man who adored her and made her feel special. That was Terry. Terry is like Jonathan. Sally's life from the moment she met Terry was like mine.

We are two parts of the same jigsaw. When we are together on our own, we are those girls from the past. We are ourselves. We have our self-worth; for the couple of short hours we are together. It's usually the middle of the afternoon as by then we have done our daily tasks and can be Anna and Sally, two giggly young women, before we are back to Anna and Sally, the dull, controlled housewives. Luckily, we are allowed to visit each other without fear of repercussion. That's most likely because Sally lives next door. Without our daily chats over tea, I'd go fucking mental. So, now you know, my life is one big area of control, except for Sally. She's my saviour.

chapter three

I've trimmed the hedge and jet-washed the path to the front door. It's a relatively short path, so it doesn't take long. I'm now walking through Brampton to the butchers to get the steak. It's more of a farm shop, to be honest. I can get all my salad things there too. I walk in. The lady I usually see clocks me and nods. She knows how important it is to get the steaks the correct weight. She only knows that because of the near breakdowns I've had previously when one looked too big or something. Jonathan has been known to weigh them before cooking. Not every time, but at random, he'll do something like that, and if they are not correct and in proportion, I suffer for it. The last time they were wrong, he made me stand for an hour with a bag of sugar in each hand above my head. Every time my arm dropped; he would stand on my bare feet. I learned quickly. Standing with two bags of sugar above your head for an hour does that to you.

'There you go, love, same as before and how you like them,' she says as she hands the two carefully wrapped parcels to me.

'Thank you,' I say and smile. She smiles back. I often wonder if she knows the life I lead or if she just thinks I'm a dizzy cow. Either way, I'm not bothered as long as they are right. I trust her. She's been serving me for long enough now. I get my other bits and pieces and walk out into Brampton's little square near Moot Hall. Brampton is a quaint, affluent market town about eight miles east of Carlisle. The population is around four thousand, with most people commuting to Carlisle for work. I like it here. People are friendly, and it's big enough that you rarely bump into people you'd rather avoid.

'Anna, Anna.' I hear someone shout. I know the voice. *Great, bloody great,* I think to myself as I turn around and see Mrs Simpson walking towards me. Mrs Simpson is someone who everyone knows in Brampton and is forever asking me to pop round for a cup of tea. I can't, though, you see. Jonathan can't stand her. She is a school governor in Carlisle. Jonathan sits on the same school of governors too. He dislikes Mrs Simpson. Calls her a *'Ten-Bob Millionaire.'* She and her husband are quite wealthy. He has dementia and is in a home. She is quite a lady, and one thing she is not is a pushover. She can't be intimidated, you see. She stands her ground. Mrs Simpson has presence, and she can cut you down without raising her voice. Jonathan says she's living on the coattails of her husband. He was a successful businessman in his day. I like Mrs Simpson, but I am tired of making excuses about why I cannot go round for tea. That's why I dread bumping into her.

'I thought it was you, Anna,' she says, panting as she reaches me. 'Ooh, let me sit down. I'm jiggered.' She plops herself on the bench and puts her handbag on her knee. She pats the bench next to her with her right hand. 'Come on, girl, sit down, have a minute, you're always rushing off home.'

'I haven't really...'

'Ooh, poppycock. I'm sure you've got a few minutes

to sit with me. I haven't seen you for ages. Now come on, sit down, and tell me what you've been doing. I would ask you for tea, but I know you'll come up with some excuse.'

I have no option but to sit down. I look at my watch. It's nearly 1:00pm. Sally is due at 3:00pm. I still need to clean the skirting boards. I cannot risk leaving them as Jonathan will no doubt have marked one of them somewhere so that he can check that they've been done. He does that. I can't be too long. I smile and sit down. Mrs Simpson smiles at me and pats my knee.

'So, my dear, what have you been doing lately?'

'Oh, nothing much, you know, this and that. How about you?'

'Who me?' she points at herself with her finger. 'I come up here most days and watch the world go by. It gets me out, you see. I only come here to visit my husband, but I see everything that goes on. I don't miss much.' She turns to me and smiles. A smile that says so much more. A smile that's not just a smile. A smile that implies there's a deeper meaning to the statement. I smile back. Mine is only a smile, though. Nothing else. We talk, we smile. We talk some more. I look at my watch 'shit' I say out loud.

'What's the matter, dear?' Mrs Simpson asks.

'It's nearly two o'clock. I've got to go. I've been here too long. I have things to do. Things I must do.' I jump up. I bend down to pick up my carrier bag. Mrs Simpson grabs my arm. I look round. 'No need to worry, my dear. The steaks are exactly the right weight. You'll be ok.' She smiles again. The same smile as nearly an hour ago. That smile that I don't do. The smile that says much more than just a smile. I stare at her for a few seconds. She lets go of my arm. She is still smiling.

'I have to go,' I say. I start to run. I keep running. I must get home and do the skirting boards before Sally pops round. Jonathan has been known to come home early. If Sally is there, he'll be fine. If the skirting boards have not been done, he won't be. I run faster. I'm panicking in my head. *That stupid Mrs Simpson,* I say to myself. *Jonathan is right. She's an old busybody. Jonathan's always right,* I tell myself.

I make it home at quarter past two. Sally will be round at 3:00pm as agreed. We are both so used to being controlled that if we agree on 3:00pm then 3:00pm it is. Even if I'm ready at two o'clock and it's my turn to go round there I won't go until three o'clock. It's how we are. We have been programmed so well that we even control ourselves, but once three o'clock comes, we can be free, but only for a short while.

I rush to put the shopping away and grab the duster and wet cloth. Now, this normally takes me 53 minutes. I know because I do it so often. It can't be a quick wipe; that wouldn't do. It has to be a thorough clean. I must crack on. Today though, thanks to busy body Simpson, I now only have 39 minutes. I must work quickly. I do not want my chores to go over into my time with Sally. It's all that keeps me sane.

Three minutes to three I finish. I am out of breath. I put the kettle on. I only have time to wash my face and gather myself. Three o' clock, knock on the door, and the door opens.

'It's only me, get that kettle on,' Sally shouts as she closes the door. I am on my way downstairs. I hear the kettle switch off—bang on time. I don't know how we do it, but whatever happens during the day we are always ready for each other.

'What a day I've had,' I say as I pour the hot water. 'That bloody busy body Mrs Simpson collared me today. An hour I was chatting to her. I couldn't believe it. I've just this very second finished my chores. You done all yours?'

'Yeah, all done. I've been sat waiting for the best part of 45 minutes. Been on top of it today I have.'

'I wish I'd known I'd have dragged you round to help me with the skirting boards. I was shitting myself in case I didn't get them done in time. You know how I hate to miss any of our time together. It's all that keeps me sane, Sally.'

'I know, bloody crackers, isn't it? You know I was sat next door thinking how silly it was that I was sat there waiting for three o'clock to come round when all I had to do was pop round early. What do I think will happen, other than Terry may come home early as he does on occasion and find out I've changed my schedule? Every morning he asks me the same question. *What time are you having tea with Anna?* But I'm scared that if I did come round early and he found out, he'd go mental. I'd have bruises on top of bruises. I daren't. I bloody hate myself for it, as you do, I'm sure. What we like, eh?'

I put two mugs of tea on the table and sit down. I know how ridiculous what Sally has said sounds, but she's right. I'm just as scared to think for myself as she is. It's amazing how two people from completely different areas of the country can end up as neighbours living the same life. We've been neighbours for nearly two years now after we moved here from Stanwix in Carlisle. Neither of us knew about each other's life of control at first, but the more we got to know each other, we could see the similarities. The fear of our husbands, the inability to think for ourselves, the way we never did anything impulsive, and the way our two homes were pristine with nothing EVER out of place. Then one day, I didn't hide a bruise well enough, and Sally saw it. She burst into tears and showed me one of her bruises. There we were comparing bruises like any other couple of friends would compare lipstick or moisturiser. That was the best thing either of us did, though, confide in each other. We were friends before that, but we would now die for each other since the revelations of that day. I trust Sally more than I trust anyone else in the world, even myself, and I know she feels the same way about me too.

'You know I dream of being impulsive. I dream of being free. Only for one day, I want to feel how I used to feel when I was younger. You know, before I met Jonathan. I want to feel alive again, even if it's for a short time. I wish I had the strength, don't you?' Sally put her hand on my forearm and leaned closer to me.

'I have the same dreams too Anna, but they are only dreams. You know that Jonathan would never let you be free. He'd kill you sooner. My Terry's the same. I also wish I had the strength. I'd do almost anything to find that strength but giving Terry a reason to kill me or beat me half to death isn't one of them. We have to make the best of it.'

Sally was more resigned to her life than I was, I think. I would often sense in our chats that my dreams were more real. I know that one day I'll be free. How I'll do that, I have no clue, but it's a knowing. I don't think Sally feels it that strongly. I half-smile and nod, as if I know she's right. 'Maybe we haven't found the reason to find that strength yet. If I find it, you'll be with me, won't you?'

'Of course, I will. You're my best mate, my only mate if I'm honest, but still the best. I'd do anything for you, Anna, you know that even it means giving Terry that reason. I'd do that for you but not myself. Funny that isn't it?'

It was strange how people would muster up the courage for someone else but often couldn't muster up the same courage for themselves. It was a bit like my sister Carol. She would stick up for me at school against anyone but could never protect herself in the same way. Similar situation I suppose.

'Anyway, you all set for Saturday night? I'm dreading it, Sal. I couldn't sleep last night thinking about it. It's a big deal for him, these two new clients are a big coup. He needs to impress them. I'm glad that he's got someone in to do the cooking. I couldn't have coped with that. Bloody hell I'd be a nervous wreck, and I'm nervous enough as it is. I'm pleased you're coming. At least you can be there for me.'

'I'll be there for you of course I will, but Terry will be watching me like a hawk too. I'm always nervous when we are in company. You know that we'll get through it together. Anyway, I've got some gossip to tell you. You'll never guess what I heard?'

'What?'

'Well, Terry told me this morning that er, ya know whatshername who's a governor at that school with Jonathan, that youngish woman, blonde hair, big tits... ooh, what's her name again?' Sally pinched her nose on top, with her thumb and forefinger, and closed her eyes, trying to think. I know who she means, but I'm also trying to recall her name.

'Rose, that's it, Rose, ' Sally blurts out. 'Well, apparently, she's been camming.'

'What?' I said, not having a clue what Sally was going on about.

'Camming. I'd never heard of it, but it's apparently, you know where they go on the internet or whatever using that camera on their computers and show off their bits.'

My eyes widen, and my mouth drops open. 'What you mean she's been getting her tits out on the internet?'

'Well yeah, whatever it is they do. Anyway, someone who knows her saw her on it 'cos he was on the website or something, you know paying to see it, and there you go old Rose is flashing her whatsit and things, doing stuff to herself.' Sally winked and nodded her head as if to say. *You know what I'm saying!* She was blushing. I remain open-mouthed and wide-eyed as Sally continued. 'So, this fella, Paul, I think he's called works with her in town and has shown everyone. I bet she's mortified. I know I would be. I mean, how can you show your face at work after that, eh? Terry heard it in the pub last night. She'll never be a governor now, I bet. There'll be a vacancy, I tell ya. Your Jonathan will no doubt hear about it at the next meeting if he hasn't already.'

'Fuck me,' I say as I close my mouth and take a sip of my tea. 'I know she's a bit flirty, but I liked her whenever we met. I've only met her two or three times, you know, at gatherings they have for the school governors. I found her quite intriguing. She was always nice to me. Bloody hell. I can't believe it. Who would do things like that, especially on the internet?'

'Well, she'd be raking it in, wouldn't she? I mean you're not gonna get your bits out for nothing, are you? The men who go on these sites will pay good money to see women flash their bits and bobs. Easy money if you're that way inclined. I mean, you could do it from home, you wouldn't even have to leave the house and the till would be ringing. Kerching! All on credit cards and that these days, isn't it? I tell ya Anna we live sheltered lives we do. We have no idea what goes off behind closed doors, even here in Brampton. I mean, who would know that we suffer physical and mental abuse, eh? I bet no one has a clue. We certainly don't tell anyone, and I'm sure Jonathan and Terry don't advertise the fact that they beat the shit out of us for not ironing the curtains properly.'

'Or shirts,' I say.

'Shirts?'

'Yeah, I didn't iron Jonathan's shirt properly this morning apparently, so he forced it into my mouth. Nearly choked me to death. Anyway, I ironed another one the same way, and that one was fine. No real harm done.'

'Bastard,' Sally shouted towards the door as if he could hear her.

'What was up with the curtains?' I ask.

'He reckoned there were creases in them, so he burnt my thigh with the iron. Look.'

Sally unbuttoned her jeans and pulled them down far enough that I see the red burn. It looks sore.

'Bastard,' I shout towards the direction of Sally's house.

We both laugh. Why we laugh, I have never been able to understand. People would think we were crazy, laughing out loud and calling them names, but it's how we cope. We know our situation. We know people would say *just bloody leave*. We would say the same thing if this were happening to friends of ours, but for all the pain we suffer, both physically and mentally, we have to laugh. We can only be that way with each other. It's what we do, and as strange as it seems, even to us, it helps us cope with it all.

'Is tea on ration today, or we having another cup?' Sally asks.

I get up and put the kettle on. As I look out of the window towards the back garden, I think of Rose. I'm shocked. Shocked that she would do such a thing, but then I think of how she must feel alive, how she must have felt the adrenalin pumping through her body and felt in control—taking all that money off the men who were paying for it. Feelings that I have not felt for years. I used to feel alive. I used to be that kind of person. I used to pole dance. I loved it. I felt in control then. I want to be Rose. I want to be the old Anna again. Oh, how I want to feel alive.

chapter four

It's Saturday morning. I'm lay in bed thinking of two things, the two things I've been thinking about for the last two days, more or less non-stop. Firstly, about tonight as it's a very important evening for Jonathan and I need to be there for him. I've been thinking about that constantly as I know how important it is that everything is just right, and then I've been thinking about camming.

Ever since Sally told me about Rose and what she's been doing, I cannot stop thinking about it. About how invigorating it would be, especially for someone like me who has no real life except for what I'm allowed to do. I have no idea what Rose's story is or why she would do things like that, but I'm dying to know. I want to know what drew her to that life, what gave her the strength to do it and what she got out of it. Jonathan did tell me about it on Thursday evening when he got home, saying how disgusting it was and how she will never be able to show her face in Brampton again. He called her a slag, a whore, and said he wasn't surprised because she was always flirting with the men, but as I said to Sally the other day, I've always found her intriguing. There was always something about her that interested me. Maybe I knew that there was more to her than was on the surface. Perhaps it was a sixth sense, but whatever it was, and whatever may come her way now, I bet she loved doing what she was doing. I think about what she might do now. I hope she walks into the governor's meeting next week as bold as brass and tells them all to mind their own business. I mean, what can they do? It was in her own home in her own time, and she's free to do whatever she pleases. I realise what I've just said, or actually what I've just thought... *she's free to do whatever she pleases.* Yes, she is, I think again, free, she's free. To my knowledge, she has no Jonathan or Terry telling her what she can and can't do, but then again, as Sally said, we have no idea what goes on behind closed doors. She can't have, though, as she lives on her own. She told me that the last time we met at the Governor's Christmas bash. The boring Christmas bash. Bloody hell, they wouldn't know a good time if it smacked them all in the face. Mind you, who am I to talk? I was stood there smiling and nodding in all the right places, just like everyone else.

I have an excuse, though, as I have Jonathan's eyes burning into me every second of every minute we are out together anywhere. What excuse did they have? Then again, they are all school governors, so I suppose they are all controlled but just by their perceived positions in society. I'm just controlled by Jonathan. He's still asleep by the way. I am allowed a lie in on weekends. When he gets up, then I get up. He doesn't like waking up in a bed alone on weekends. This at least gives me time to think some more about Rose and camming. I'd never heard the phrase until Sally told me, but it's all I can think about. I'm trying to work out how I can bump into her. I can't just go and see her. I think I know where she lives at Lanercost near the Priory, but I dare not go up on my own. Jonathan would be bound to find out. Lanercost is a hamlet just outside of Brampton. It has a sprinkling of properties nestled around the priory. Lanercost Priory is a very beautiful medieval building that stands so proud in the countryside surrounding it. It is an idyllic setting with a primary school just along the road.

It occurs to me how I've never seen Rose in Brampton. I've only ever met her at school governors' shindigs. I wish I knew more about her. I sit up bolt upright in bed. That's it, I remember. She told me she works in Carlisle, in a cafe. I lie back down. I try and recall the conversation. Yes, she did, definitely. She works in a cafe near to the cathedral. I need to go there. I can do that. I can tell Jonathan that we need to go into Carlisle to top up his favourite red wine. He's playing squash later today at the Sands Centre. He'll drop me off; I know he will. As long as I can get him to agree to the wine, I know I'll be able to swing it. He's done that before.

As long as I'm straight there and straight back, I'll be waiting for him in reception at the Sands Centre when he comes out of the squash court. I'm so excited. I look over at Jonathan. He's still asleep. It's 7:35am. He'll be asleep for a bit yet. I have no idea why I want to meet with her, but I just do. I'm excited. I'm never excited. I'm usually just nervous and scared or apprehensive, but as I lie here, I'm excited, but I have no idea why. Yes, I do; what am I thinking? Of course, I do. I want to know all about this camming lark. I want to know how she felt when she did it in her own home. I know what I want to think, but I can't bring myself to think it. Can I? Yes, I can, of course, I can. I want to do it; I want to know what it feels like to take my bra off on camera and show my boobs to men on the internet. I want that excitement from my own home. I want to feel alive. I want to feel excited like I do now but 100 times more. I want to be just like Rose but without getting caught, but first of all, I want to know what it was like, how she got into it, and more than anything, I want her to tell me she doesn't care what anyone thinks. I want Jonathan to come home on Tuesday night and say she was there bold as brass.

All of a sudden, I feel deflated. What am I doing? What am I on about? I can't do any of that. I'm weak, and I'm useless. Without Jonathan, I'm nobody. *Give yourself a shake, Anna, and wake up. You can't do any of that. It's just a dream, just a pipe dream.* I begin to feel nervous again as I think about tonight. What if I say something wrong? What if I mess up in some way? What if they don't like me? I know it will go wrong; I know I'll let Jonathan down. I'm just a stupid, useless insignificant woman. Just someone who needs telling what to do all the time. I'm not Rose; I'm Anna. I can never be Rose. For a few moments there, I thought I could be. I thought I could be that person, the one who has excitement, the one who has adrenalin pumping around her body, but I'm not. I'm the one who is afraid and nervous. *You stupid woman,* I remind myself.

It's now 5:15pm on Saturday afternoon. Of course, I didn't go to the cafe earlier today. I totally bottled it. I had that brief moment of courage as I lay in bed first thing this morning, but that soon evaporated. I hated myself earlier this afternoon when Jonathan was playing squash as I knew I had missed my chance. It could be a while before I get the opportunity to suggest me going into Carlisle on my own. I can't even use the red wine excuse as Jonathan said he would get some himself today to top up his stash. So that's probably the end of that little idea. I'm still hoping that Jonathan says she was at the governor's meeting. I hope she doesn't crumble under the pressure. I've just come out of the shower. I need to dry my hair and then press Jonathan's clothes for tonight. I pray that there's no repeat of the shirt incident from a few days ago. I don't think there will be, though, as I'm sure he won't want any tension in the house.

They'll be eight of us here plus Jonathan's secretary Marie. She's doing the cooking. She's downstairs now. I know she is Jonathan's secretary, but she's a marvellous cook. She's done it before. I've told her that she should go into catering, fine end stuff, but Jonathan was furious when he found out. He dragged me round the living room by my hair for that. She's a good secretary, you see. She's been his secretary for nearly a year now and looks after him well, so I know I was in the wrong to suggest that to her and give her ideas to leave his side. I just wish that he'd not pulled at my hair so hard. I'm sure it doesn't grow as well in some places. Marie stayed at the firm anyway, so I didn't suffer any further. She adores Jonathan and was never going to leave; I don't think. She's cooking Chicken in a white wine sauce tonight for mains and then a lemon cheesecake for afters. I love her cheesecakes, divine they are.

I go into the spare room upstairs, where I have set the ironing board up. I have hung one of Jonathan's suits up and only need to press his shirt and then polish his shoes. His toiletries are already all laid out for him. I've only ironed his collar when he walks in. He stands in the doorway and just stares at me.

'Take off your dressing gown, sweetheart,' he says.

I know better than to argue. I undo the belt and let it fall to the floor. I'm stood there naked. He stares at me. I look down at my naked body. He walks over to me. He caresses my breasts whilst all the time looking straight into my eyes. Not like a loving husband would, but more in a controlling kind of way. He stoops down and takes one of my breasts in his mouth and kisses my nipples. He cups my other breast in his right hand. I should be feeling erotic right now, sexy, and ready for an explosive session of sex, but instead, I cannot take my eyes off the hot iron that is still standing on the ironing board. That's all I can concentrate on. He lifts his head up. He stares at me, saying nothing. I know what I have to do. I undo his flies and button and take out his erect penis. His jeans fall to the floor. I get down on my knees and take his penis in my mouth. I am still conscious of the hot iron. I try to concentrate on the job in hand, or rather the job in my mouth, but I'm tense, ready for any unexpected blow. I carry on. I let him finish and swallow it down. I hate swallowing. I'd rather spit it out, but that would be a major embarrassment to him. I've only done that once since we were married. I used to do it all the time, but after the humiliation of him rubbing my face into the wet patch I'd just spat out and making me lick it up, I learnt very quickly to just swallow. Having your face rubbed into a patch of your own saliva, and a man's sperm does that to you.

I stand up and lick my lips. I have to do that to show him how much I've just enjoyed him coming in my mouth and swallowing it down. I then bend down and pull his jeans up, and put him back in. I fasten his jeans as he strokes my hair. He's still not spoken a word. He turns his head and picks up the iron. He licks his finger and puts his finger onto the bottom. It sizzles. He grabs my hair and pulls my head back. I can feel the warmth of the iron on my cheek. It can only be millimetres away. I have my eyes closed.

'Open your eyes,' he whispers. I open them and look at him. I can see the iron in my side view. I can still feel the heat. 'Be a good girl tonight, sweetheart, won't you? Don't embarrass me, will you?'

I don't know whether to nod my head in reply to being a good girl or shake my head in reply to not embarrassing him. I plump to shake my head in reply to the second question. He puts the iron down and walks out of the room without another word. I want to gag with the taste of semen in my mouth, but I resist the urge and just carry on ironing his shirt as if nothing had happened. As if all that was the most natural thing in the world to happen between a married couple. Mind you, for me, it was. Things like that happen quite frequently. Not embarrassing him means keeping up with the conversation, not drinking too much wine, and complimenting him at every opportunity. Being a good girl means all of the above, plus complimenting his guests at the right moment. I know the score. I've done it all too often.

I finish the ironing and continue to get myself ready. The guests are due at 7:00pm, which means Sally and Terry will be here around a quarter to seven. Jonathan comes out of the shower. I can smell the food from downstairs. It smells lovely. Jonathan takes a deep breath in.

'Wow, that smells good, doesn't it, eh, smell good? He says.

'It does. I can't wait to taste it.' I reply, reminding

myself that it will taste a lot better than the salty taste I still have in my mouth.

'These are important to me you know Anna tonight. They are directors of the new charity for battered women that opened up over in Newcastle last year. I can get the contract for the whole of Cumbria and southwest Scotland if I play my cards right. I want that contract. Understand?'

'Yes, darling, I know. I will do whatever I can to help you tonight, you know that.'

'Mmm, I know you will. Well, you'd better anyway. If I don't land it, I'll hold you responsible. It can only be your fault if tonight does not go to plan. I've met them on three occasions already, and this is the last hurdle, so they must like me. Stands to reason that if they go cold on me after tonight, it will be your fault, so make sure they go away happy.'

'I will, of course I will.'

I try to sound convincing, but I'm now more nervous than ever. Why does he not see that making comments like that makes things worse? I take a deep breath trying hard not to hyperventilate. I get up and walk downstairs to join Marie. Maybe she can calm me down. I need a drink, wine, anything. I know that's not a good idea at this stage in the evening, but I need one. Jonathan calls me back. I've not pulled down his collar at the back after he's put his tie on. I do as I'm told and then hurry downstairs to grab a wine before Jonathan comes down.

Marie is standing over the cooker when I walk into the kitchen. She tastes something with a spoon and closes her eyes and licks her lips. Whatever it is she has just tasted must taste really good. She opens her eyes and looks across.

'Hi honey, how are you today?' she asks. 'You look gorgeous Anna, I bet Jonathan can't keep his hands off you.' she remarks with a wink. I recall how he had one hand on my breasts and one hand on the iron just a few moments ago. I smile as if what she has said is a compliment.

'You look stunning too.' I say as I walk over and pour myself a small glass of wine. I drink it down in one go. I can feel the warmth of the alcohol as it travels down my throat. It tastes good. I instantly feel better, less anxious. I'd love another one, but I know better than that. I look at Marie as she continues to cook. She looks good for her age. She's 43 I think, but looks mid-thirties. She's very slim with dark hair cut into a very neat bob. She looks like a secretary even as she slaves away over the cooker. She adores Jonathan, can't do enough for him. She's always there for him, and I know she'd defend him to the end. I often wonder what her reaction would be if I told her what he was really like. She only sees Jonathan, the brilliant solicitor, the knight in shining armour who comes to the aid of Cumbria's most vulnerable women. She has no idea that behind that charade is a manipulative, nasty bully who makes my life hell at times, but all told, she is a nice lady.

I've never once thought that there might be anything between her and Jonathan. I just don't think she's the type. Jonathan walks into the kitchen and pours himself a glass of red wine. He asks Marie if she'd like a glass. She accepts, and I watch as Jonathan pours her one and passes it to her. He looks at me and smiles.

'I know you won't want a glass yet, darling,' he says as he puts the bottle back on the worktop. 'You'll want to keep a clear head, won't you? To make sure you are able to look after our guests.' I nod my head and reply.

'You know me too well. Always playing the host.'

'I'm such a lucky man, Marie, aren't I,' he quips. 'I don't know what I'd do without my Anna.' He walks across and puts his arm around my shoulder and kisses me on the cheek. Marie looks up.

'You are indeed a very lucky man, Mr Fox; you have women looking after you from all angles,' she giggles as she speaks.

'I keep telling Anna to get a job, don't I, sweetheart?' He kisses my cheek again. 'But she just says she'd rather just stay at home and look after me, don't you my little angel?'

Jonathan knows I'd much rather have a job of my own with my own money and my own circle of work friends. It crosses my mind in a flash to say, *actually, I'd love to get a job, darling, but you won't fucking let me,* but of course, I don't say that.

'I love looking after you. It makes me happy. You know that.' I say.

'You've been out of work for so long now, though that you'd probably be unemployable. Employers want experience, and I know that from speaking with my business associates, so it's a good job you're happy doing it.' Jonathan says, laughing loudly. I don't laugh, and I'm glad to see that Marie only manages a customary smile, an awkward one at that. She returns to the cooking.

'What about kids, though, eh?' she asks without looking back round. There's no reply, just a silence that goes on a little too long and prompts Marie to turn her head towards us. She's only been with Jonathan for just under a year, so we've never discussed children yet with her. There's silence because I never know what to say when this question is asked of us. We could have had children. I wanted them, lots of them. Jonathan did too supposedly when we first met. That was always part of the grand plan for us to have three or four children, but it soon became apparent that children were never on the agenda after our marriage. Jonathan made that very clear. He was not prepared to share me with anyone else, our own children included.

I got pregnant soon after we'd tied the knot. I was over the moon, and I assumed Jonathan would have been too, but he persuaded me to get rid of it. He paid for a private termination. He said it was too early. At first, I refused to go, but he made it very clear to me that it was too early in our marriage. He said we had so much to do together and that he wanted us to experience so many things. That may sound plausible to anyone who heard my story, but he also said that if I didn't go along with his termination plans, he'd make sure I lost it another way. I knew what he meant, and I could not put myself or our unborn child through that trauma. The worst thing about all of this was that I had to make out it was me who wanted to get rid of it. He played the victim so well at the time. Everyone thought I was heartless; you know, not giving Jonathan a child. I had to play along with it, though. Soon after, he went to have the snip, privately, of course, but only I know that little secret. He wanted to make sure that we never have kids, and I have to resign myself to the fact that they'll never be any little ones running around our house. The worse thing about it all is that everyone thinks it's my fault we can't have children.

Marie looks nervous as she catches our faces. 'Have I put my foot in it?' she asks with a somewhat worried look on her face. Jonathan lowers his head, as he always does. He looks up with eyes so sad that even the most heartless person in the world would be hard-pressed not to feel some kind of sorrow for him.

'We can't have children, Marie. We were blessed with a pregnancy once a few years ago, but sadly, Anna didn't feel it was the right time for us, so she decided she wanted an abortion. I, of course, supported her with her decision even though children was the one thing I wanted most in my life.' He lowers his head again. I bow my head. I can't help it. I feel ashamed that I let this man do what he did to me, but of course, it just appears that I am bowing my head in shame of having that abortion.

'Sadly, the abortion was a little complicated, and as a result, Anna can no longer have children. We just have to accept that God has decided that maybe as some sort of punishment for Anna making that decision, he will not bless us with a child again.' Jonathan pulls me closer and kisses the top of my head. 'I don't blame Anna, Marie. We all make decisions in life that we may later regret, but we are a strong unit, and together we get through it, don't we, darling?' He again kisses the top of my head. I remain silent. I cannot play any part in this charade other than to say nothing and feel the shame and resentment directed my way. I cannot even look up at Marie as I know what she will be thinking. *Heartless bitch* or something similar I suspect. I can see that Marie has turned back towards the worktop.

'Well, that's nothing to do with me. I'm sure you can both live with that decision, as I say nothing to do with me.'

I want to run and never stop running. I want to scream and never stop screaming. *I can have children,*

I didn't choose to have an abortion, you've had the snip, you did all of this, but I can't. I have to just accept that everyone thinks I am a heartless cow who killed my own flesh and blood. Sally is the only one who knows the truth. I look at my watch. 6:35pm, she'll be here soon. I just hope that she and Terry have had a good day as that way she will at least be some comfort to me tonight, but if she's upset him, she'll be very distant all evening.

The atmosphere in the room has changed. I suspect Marie now hates me and thinks that the fact that I can't have children is poetic justice on me. I only wish I could tell her the truth.

Sally and Terry arrive just before 6:50pm. Sally is in quite a jolly mood, so today must have been a good one. We don't have our daily catch-up at weekends, only in the week. I'm glad she's quite upbeat. I'm still nervous, but all the talk about abortions and that had taken my mind off the evening's events. I must refocus. I must put all of that behind me. I walk into the kitchen and hear Marie telling Jonathan that she has great admiration for him with how he handled the abortion, supporting me back then and still not blaming me. She tells him he's a hero. He plays the victim once again. He knows I can hear, but Marie has her back to me. I walk out. I block it out as I need to be at the top of my game tonight. I can't let Jonathan down. He needs me to help him win this contract.

Bang on 7 o'clock, the doorbell rings, and I go out to let our guests in. Jonathan likes to be in the lounge to greet them when we have guests. He likes me to let them in, take their coats, and all that. I open the door to find two middle-aged couples stood there. I invite

them in and introduce myself and take the ladies'
coats. They, in turn, introduce themselves. Dominic
and Cara and Max and Fiona. Max is quite fat and
short with hardly any hair; Fiona is slim with naturally
greying hair, but it suits her. Both are from Newcastle.
Dominic is rather rugged-looking, and it turns out he
is Australian, and Cara looks Eastern European, but it
turns out she is from Gateshead and has the broadest
Geordie accent I've ever heard. In fact, I struggle to
understand her at times.

As I take them through to the lounge, I can feel Max's
eyes undressing me constantly. He's checked out my
breasts three times already in the thirty seconds I've
been in his company, and I feel rather uneasy in his
presence. Anyway, we all go through, and everyone
is introduced to each other. Pleasantries are coming
thick and fast, and the drink is starting to flow. As
I drink my glass of wine, I can feel Jonathan's eyes
burning into me, saying, *make that your last,* and I
can feel Max's eyes burning holes into my bra. The
subject of the contract has not had a mention yet, but
then again, I suppose it won't come up in conversation
until later in the evening, if at all. Marie walks out into
the kitchen, and I follow her. I want to see what kind
of reception I get from her. I like Marie, and I'd hate
her to think badly of me that we cannot continue to be
friendly.

'Everyone seems to be enjoying themselves,' I say as
I walk in.

'Yes, life can be great at times, Anna, that's when
you get a chance of life, that is.'

It cut through me. I stop in my tracks. I look straight
at her, desperate to tell her the truth, but I know there
is no way I can do that. She just stares at me. I turn on

my heels and walk back into the lounge, trying hard to stem the tears. I find it hard, though. I fill up my glass. I don't look at Jonathan. I know he is glaring at me.

'Take it steady, sweetheart, we have all night, you know,' I hear him say. I ignore the remark. I know I will pay for it later, but it won't hurt me any more than I am hurting now. Max moves to stand beside me. 'You carry on, Anna. A glass or two of wine didn't hurt anyone.'

I smile at him. Then I feel his hand on my bottom. He pinches my right cheek and then rubs it with his hand. Without thinking, I throw my entire glass of red wine in his face. He gasps. Everyone looks round in horror. Fiona squeals. Then the room sort of freezes, and then things seem to happen in slow motion as I slap him across his face. I drop my glass as I realise what I've just done. I hear the glass smash, but everything else is just a drone. I want to turn back time. I didn't mean to do that; I mean he only pinched my arse. What was I thinking? *Fuck* I think to myself as I come back into the room, and the enormity of what I've done hits me like a ten-tonne truck.

chapter five

Two days later...

I get out of bed and walk to look out of the window. It's raining and cold as usual for this time of year. It's not yet fully light, and it's nearly lunchtime. I'm ready to go, all packed and ready to go home. I look at the ambulances pulling into the yard next to the A & E department and thank my lucky stars that I am able to go home. Don't get me wrong, I'm still in pain, all over. I still hurt from head to toe, but the pain has subsided somewhat. I fell down the stairs you see on Saturday evening after everyone had left. After the incident, they all left pretty quickly, where I threw my glass of wine over Max and slapped him in the face. That didn't go down too well. He told me I was a stupid cow; he wiped the wine from his face and marched himself out of our house with his wife Fiona in tow, following a step behind him. Dominic and Cara left at the same time. Dominic smirked at me as he passed, I think giving me a little bit of a nod to say *that was a brilliant stunt you pulled there,* Anna, but, of course, he had to save face and support his business partner.

The last thing I heard before I managed to look up at Jonathan's face was Max shouting from the doorway, *the deals off, don't bother to contact us again.* I could see the anger boiling up inside Jonathan. I could even feel the heat from the steam coming out of his ears. I knew what was coming, but I also knew it would have to wait as Sally and Terry were still in the lounge, as was Marie. I stuttered that he'd felt my bottom and pinched it. I stammered that it wasn't my fault. Sally and Marie consoled me as I began to cry. I wasn't crying because of what would follow later but because I genuinely felt violated by that fat, bald horrible creep. As I was consoled by Sally and Marie telling me I did the right thing and that it was totally unacceptable, I looked over at Jonathan. His face was void of any emotion, and then as quick as a flash, he seemed to come back to life and came straight over to console me too. He told me and everyone else how wrong it was and that if he'd seen him do it, he'd have punched his lights out. That prompted a comment from Terry, who said that if I wanted to press charges, he would see to it that Max was dealt with swiftly with the full force of the law. He's a police inspector is Terry; I don't think I've mentioned that, but before I could answer, Jonathan told him to leave things be as there was no real harm done.

Marie interjected and told Jonathan that some real harm had been done and we should think long and hard about pressing charges. Jonathan didn't answer her. He was too busy comforting me. For a brief moment, I thought he was genuine, but then he asked everyone to leave as he just wanted to put the events of the night behind him and concentrate on me. I knew what he meant by that comment, as did Sally as she immediately asked if she could stay to comfort me too. Jonathan told her that would not be necessary. Marie offered to stay and help clear up, but Jonathan was insistent that everyone should leave as we just wanted to be alone.

I didn't want to be alone with him, I was sure of that, but I knew better than trying to argue the point. Marie made sure the oven and appliances were turned off and left things as best she could, but in the end, Jonathan was more or less man-handling her out of the door. Once he'd waved her off and had seen that Sally and Terry had gone into their house and shut the door, he closed ours and immediately flung himself towards me. I turned and ran towards the stairs and began climbing them two at a time. He caught me halfway up and then dragged me to the top by my hair. I struggled with him, and then he pushed me down the stairs. Yes, he pushed me. I didn't fall, I know what a push feels like, and he pushed me.

I can remember falling down every step almost in slow motion. I must have blacked out as when I came around, Jonathan was sitting on the stairs a few steps up with a glass of wine in his hand, just staring at me. I have no idea how long I was out. I hurt all over. I tried to move, but I was in such pain I just relaxed back into the floor. All he said was *if I call an ambulance, then you fell. Got it, you fell. Say anything other than that, and I'll kill you. Do you hear me? I'll kill you?'* He said it so coldly and calmly that I knew he was serious. I just replied, *deal.* I needed an ambulance, so that seemed the best option. No one believes me, of course, maybe except a couple of the nurses. Only this morning, a nurse told me that if I were in any danger, there were people I could speak to. I would be safe, and no one would be able to get at me if I didn't want them to. I told her I was fine. I was still in a lot of pain, but it had subsided a little, and I was able to go home. I've had worse than this for answering back. A few bruises? I'd have taken that deal in an instant. When I was stood in the lounge, having just slapped Max around the face, I'd have taken a few bruises without a second thought. I think Jonathan panicked a little when I fell and was sorry when he pushed me down the stairs. He knew he'd have to leave it there; he knew that he couldn't inflict any more injuries on me, and he also knew that he'd have to call an ambulance. Unfortunately, he also knew I'd keep my mouth shut.

Jonathan is coming to pick me up after lunch. He'd put the charm act on of course when the ambulance arrived, and with the nurses here in the hospital, but I don't honestly think he's fooled anyone. The strange thing is that as I stare out of the window, watching the comings and goings of the Cumberland Infirmary, I feel as though this is a turning point in my life. I feel positive about the future. I've had some time to think over the past couple of days, and I've thought a lot. I'm better than this. I don't deserve this, and I'm getting out of this shit life. Not just yet, I haven't got any money, but I'm going to make some, and I'm leaving that bullying bastard.

I've been thinking about Rose and how she must have made a mint doing what she's been doing. I can do that. I know I can, but most importantly, I must do it. I was the queen of pole dancing, remember. Ok, it was a long time ago, but that Anna is still inside me. I know she is. I just need to let her out. I think I could do it from home without Jonathan knowing, but I need to speak to Rose first. I hope that when Jonathan comes home from the governor's meeting tomorrow night, he tells me that she waltzed in bold as brass and didn't give two hoots about what people thought. I decided as I lay in my hospital bed that if she turns up tomorrow with her head held high, I will contact her somehow and do it, and Rose will show me how.

'Cup of tea, Luv?' I hear someone shout. I look round, and there is the lady in the hallway who brings the tea. 'Yes please,' I say as I walk back to my bed.

'There you go, Luv, nice and hot. Biscuit?'

'Mmm... go on then, just the one. I have to watch my weight, you know.'

'Give over lass; there's nowt on ya. You're like a skinned rabbit. No one would get much nourishment from eating you,' she says, laughing.

I look down at my slender frame and agree that there's not much on me, but until I make my money and get out of this life, I'm going to play the game and keep myself as safe as I can. I need to look my best for my clients after all. I chuckle as I picture myself posing for the camera, taking off my clothes, and maybe a bit more. I'm excited, nervous, but raring to go all at the same time. I haven't felt like this in a long time. Nervous, yes, but excited and raring to go? It's been a while, but as I sit back and enjoy my hot tea and a digestive biscuit, I just hope and pray that Rose doesn't let me down.

chapter six

It's Tuesday Morning. I came out of the hospital yesterday afternoon. Jonathan was very charming, of course, and to be fair, he's been very attentive since we got home. He even offered to stay home today, but I insisted I was ok. Normally that would raise suspicion with him, but he seemed fine with it and went off to work happily. I didn't have to make his breakfast or iron a shirt or anything. I can't recall the last time that happened. Either this is the new Jonathan, or he really is nervous after the questioning from the nurses. I put on a convincing show, though, so I doubt he'll have anything to worry about.

The doorbell rings, and then I hear Sally's voice.

'It's only me, Anna.' I look at my watch. It's only 10:40am. Sally is over four hours early. She comes bouncing into the living room.

'Bloody hell Anna, I've been a nervous wreck since Saturday night. All Terry told me was that you'd been taken to hospital after falling down the stairs. That's all I could get out of him. I wanted to come and see you. Honestly, I did, but Terry wouldn't let me. He said it was none of our business and that Jonathan would take care of you. well, did you fall?'

I smiled, only because she was like a whirlwind at times was Sally. She's not even said good morning yet.

'What do you think?'

'I knew it, the bloody swine. I knew it. I tell you something Anna, I know Terry gives me a few backhanders and knocks me about a bit and well, controls my life entirely,'... she turns her palms over as if to say *well you knew all that...* 'But he would never push me down the stairs, never. I mean, he could have bloody killed you. How are you feeling anyway?'

'Nice of you to ask at last,' I say. She knows I'm only teasing. 'I'm ok, actually. All things considered. I think I got off lightly. I mean, I threw a glass of red wine in the face of the man that Jonathan was trying to impress the most, and to cap it all off, I slapped him round the face. As I told myself when I was lying in the hospital bed, I'd have taken a trip down the stairs with a few bruises any day. I mean, I dread to think what he'd have done otherwise. He knew he'd overstepped the mark, though. He was so sheepish at the hospital.'

'Shitting himself, I'd say, more like,' says Sally.

'Probably. He's been ok since, but I'm not fooled. I'm getting out of here. As soon as I can, I'm off. I made my decision in hospital. I'm worth more than this, Sal. I don't deserve this life. I mean, I sometimes struggle to comprehend how I've got here. I think back to when we first met, to before we met, and I was such a lively, glass half full kinda girl, but look at me now.' I look down at myself. 'I'm a battered wife, Sally, a battered wife. How the hell did I get here, eh?' I know how I got here. I let Jonathan control me. It all happened slowly, but I have allowed it to happen, and I've been stuck here ever since.

Sally puts her hand on my knee. Her eyes fill up. She sniffles.

'We're stuck here, Anna. We've had this conversation before. How can you escape, eh?... you have no money and no access to any. Where would you go, eh? He'd find you.'

'I don't care, Sally. I've made my mind up, and I need one more piece of the jigsaw to fall into place tonight, and I'm off and running. It'll take a while, but I can wait. I've been here long enough to be able to wait a few more months, even a year. I don't care, but I am going to do this, Sally. I mean it.'

'What you are gonna do?' she asks.

'I know I can trust you, Sally; I know I can, can't I?'

'Hey, that's insulted me. I'd die for you; you know that. You're the only one I'd die for, mind you, but seriously you can trust me 100%, always.'

'Well, remember Rose?'

'The lady who they caught getting her kit off?'

'Yes.'

'What about her?'

'If she turns up at the governor's meeting tonight bold as brass, head held high, then I'm going to contact her, and I'm going to get her to show me the ropes on how to get into this camming lark, and I'm going to do it.'

Sally coughs and nearly chokes.

'You what? Are you bleeding mad?'

'No, Sally, not mad, just alive. Why not? She did'

'Yeah, and she got caught, remember? Bloody hell Anna don't do this, please. He'd kill ya.'

'Listen, I'd do it from here during the day. All I need is a laptop and something to take payment, but Rose will sort that for me, well I hope she will. Anyway, I'd do it in disguise.'

'How? You've got nothing to disguise yourself with.'

'I'd ask Rose to get me all the gear. I'd then pay her back out of my initial takings. Look, I know it may seem a long shot but, and don't ask me why but I just know that she'll help me. I know she will.'

'And what if she doesn't?'

'Then I'll just have to either figure another way, or I'll just have to do a moonlight flit and disappear, but if I do that, I'd have no money. I need to earn money, Sal. I need to give myself half a chance to do it right. I'm not giving him the satisfaction of me going without a penny in my purse. When I go, I'm going with a few quid.

Sally stands up and paces the room. 'Bloody hell Anna, you've given this some thought, haven't you, but how the hell is a girl like you going to be able to do that?'

I've never told Sally about my pole dancing in my youth. It's just never come up in conversation.

'I used to be a pole dancer.' I blurt out, looking for her reaction.

'A what, when. You've never told me that before,' she replies, looking surprised. Not shocked, just surprised.

'I know, but I did it at uni. I did it for a while, and you know what, looking back, I bloody loved it. It seems like it happened to someone else. I'm so far removed from that girl it's quite amazing, but she's still in here, Sal,' I say as I put my fist onto my chest. 'She's in here, and she's ready to come out. That Anna can do it and that Anna is me. I have to keep reminding myself that she's still in me, but I know she is.' I take Sally's hand. 'That stay in hospital was the kick I needed, or should I say it was the push I needed.' I laugh out loud as I realise the irony of what I've just said. That push from Jonathan is what made me think. 'This is the start of the rest of my life.'

Sally paces some more. She rubs her face with both

of her hands and then runs her hands through her hair.

'No, Anna, you're wrong.'

'What do you mean I'm wrong?'

'It's the start of the rest of both of our lives. If you're doing it, then so am I. If you bugger off, there's no way I'm staying here. I'd never get through the days.'

I sit, mouth open, speechless.

'Well?' Sally asks; I stand up. It still hurts but not too much. I squeal with delight.

'Seriously?' I say as I hold out my hand. Sally shakes it. 'We're gonna do this, Sally. Me and you, together. We're gonna get out of this life. I don't know where we're going, but wherever it is, we'll be there together.' Sally hugs me, and we jig up and down. It hurts, but I don't care.

I spend the day so excited, thinking about the future. I can't sit still. Me and Sally were like two giggling schoolgirls as we talked about what we could be doing in a few weeks. A few weeks seems so soon, but we are so excited we just cannot wait. We both remind each other that we've not felt this alive in years. Sally stayed the rest of the morning, through lunch and right up until nearly 2:30pm. She then had to go and do her chores. She'd taken a bit of a risk leaving them so late, but she just didn't want to go. I didn't want her to go either. She knew that I would find out tonight if Rose had gone to the meeting. I was so excited to hear about it all. I could not stop thinking about it all afternoon. It was all that occupied my mind. I just had to know.

Jonathan comes in from work around 5:40pm. He kisses me on the cheek and asks me what time dinner

will be ready. I say it will be ready for six o clock. He
seems ok with this. He runs upstairs to have a shower.
I then remember I've not left his things out for him to
change into. I run upstairs to find him staring at the
bed.

'Where are my things?' he asks rather sharply.

Shit, I think to myself. *This will not bode well for
what I want to happen later.*

'I'm sorry darling, I've just been so tired today, you
know, with what I've been through over the last couple
of days. Look, you jump in the shower, and I'll get your
things out.'

'So, who's looking after dinner while you're sorting
my things?' he asks.

Shit, the dinner, I think to myself.

'Erm, it's fine. I'll run down and turn it down, and
then I'll come back up here to sort your things out.
They will all be laid out for you when you get out of the
shower.'

Jonathan says nothing and turns to get in. That is
my cue to crack on. He's not happy, though. Silence
is not a good thing. That always means something will
follow. I pray that he will be lenient because of what has
happened. I run downstairs and tend to our dinner.
I then run back up. He's already showered and is
standing there naked. This is to make a point. He never
showers that quickly. He can't have even have washed
himself properly. He remains silent and watches me
as I get his things ready. When I've finished, I stand
back and look at him. I feel like a soldier in the army
standing by their bed. I can't leave the bedroom until
he's dismissed me. As I stand here, I cannot believe
how much I hate him and how much I cannot wait to
leave this shitty life. But for now, I play the game.

'You have nothing to do all day, and yet I have to come home and stand here naked whilst I wait for my wife to do her duties to me as a husband.' he says to me as I stand to attention. He then walks towards me. 'Do you realise how that makes me feel? It makes me feel humiliated. Do you do this to humiliate me?' he asks in a rather raised voice.

'No darling, honestly I was just so tired it slipped my mind.' I am now thinking about our dinner and just want to be able to go and see to that as I know that a ruined dinner would be a disaster for me. He runs his finger down my cheek.

'I think you do like to humiliate me. I think you wanted to humiliate me on Saturday night. I think you planned it all. Did you?' he asks.

'Of course not. He sexually assaulted me,' I say in reply.

'Did he, did he eh? He pinched your bottom. Would you like me to show you what sexual assault really is, eh, would you?' He is now shouting.

I remain silent. He walks away. 'You've always been useless as a wife, Anna. Sometimes I'm embarrassed by you. I lie for you and tell people what a good wife you are.' He laughs. 'You're so useless I can't even be bothered to shag you. I think dinner needs looking at.'

I run out of the bedroom and downstairs to save our dinner. I check it, it's fine. We eat in silence. As I wash up, I try and pluck up the courage to suggest I need some air and that I could go with him and maybe just sit in the car. Anything to see Rose and she how she is, but I can't. I'm too scared. Jonathan goes to the meeting alone.

I sit and try and play my guitar. I can just about play it with my sprained wrist, but it sounds pretty awful. I watch a bit of telly and try not to get too excited about what Jonathan might tell me. I feel deflated. When he tells me I'm useless, I find it hard to remain positive. It has always struck a chord with me, more so than the physical stuff. I try and work out why it does, but I do not have the skills to do it. Maybe I am useless, especially if I can't even work out why. Maybe he's right. Maybe this Rose thing is just a fantasy, and I won't actually do it at all. I think about how I was stood in the bedroom, scared to even move, and I ask myself how I could possibly do this camming lark and muster up the courage to leave him. As I sit there waiting for him, I wonder how I have gone from taking on the world this afternoon to feeling so low as I do now. What a difference a few small hours make.

Then I realise what it is. I've allowed him to make me feel this way. It's not Jonathan; it's me. He doesn't do this to me. He doesn't make me feel like this. It's only because I allow him to. He can't make me feel anything. I do this to myself. I remember a friend of mine who was doing Counselling and Psychotherapy at university, and she told me that no one could make you feel anything. It's your own stuff that is the trigger... yes, that's the word, trigger. I remember it now, what she told me. Why have I not remembered this before? She told me it was all to do with someone's self-worth, where they put their worth. I sit up. I recall the conversations we had. It's a blur, but the more I think, the more I can recall. I am putting my self-worth on Jonathan. I must think so poorly of myself that the way he treats me, or actually the way I allow myself to be treated, is how I value my self-worth. I then remember the conversation I had with Sally earlier... *I am better than this. I am worth more than this. I do not deserve to be treated this way.* I stand up and walk around the room. I stroke my chin. 'Come on, Anna, that's right,' I say to myself out loud. I realise that whilst I continue to allow myself to be treated this way, I will feel like I do. I tell myself over and over again that I need to play the game still, but whenever he tells me I'm useless, I can just smile inside and remind myself about self-worth. I feel better already. I feel like I did earlier this afternoon with Sally.

'Wow!' I say out loud. I've never pushed away those feelings of sorrow and pity so quickly. I did that myself, and I can do it again and again. I hear the door go. It's Jonathan. He's back. I sit back down and look pitiful. I'm strong inside still, but I look pitiful on the outside. Strong on the in but pitiful on the out. That's me from now on. Jonathan walks into the living room.

'She's going abroad,' he says.

'Who is?' I ask.

'That whore Rose, she walked in tonight bold as brass without a care in the world. Sat in on the meeting, said nothing about the rumours, and then announced she was resigning as she was selling up and moving to Portugal, bloody Portugal. Buying a villa by all accounts. She then had the audacity to tell us all that she's made so much money taking her clothes off she can sell up and retire in the sun. Unbelievable.'

I sit there aghast. I can't believe what I've just heard. I sit there strong and excited on the inside while still looking pitiful on the out. Ooh, I like to feel strong and excited on the inside. I like it very much. Anna Fox, you are getting very good at this, I say to myself.

I need to see Rose quickly. My mind is racing. Jonathan is still stood shaking his head. I get up to pour him a whisky. I'm trying to think. *I need to view her property,* I think to myself. I need to arrange a viewing. Well, me and Sally do. I can't wait to tell Sally tomorrow.

I'm sat in my lounge on Wednesday afternoon. It's 10 to 3. I'm to be at Sally's for 3pm. I've been itching to go round all morning, but Jonathan was in a foul mood this morning, a mixture of me forgetting to have his clothes ready last night, and he was still taken aback by Rose. Either way, I'm not going to risk stepping out of line as when he's annoyed, he's more likely to come home unannounced to try and catch me out at something. I can wait a few more minutes. I look at my watch again, 2:53pm. I get up to put my shoes on and look out of the window. It's stopped raining, so I decide against putting my coat on, especially as Sally only lives next door. I can risk leaving at 2:56pm. I check my watch constantly. I pace up and down. My watch says 2:56pm. I bolt out of the door and run to Sally's. I get there before it's even got to 2:57pm. I'm three minutes early, but hey, this is the new me isn't it. I smile to myself as I say the words and the irony of it all. The new me, eh? I daren't leave the house until it's 2:56pm as in my head that's acceptable. No one has told me that, no one has said that I can leave at 2:56pm, but in my head, I could try and justify that to Jonathan if needed. Yeah, this is the new me. *Go girl,* I think to myself; *you really are living dangerously these days!*

Anyway, I knock on Sally's door and let myself in. I shout; she shouts back the usual reply, kettle's on. I barge into the kitchen, a little breathless.

'Where's the fire?' Sally asks as she pours the water into the mugs. 'How're your bruises, they any better?'

'Err, yes they are not too bad, pains easing, still a bit sore and tender though but forget that, listen to this, guess what happened at the governor's meeting?' I reply. I stand and lean onto the kitchen worktop.

'Eh?' Sally responds, looking confused as she turns round to face me.

'She's moving, selling up, going to Portugal,' I say without explaining what or who I am going on about.

'Who is?'

'Rose. She walked in last night at the meeting bold as brass and told them all she's resigning and buggering off abroad. She's made so much money she's going to live in the sun. Buying a villa apparently.'

'Bloody hell,' Sally says very slowly as she sits down at the table. 'Portugal, eh! What did Jonathan think of that?'

'He thinks it's disgusting. Says she's a whore and nothing more than a stripper. Good riddance, he says. He said the school does not need people like her, and apparently, everyone is glad she's going.'

'I know, but Portugal. Just think, Anna, that could be you and me.'

'I know,' I say dreamily. 'But she's selling up, and I don't know if she needs to sell before she goes or what? So, we need to get a viewing of her property and quickly. We need to speak to her soon. Without her input, we have no idea how to go about doing this.' I look at Sally, she ponders.

'How the heck we going to swing that one then?' she asks. I get up and pour the milk in the tea and take out the teabags.

'How?' Sally asks again.

'We're going to just have to put our big girl pants on and buckle up, girl.'

'Put our what on?' Sally asks, narrowing her eyebrows and looking confused. I have no idea where that statement came from, but I like it.

'Our big girl pants, you know, like *man up*, but for girls. We need to take the bull by the horns, Sally, and just go for it. If we dither, we'll miss the boat, and we'll be stuck here forever, and I for one, am not doing that.'

Sally smiles. 'Don't worry, mate, I've got some big pants. So, what's the plan?'

'No idea,' I say, 'But that's what we're gonna do now, make a plan, yeah?'

'Like a brainstorming session?' Sally replies excitedly, 'You know like what they do in those big meetings. Terry talks about how they 'brainstorm' at work all the time, especially if there's a case on that's a bit meaty.'

'Yeah, if you like,' I say. 'Whatever it's called, we just need to know what we are doing. I'm sure I know where she lives, near Lanercost Priory it is. I'm not sure of the house, but it's more or less opposite. There can't be many houses for sale in Lanercost on that road, so fire the laptop up, and we'll have a look.' Sally looks nervous all of a sudden. 'What's up?' I ask.

'Terry will know I've been looking at houses if we use the laptop. He checks the history whenever he uses it. I don't know how he does it, but he always knows what I've been looking at.'

'Bloody hell,' I say out loud. 'Jonathan's the same, but we have two spare laptops. They are in the loft. He never chucked them out when he bought a new one. I was planning on using one of them when we start to do the camera stuff online as he never looks at them. They're just gathering dust. I know he's not turned them on since they've been up there. I'll be back in ten minutes.'

I run back home and as quickly as I can I get one of the two laptops. I get the newer one of the two. Hopefully, it will be the better one. I get back to Sally's and put it on the table. I open it up to turn it on. It's flat. I'd not thought of that.

'Where's the lead?' Sally asks.

'No idea,' I reply. I stand up. 'For fuck's sake!' I shout in frustration. Sally goes out of the kitchen and returns 30 seconds later with a lead.

'It's the same brand laptop,' she says. 'Maybe it's the same lead connection.' We try it. It is. 'YES!' I shout, and then I hug Sally. She hugs me back. I feel good.

We watch as the laptop bursts into life. The screen comes on. We wait a few seconds and then try to load up the internet. Nothing. 'Of course,' I say as I hit my forehead with the palm of my hand. We need your password to connect it up.'

'Where's that?' Sally asks.

'On your router, you know the little machine you got from your internet provider.'

'Is this it in here?'

I follow Sally into the lounge. Behind one of the chairs is a little router. 'That's it.' I say. 'We're off and running, Sal.'

We connect it up and load the internet. We then type in *houses for sale in Lanercost*. It brings up three properties.

'Which one is it?' Sally asks.

I don't reply. I'm trying to recall if Rose ever said anything to me about her property. I can't think of anything.

'Well, it can't be that one, Anna,' Sally says, pointing

to a property. 'That one's not in Lanercost, that's definitely in Brampton, so I'd say that one's out of the question. It's on Lanercost road, but it's not really in Lanercost.'

'Maybe they wanted to put Lanercost on to try and lift the selling price.' I say, still trying to recall anything. 'She's got a garage,' I shout out. 'I remember she said she parks her VW Beetle in the garage. I remember because I love Beetles too.' I check the houses. Only one has a garage, and it was only listed three days ago. 'That's it.' I say, 'that's the one.'

We both look at each other and laugh.

'So, let's make a viewing,' Sally says, nodding to the laptop. I'm nervous all of a sudden, anxious almost. I then tell myself I am worth more than this. I tell myself my self-worth is worth more than this. 'When for?' I ask.

'Well, tomorrow I'd say Anna before we back out. Big girl pants, remember!'

'You're right.' I dial the number of the estate agents. Sally snatches the phone. 'Terry might check the last number re-dial when he gets in.' I snatch it back.

'Who do you ring regularly?'

'My mother,' says Sally.

'Then ring your mother after I've rung the agent.'

'Ok, good idea.'

I ring the agent. I ask to make a viewing for tomorrow. The agent says she'll have to ring me back. I panic and give Sally's details. I put the phone down, and we look at each other.

'What if they ring back when Terry's home?' Sally says in a rather tepid, fearful tone.

'We didn't think of that, did we?' I say.

'No, we bloody didn't, but you gave my number,

didn't you. If Terry finds out Anna, I'm in big trouble. You know that. Why did you do it?'

Sally appears quite frantic. I don't know what to say. What can I say?

'I didn't know what to say, Sally. I'm sorry, I'm really sorry.'

'This is a bloody stupid idea. What the hell are we doing. He'll put me in hospital for this Anna, I'll be in the bed you were in, but I'll look a hell of a lot worse. Bloody hell, what am I going to do, eh?'

I try and comfort her. The phone rings, Sally answers it. It's the agent. Tomorrow's on. 2:00pm. We sit in silence and stare at each other. Then a smile comes across both of our faces.

'If Terry doesn't kill me, then the stress will. I'm telling you. I wish I still bloody smoked.'

I bite my lip as I smile. I tell myself again about my self-worth. I then tell Sally about it all. I tell her that she needs to do the same. Whenever she feels like she's going to buckle, she needs to remind herself of what she's worth.

As I lie in bed that night, I can't sleep. I have so much emotion whirling around my body I can't even blank my mind to fall asleep. I feel so alive, and I'm amazed at how the pain of that trip down the stairs has eased. My mind is so preoccupied I'm not even thinking about it. I look over at Jonathan, and in my head, I say to him, *I'm leaving you soon, you Bastard.* I then get brave, and I mouth it silently. I stare at him a while longer, and then I do the bravest thing I've done in a long time. I whisper it. It's only a whisper, but I'm actually saying it. I'm actually bloody saying it. I turn over and try to fall asleep. I look at the clock. It's 1:17am. Just over twelve hours to go.

I eventually fall asleep.

It's Thursday morning, and I'm eating my breakfast. Jonathan has just left for work. I've cleared up his breakfast pots and am now eating fruit and yoghurt. I can hardly eat it; I'm so nervous. I'm excited too, but hell am I nervous. I repeatedly remind myself of my self-worth. It works. I feel instantly more confident each time. I eat my breakfast slowly as I again, for the thousandth time, think about what me and Sally are about to embark on. Mind you, that's if Rose will play ball. I have to push the thought of *'what if she tells Jonathan all about our plan'* to the back of my mind. That is unthinkable and my newfound strength and confidence, no matter how small it is at the moment, allows me to push that thought away. She has to *help us;* I keep saying to myself. *Why wouldn't she?* She has no reason not to try and help us. I mean, I doubt Jonathan was very sympathetic on Tuesday night at the meeting.

I finish my breakfast and continue my day as normal. I do the chores that Jonathan has left me, and I look through the cupboards and fridge to see what we need when I go shopping. Today is shopping day, you see. Every Thursday, without fail, Jonathan leaves me £100 in twenty-pound notes to do the shopping. I go to a supermarket in Carlisle, every week, same time, just after lunch. I have to account for every penny and leave Jonathan the change and receipt. Sometimes he will check the mileage when I get back to see how many miles I've done just to make sure I've not been anywhere else. Sometimes I will detour into Brampton to go to the butchers which will account for a couple of extra miles. He doesn't always check, but I never know when he will or when he won't. It's very sporadic. That way, he keeps the control, you see. I have no idea if he will check the mileage today or not, but as it's Thursday, I can swing back to collect Sally and then go the three miles or so to Lanercost and back. That will be about six extra miles, enough for questions and interrogation if he checks the mileage today. I pray he won't.

I leave for my shopping trip at 11:30am. I happily browse the isles taking a little longer than normal as I want to time things just about right. I want to be back home with just enough time to put the shopping away and then get straight off with Sally to Rose's house. I can't afford to have much spare time to think, as that will just set my mind racing, which could mean allowing doubts to creep in. I must stay focused and keep my mind active. I look around at the people browsing the same isles as me, and I wonder if any of these ordinary-looking people would ever dare to even contemplate taking their clothes off on camera. I giggle to myself, and I feel electric. I feel as though I could strip off right here in the middle of my shopping.

I glance at a young man, maybe in his early twenties, and see him check me out. He looks at me up and down, and I feel a tingle in my stomach. I feel sexy. I imagine what I could do with that man, and I feel a stirring of adrenalin run through my body. I imagine what I would feel if I were stripping off for him. I have to focus myself back on the job in hand and reach for the mayonnaise. I look round, and he's gone. He was probably just getting a sandwich for lunch and going back to some boring job in an office somewhere. I finish my shopping and drive back home. I still feel sexy; the feeling hasn't gone. I haven't felt this feeling in my undies for so long now I'd forgotten what it was like. I rush to put the shopping away, and I rush upstairs. I need to pleasure myself; I need the release that I'm craving. I have time before I collect Sally. It's a long time since I've done this, as I never feel sexy with Jonathan. I know I don't have much time, and I give myself the best orgasm I've had in years. *Wow that feels good,* I tell myself.

As I fasten my jeans, I wonder if I could do that on camera for anyone paying to see it. I tell myself I can, but whether that's true or not will remain to be seen. I look at my watch. I'm two minutes late for Sally. As I run downstairs, I hear a knock, and Sally comes in.

'It's only me, you ok?' she shouts as she comes through the door and instantly sees me running downstairs. I'm a little breathless.

'What you been up to up there eh!' she says mockingly. 'We're late, you know.'

I look in the mirror and check my hair and make-up.

'I know Sally, sorry. I was bursting for the toilet, and then I decided to get changed. It's only a couple of minutes, though.'

'I'm only winding you up girl, what you do up there is your business,' she says, laughing. I know she's only teasing, but I feel myself colouring up, blushing slightly. I hope she doesn't notice.

'Right,' I say as I straighten my clothes, 'let's go.'

As we walk out to the car, Sally links my arm. 'I hope my Terry or your Jonathan don't come home while we're out,' she says. I can tell she's anxious. So, am I, but I put it to one side as best I can? We sit in the car, and before I start the engine, I look at Sally.

'Let's not even think of that Sal, have you got your

big girl pants on?' She smiles.

'I have Anna, the biggest ones I could find. The way I feel, I need a bloody tent wrapped around my bits. I'm a nervous bloody wreck but come on, let's go before I chicken out.'

I start the car, and we drive the three miles or so to Lanercost. We get to the Priory and turn the corner, and 100 yards or so up the road, we see the for-sale board. I pull up outside and take a deep breath. I again look at Sally, who does the same. I open my door and am relieved to hear her do the same. As we walk through the gate, I look at the very neat, if a little small-detached sandstone cottage. It's quite picture postcard, and I picture the horror on the faces of the neighbours when they found out what had been going on here, but then I turn and walk back to the gate, and I look out up and down the road. There are no neighbours, well, not for a good 200 yards or so anyway, so perfect for working from home. As I walk back through the gate, Rose opens the door.

'Hi, I'm.... Anna? What a surprise,' she says as she realises who I am before she's even managed to tell me her name. 'It is you, isn't it, Anna?'

'Hi, yes, and this is my friend Sally.'

'I didn't know you and Jonathan were thinking about moving; he's never said.'

'Well, er, no er, can we come inside?' I ask, desperately trying to get in off the path.

'Yes, of course, sorry, what must you think of me.'

We go inside and walk through a very cute hallway with exposed beams into a deceptively spacious kitchen that looks out onto a very neat typical cottage-style walled garden.

'Would you like a cup of tea?' Rose asks, having

already started to fill the kettle with water.

'Yes please, no sugar but milk for me.' I say.

'Same for me, please.' Sally says rather meekly.

'So, is it for you and Jonathan, Anna, or is it for yourself, Sally?' Rose asks. She's still getting the mugs from the cupboard and has her back to us both.

There's a silence that I become aware of and feel the need to fill quickly before it becomes awkward. I inwardly take a deep breath and blurt out, 'Neither, we want to talk to you about that camming business. We want to do it, Rose, me and Sally here.'

I can't believe what I've just said. Rose stops doing what she's doing and stares out of the kitchen window. She remains with her back to us.

'I thought you were better than this, Anna. Now can you both just leave? That's my business, and I'd thank you both not to come here fishing so you can both gossip it all around town.' She turns round. 'That's pretty low, Anna. Jonathan, send you, did he? That wouldn't surprise me, the smarmy Bastard.'

'No, I mean you've got it all wrong. That's not why we are here at all. I'm serious. Me and Sally want to know all about what you did to earn your money. We want to do it and earn the same. We're both trapped, you see, battered wives and all that, you don't understand, I want to be free, I don't want this shit anymore.'

I sit down at her table, and I start to cry. I then hear Sally speak.

'It's true love, all of it. I wasn't planning on pouring my heart out to you today, but hey, I've got me pants on, so fuck it.'

Sally and I then proceed to tell Rose the whole shebang, the whole story, well, two stories if truth be known. Abbreviated versions but enough so that she gets the gist of it all. Rose lets out a huge sigh.

'Bloody hell, ladies, I didn't see any of that coming.' She looks at Sally. 'I don't know your husband Sally, but I know Jonathan, and I must say Anna, I'm not surprised. Always came across a bit too nice for my liking, did old Jonathan. People aren't normally that nice; he was always smarmy too. I'd never put myself in a room alone with him.'

I look her straight in the eye. I can see she's aware of my gaze. 'You know it all now, Rose. No one else knows anything. We're the only three people in the world who know what solicitor Jonathan and Police Inspector Terry are really like. We've poured our lives out onto your kitchen table. Will you help us. Will you show us how to make money from doing what you did, show us how to get enough money to break free from the shit lives we lead?

Rose gets up and stands at the kitchen window, and stares into her garden. Sally and I look nervously at each other. The thought of whether she will tell Jonathan comes back into my mind. I don't have the time to put that thought anywhere. I'm too transfixed on Rose. Without turning round, she replies, 'Too bloody right I will ladies. I'll make you enough money to break free within six months, and you know what?' She turns round and leans on the table with both of her palms. She has a determined look on her face. 'I'm going to take my house off the market and postpone my retirement to sunny Portugal. I'll do it with you ladies. I have all of the equipment here; it's all set up. We'll split the money three ways. All you two have to do is decide whether you can get up here to my house every morning for two hours while your hubbies are at work.'

I look at Sally, and she looks at me. We are like two rabbits caught in headlights. I'm suddenly nervous. So is Sally. I can see it in her.

'It's all here for you ladies. I'll do my bit; I'll show you everything, and believe me, there are things you can do to make serious money that won't have even entered your little heads.'

My heart is pounding so hard; I think it's going to jump right out of my chest. I can hear it pumping away.

'We can't do it every day. Five days a week?' I say with trepidation in my voice.

'Why not?' Rose asks.

'That's too much. Look, Rose, we are serious, believe me, but there's no way we can risk it every day. Can we not just do three days a week?'

'We can, but it will take you longer to get away,' she replies. I look at Sally.

'What do you think?' I ask.

'I agree,' she says, 'Three days a week would be far better for me. You have to understand the lives we lead' she says, looking at Rose. 'Try and put yourself in our shoes. I know it's hard for you to understand, but every day would be a huge strain on our lives, our lives with those two bastards we live with.'

Rose nods her head in some sort of approval and says, 'I understand, ladies, I get it, whatever you think is best. I'm here to support you, not make things worse, so sorry if I come across a bit strong. That's just who I am at times. Agreed then. Three days a week in the mornings before lunch.' She smiles. Me and Sally smile at each other and then smile back. I then realise what we've just agreed to, and a wave of panic comes over me. I thought I was already nervous, but now. Wow, now I really am panicking. I feel like I'm going to hyperventilate, but at the same time, I'm excited. It's a wired feeling. I hate it when it happens as it's so overwhelming.

'Jonathan sometimes comes home unexpectedly,' I say. I can hear the nervousness in my voice.

'So does my Terry.' Rose stands up.

'When was the last time either of them came home unexpectedly before lunchtime?'

I think. I think hard. I can't ever remember Jonathan coming home before lunch. Whenever he has, it's always in the afternoon, an early finish. 'I can't,' I say. 'It's always in the afternoon.' We both look at Sally.

'I think he's only ever done that once, and that was because he'd forgotten his diary, which was my fault, of course, and I got a backhander for it, the swine.' Sally says. 'Other than that, it's like with Anna, only in the afternoon.'

'So, are we in this together?' Rose asks. She has a real sense of leadership about her, a real determination that I like. I like it a lot. I'm fascinated by her. I know I will need her. I know we will both need her leadership and authority. Without Rose, I know we'd never do it.

'I'm in,' I say. 'I have to be.'

'Then so am I,' Sally responds. We all put out hands in the middle of the table, one on top of the other.

'So, we start tomorrow.' Rose states. She doesn't ask; she tells. I like that. I need that.

'Tomorrow's Friday, so we can do the first day, then come back Monday after you two have had the weekend to get over it.' She continues in between a giggle, a schoolgirl-type giggle. I put my head in my hands.

'Oh don't, Rose,' I say, 'saying things like that just makes me even more anxious, but yep that sounds ok to me. Let's just do it, eh. We have to. This is what will get me away from here.' I look at Sally. 'Well, it's what will get us both away from here.' I smile, as does Sally, but I feel mine is a little bit more confident than hers. We then both nod. I look at my watch.

'Come on, Sal, let's go, or else we'll have trouble before we start.' We all laugh, but Sally knows the seriousness of what I've just said. We all hug each other, and Rose tells us both she will be with us all the way. I trust her. Even though I hardly know her, I can see that I can trust her. As we leave, she taps my shoulder.

'No big pants tomorrow ladies, in fact, no pants at all would be best.' I'm halfway down her path, and I stop and turn around to face her.

'What about disguises? We've not discussed disguises.' I run back to her door so as not to say anything too loudly. Sally follows me. Rose takes us just inside the door.

'Leave that to me,' she says. I'll sort it. Everything will be here tomorrow.'

I feel that adrenalin rush through my body again. I feel alive once more. I feel scared shitless, but wow, do I feel alive too. This is what living must be all about, I tell myself.

chapter seven

It's Friday morning. I wave Jonathan off to work. He suspects nothing. Well, if he does, he doesn't show it. I'm amazed at myself at how calm I am, how calm I was last night. When me and Sally left Rose's house, we were on a high. A nervous high, but a high all the same. By the time we both got home ten minutes later, we were nervous wrecks. All we did on the short journey home was fixate on what we would do if our hubbies came home to find us gone. We were on the verge of calling the whole thing off, but then as I sat with my cuppa on my own after Sally had gone home, I again found that inner strength that I have, that inner strength that I have to now call upon more and more to keep me from falling by the wayside. I just hope that Sally did the same thing. I can't do it without her; I'm sure of that. I need her, and she needs me. That's how it's been with us since we first met since we first realised, we live more or less identical lives. I have my inner strength, but without Sally, it wouldn't be quite strong enough.

I sit and have my breakfast as usual now Jonathan has gone to work. I remain strong. I'm still calm, remarkably so. We are due at Rose's at 9:45am. We will leave at 11:45am and be back at home for midday. Unless Jonathan or Terry suddenly decide to come home unexpectedly before lunchtime, which Jonathan has never done, and Terry has done only once to pick up his diary, we will be fine. That's all I keep telling myself. I am not allowing any negative thoughts to come into my head. *I am worth more than this.* I keep telling myself over and over again, and I am really starting to believe it.

I clear up my breakfast pots and quickly start on the chores Jonathan has left me. I can get half done now and the other half done when I get back. I wonder what we will be doing this morning. *Will Rose ease us in gently?* I've not had much time to stop and think about what we will be doing today. *Will I have to take my clothes off today? Will Rose just be giving us the low down, so to speak?* I feel like I'm starting a new school or a new job. Well, I am, I suppose, starting a new job. I've certainly never done this kind of work before. *Work?* I say out loud. Is it work? Well, I'll be earning money from it, so I suppose it is work at the end of the day.

I rush through the first half of my chores and check my watch. It's just approaching 9:00am. Sally will be here for 9:30am. We agreed to 9:30am so that we won't have time to do anything else other than jump in the car and get there. We don't want to be late, not on our first day in our new jobs, that would not give a good impression. We need to show Rose that we are serious.

I jump in the shower. I shave my vagina, not entirely, but just so it's nice and neat. I have no idea who will be seeing it today. Maybe no one, maybe twenty guys, who knows. I laugh out loud and scream with excitement as I let the hot water run down my back. Wow, this feels good. I feel excited, nervous, anxious, sexy all mixed together, but above all else, I feel alive. I feel as though I am finally living and not just existing in the miserable fucking world I have allowed someone to create for me. I cannot believe I am going to do this. It seems so alien to me, but somehow, I've allowed myself to realise and understand that the only person keeping me here is me.

Yes, I could just go now. I could run away right now and never come back, but I have no money. It's money that is the driving force. That and feeling alive, of course. I want to earn the money so that I can go and make a life for myself elsewhere. That's what I deserve. I do not want to have to go into a shelter for abused women. That is not where I want to be. I want to leave with a shit load of cash and stick two fingers well and truly up to the miserable life I will leave behind. That's what I want. I want it all with Sally, too, though. I want us both to walk away and never look back. Together we are strong. I need her. She needs me. We are two peas in a little pod. Our pod. I just hope we have the strength to see it through.

I get myself dried and put on the sexiest underwear I have. I do not possess anything that's overly sexy, nothing too racy, but I do have good-quality lacy underwear. Jonathan likes me to have nice underwear. Not for me, of course, only for his benefit. I dress and do my make-up. Not too much, just enough to highlight my cheekbones and my lips. I want to make my lips full, but I want to look classy and sexy, not like someone who takes their clothes off for a living. I smile to myself at the irony as I stand up and look at myself in the mirror. I look good, I feel good, I feel powerful. I'm not sure why or how, but I do. I feel powerful and sexy, and confident. Yes, I feel confident. I can't believe it; I feel confident. I can take on the world. I hadn't felt confident since I was at university, since before I met

Jonathan.

Back then, when I was pole dancing, I was the optimum of confidence. I oozed it. It makes me sad to recall how I was. I think of the happy-go-lucky young girl ready to take on the world, and I'm sad. I ask myself how I let him do this to me. Has it really been that long? I hear the front door open. For a split second, fear rushes through my body. *Is it Jonathan?* I think to myself. Then I hear Sally shout.

'It's only me. Are you ready?' I exhale a long breath and puff out my cheeks.

'I'm coming,' I shout back.

I rush downstairs. I don't know why I'm rushing, but I nearly fall down the stairs.

'Where's the fire?' Sally asks as I reach the bottom and steady myself on the handrail.

'It must be my nerves.' I say as I look at her. She looks beautiful. Like me, she looks classy. Minimalistic make-up and a nice dress. We look like we are going out to an office party or for a meal with our husbands. We certainly don't look like two ladies who are going to probably take their clothes off for a camera for the whole world to see.

'Are we dressed right?' Sally asks. 'I mean, I wasn't sure what to wear.'

'Me neither, Sal. Who knows? We'll find out soon, though. Come on, let's go. No time to stand and think.'

I pick up my car keys, grab Sally by the arm and close the front door behind me. I'm shitting myself all of a sudden. I know why. It's because I feel as though I'm doing something wrong just by leaving the house without Jonathan's approval. I need to just go, though. I can't think too much about it. I start the car and look at Sally.

'I hardly slept,' she says, 'Did you?'

I smile. I did sleep well, actually. Surprisingly well. I was amazed at how well I slept. I woke up fairly early, though, around 5:30am, and then I couldn't stop thinking about the day ahead.

'Well did ya'?' Sally asks again.

'Yeah, I did, actually. I slept well.'

'I can't have had more than three hours all in all,' Sally tells me. 'I talked myself in and out of this more times. I'm sure Terry suspects something.'

'How can he, Sal?... you haven't said anything have you?'

'No way, but he's a copper, ain't he. He can smell something fishy a mile off. Every time he looked at me, I felt as though I had a tattoo on my forehead saying *I'm going to be stripping tomorrow.'* I laugh so much; I flick my head back.

'Oh Sally, if we get through this unscathed, we'll have one hell of a tale to tell. Maybe we could write a book or something. It'd make a blinding read.'

We drive past Lanercost Priory and turn up towards Rose's house.

'How are you feeling?' I ask Sally.

'Bloody terrified,' she replies.

'But excited too? I ask.

She laughs. 'Oh yeah, excited too, most definitely excited too, but I'm bloody terrified more.'

'Me too, but that's normal. I'd be more worried if we weren't. Remember, we've never left the house before unless we were told we could. This is huge, bloody massive, in fact, for us, but we are in it together. I can't thank you enough for doing this with me. I need you with me.' Sally smiles. She says nothing. She just smiles an assuring smile that says, *you're welcome.*

I pull up and switch off the engine. I look at the clock in my car. 9;38am. We're early, which is good.

'Come on then. Here we are. The start of the rest of our lives.' I say. Sally gets out without saying a word. We walk through the gate and up the path. Rose opens the door and smiles.

'Morning,' she says.

'Morning,' we reply in unison.

'I'll just get the plates out of the oven,' she says. 'And then I'll pour the wine.'

Sally and I look at each other quite confused as Rose shuts the door.

'Well, you have come to a dinner party, haven't you?'

'Eh?' I ask.

'Well, you look like you have—both of you. You look like you're either going to the local Tory party AGM or a dinner party. Who dressed you two this morning?''Well, we were unsure what to wear.' I say, feeling like I've just been told off at school.

Rose walks through to the kitchen and pours the hot water into three mugs of tea. She says nothing and then puts the mugs on the table. She nods and says, 'Come on, sit down.' We do as we are told. 'Look, you can wear what you want, ladies, but no-one's gonna see those dresses on camera. You'll have to be at least down to your undies for when the camera is rolling, so wearing dresses like that is a waste of time, plus you must want to remain fairly inconspicuous given the secrecy of all this from everyone, including and most importantly your husbands. Am I right?'

We both nod, saying nothing whilst being totally in awe of Rose's presence and confidence.

'Right then, so when was the last time you two went

out looking like you are going to a dinner party at 9:30 in the morning?' I look at Sally, who looks back. We both nod.

'You're right. We stick out like a sore thumb, don't we?'

'Yep, and that's exactly what you want to avoid, so tomorrow, just dress as you would normally as if you were going to the butchers or going to the supermarket. Have your nice underwear on, of course, but outwardly just look completely normal.'

'Gotcha boss,' Sally says as she takes a sip of her tea. We all laugh.

'Right once we've finished our tea, we'll get straight to it. I've set up the laptop upstairs. It's all ready to go. We'll log on and wait for our first client to link up. Once we have one guy online, it will encourage others to do the same. The beauty of this game is that you can have many men watching you all at once, all paying with their credit cards. Sometimes it might only be one guy, but sometimes it can be quite a few.'

'So, what are we going to do?' I ask.

'Initially, you can just be sat there in your underwear, but to keep them online, you need to give them something. At the very least, you'll be taking your underwear off but probably be playing with yourselves, you know, playing with your boobs andpark with your fanny. I have some sex toys up there which you can use too, and if you want to earn the big bucks, you can play with each other or with me if you like.' I spurt my tea all over the table. I look at Sally, who is sat there open-mouthed. I wipe my mouth. 'I thought that might get a reaction.' Rose says, remaining in a serious mood.

'Play with each other?' I say.

'Yep...... look, ladies, this isn't a game. It's a serious business. Now you don't have to, of course, but there are three of us here, and surely you know that most men will pay handsomely to see two or three ladies play with each other and pleasure each other. You didn't think that you were just going to sit there and take ya bra off, did ya?'

I look at Sally. I need some support here. Sally looks back, her eyes still wide. I know I'll have to do the asking.

'Well, we weren't sure, to be honest. Yeah, we knew we'd be getting naked and all that, but erm, we'd not given much thought to doing that sort of thing.'

'Well, as I say, you don't have to, but you'll get away from those husbands of yours a lot quicker if you do. You might even like it.'

My mind is now racing. I'd never thought of doing anything like that, but then I suppose it should have been fairly obvious given what we were going to be doing. I haven't done anything intimate with a female since that fling at Uni. I doubt Sally has ever. I know as much as anyone how men liked to fantasise about women doing things together. It's all most of the lads talked about at college and university. They were always trying to get the women to do things. Some did and thinking about it; they were the ones who were the most popular, especially after they'd put on a bit of a show for the lads. It was mostly just kissing, but that alone made the lads go wild, so thinking back, I'm sure they would have paid good money for a bit more. I never took part in anything like that. My lesbian fling was just that—a fling. An experiment, really. One that I enjoyed, but it's not something I've done since. As I sit here, though, I'm not sure I could ever do that with

Sally or even Rose. Sally's my best mate. I've seen her semi-naked a couple of times, so I know what she's got underneath, but I'm not sure I could do it. I don't think we'll get that far today anyway, so we could probably park that for another time.

'Right then, come on, let's go upstairs. No point in sitting down here any longer.'

My stomach is churning. All the emotions I'd ever felt were here now, well, all the softer emotions anyway, like anxiousness, excitement, those sorts of feelings. I'm not fearful or angry or anything like that. Scared, yes, but scared like you are if you are sat in a plane ready to do a skydive, not that I've ever done a skydive, but I can imagine the adrenalin going through your body, and that is how I fell right now.

We enter what I assume is a spare bedroom. The laptop is open on the dresser with a camera attached to it. The camera is pointing at the bed. On the bed are two dildos and a tube of what looks like some sort of lubrication. I suddenly feel dirty, not dirty as in unclean but dirty as in sexy dirty. I get a wave of emotion run through my knickers. A feeling I don't get very often but the same feeling I had yesterday when I made myself cum in the shower after my trip to the supermarket. I feel excited above anything else. I whisper to Sally, 'I'm all excited, Sal... are you?'

She whispers back. 'I don't know what I am, but whatever it is, it's all new to me. If my legs weren't like jelly, I think I'd run back down those stairs.'

Rose laughs. 'I was just the same, Sally. Remember, I had no one to show me the ropes, so I was scared shitless, but once you get into it, it's like anything else... it just becomes easier.'

'I hope so, Rose. I bloody hope so.'

Rose starts to strip off. I look away. I don't know why; it's just instinctive. Sally does the same. She's now standing in just her bra and knickers. She has a good body for her age. All toned in the right places, and I wonder if I will look ok. I'm ok for my age, but I do have a few wobbly bits here and there. Rose looks like she works out regularly. Her wobbly bits are there but just not as wobbly. I can tell Sally feels the same. Sally is a bit curvier than me, but she has a great pair of boobs on her. I giggle. I'm like a schoolgirl.

'What's so funny?' Sally asks.

'I'm just taking it all in Sal... I mean, what the hell are me and you doing here. We're two bored housewives scared to even think for ourselves normally, and here we are about to take our clothes off and parade our wobbly bits in front of that camera. This time last week, I was probably mopping the kitchen floor.' We all laugh, including Rose.

'I know why you are both here, ladies... to make some bloody money and get you away from those abusive husbands of yours.'

'Too right,' I say, 'This time next year, we'll be out of it all, Sal.'

'It better not take a year. I'm not playing with your fanny for a year,' she says, laughing nervously. I scream with laughter.

'Look at you Sally, all sexy and provocative. Where has this Sally come from?'

'Sod knows, but she's here to stay, I suppose, well whenever we're in your house Rose anyway. It's the only way I'll get through it. You know to put on an act.'

'That's exactly right, Sally,' Rose chips in. 'It's all an act. If you can leave normal Sally at my door and change into this sexy, confident, provocative Sally when you are here, you will find it easier. Pretend you are playing a part in a movie; just be an actress. In fact, we need new identities for you, don't we? I nearly forgot what with all this sexy talk.'

She leaves the room and returns a few seconds later with two wigs, one for me and one for Sally. We put them on. I look different, as does Sally. I stand and look in the mirror.

'Do I look different enough?' I say as I turn round. No one answers me initially. Sally looks in the same mirror. She plays with the wig. She then opens her handbag and takes out two pairs of glasses.

'I brought these, Anna, just in case we needed them.' She throws me a pair. I put them on. Now I look different enough.

'Perfect,' I say as I put my hand on my hips and pose as if I'm posing for a catalogue shoot.

'Perfect,' says Sally as she does the same.

'Right then, we need to decide on your names. Mine is Louise,' says Rose.

'Why Louise?' asks Sally.

'No reason other than my best friend at School was called Louise, and I just kind of liked it.'

'Well, my best friend at School was Jenny. Is that fitting?

'As good as any,' Rose replies. 'It doesn't have to be sexy. Just normal and something different from yourself.'

'Right then, Jenny, it is for me. What about you, Sally?'

'Well, my best friend at school was Suzanne, so I suppose Suzanne will do for me.'

Rose steps forward. 'Here we are the girls, Louise, Jenny, and Suzanne.' She raises her hand as if she has a glass of wine in it. Me and Sally do the same.

'Louise, Jenny, and Suzanne, ' we all say in unison.

'Right, you two stand here.' Rose orders. She points to a spot out of view of the camera. 'There won't be any great training sessions, no hand-holding. Watch what I do, and then when it's your turn, do something similar.' She looks at us, obviously looking for signs of fright. I try to look calm. Inside I'm in knots. I daren't look at Sally.

'The best way to learn ladies is to jump in and start swimming. If you start to sink, I'll throw you some armbands, but you need to get to the other side and quick, then the second length is a lot easier. Make sense?'

I nod. I can see Sally nodding too out of the corner of my eye. It did make sense; the analogy was easy to understand. It really was sink or swim. At the end of the day, we couldn't do any harm, well, only to ourselves if we mess it up, but we're not going to. I'm a good swimmer. I look at Sally.

'Can you swim?' I ask.

'I got my 50-length badge at school.'

'Great, so did I.'

Rose starts to press a few buttons on the laptop. She then sits on the bed. She waits. Nothing. She waits some more. The room is silent. I want to speak, but I daren't. I look at Sally. She looks at me. I raise my eyebrows and stick my bottom lip out. I want to shrug my shoulders too, but I don't. I don't want to put Rose off. Then I hear a ping on the computer. I look at her. She sits up.

She speaks to the laptop.

'Well, I was wondering where you all were today, you naughty boys. I've been waiting here all wet and hot for you guys.' She sits up on her knees and takes off her bra. She rubs her breasts and plays with her nipples. Her tongue is circling around her lips. 'Come on boys, don't be shy. If you want more, then so, do I.'

She clicks the mouse on the bed that must be connected to the computer. The computer makes a click sound. She waits a few seconds; then it pings again.

'That's better boys, I was thinking for a moment there I would have to make myself cum all on my own. Now you know I like to orgasm in front of all of you. Being on my own is not as much fun.'

She lies on her back and slides her hand inside her knickers and rubs herself. She starts to moan. She then sits back up and puts her hand back into her knickers whilst playing with her breasts with her other hand. She does this for about a minute before she takes her knickers off. She is totally shaven down there. She then continues to play with herself. She clicks the mouse again and then stops for a few seconds. The computer pings again, and she continues. She then turns around so that her bottom is facing the camera. She picks up one of the dildos and inserts it into herself from behind. I want to look at Sally, but I daren't. I don't know what I'd do if I did. I might colour up, I might laugh, I might just burst out laughing out loud, I have no idea, so I just look straight ahead. Rose is really going for it with this dildo and is moaning and groaning like someone who is about to explode. I want to put my hands down my own knickers as I feel so sexy and horny. I just want to rip my clothes off and give myself a huge seeing to, but again I can't. I'm transfixed. Rose has now turned back round and is lay legs spread facing the camera. She has turned the dildo on to make a humming sound, with the end making a circling motion. She is now screaming in ecstasy, and from what I can make out, is about to finish. She is breathing heavily, has put the dildo down, and is just using her fingers. She lets out one final scream and then takes her hand away. She is still breathing heavily but manages to sit up. She looks straight into the camera and looks into it and smiles.

'Now, if you liked that boys, I'll be back in half an hour, and I may not be alone.' She winks at the camera and double clicks the mouse. She then looks at me and Sally. 'What you reckon then? Still think you can do it?'

chapter eight

'Bloody hell Rose, that was unbelievable. I mean, just unbelievable. Wasn't it Sal?' I look round to face Sally. The first time I've looked at her since that computer first pinged. She looks mesmerised, in some sort of trance. 'What did you think, Sally?' I ask again. She turns to look at me and then back at Rose.

'I'm speechless, bloody speechless,' she says. Rose gets up as if nothing has happened and walks out of the room. I hear her running the tap in the bathroom.

'What you reckon? I ask Sally.

'I can't do that, Anna. I wouldn't know where to start. How to start, I mean, could you?'

'I reckon I could, yeah. I was that excited, I was about to jump on there myself; in fact, I reckon I could right now. If I don't have an orgasm here before we go, I'll sure as hell need one when I get home. Didn't you feel the same? You must have done Sal. How can you watch something like that and not feel like you want to have a go? I'm telling ya I could have jumped on that bed and put that dildo up Rose myself.' Sally bursts out laughing.

I now remember how I felt at Uni when I was pole dancing. The provocative dances. The men lusting after me, whilst all the time I was in control. It always amazed me how powerful I used to feel. I feel that now. All of those emotions and feelings have come back.

Where have I been all these years, I ask myself.

'Bloody hell, Anna, I'd have paid good money myself to see that. Could you honestly?'

'Too right I could. This is what living is all about, Sally, not stuck at home, petrified to breathe without someone telling you to. I was still wondering beforehand whether I could do it, but I've got so much adrenalin running through my body at the moment I know for sure I can.' Sally paces the bedroom.

'Bloody hell, you're hooked, aren't you?' she says.

'Yep, I'm doing this, Sal, and if you know what's good for you, so will you. Don't let me do it on my own. I need you, Sally, and you need me too.'

Rose comes back into the room. She's been washing her dildo, and herself no doubt. 'I heard what you've just been saying. It sounds like you are up for this, Anna.'

I look at her and immediately say, 'I am. 100% I am. How much did you make in that ten-minute slot?' She walks to the laptop and taps a few buttons.

'£317.'

'What... £317?' shouts Sally

'Yep... here take a look.' She shows Sally the screen. 'There it is £317 deposited into my screen account. What can't speak can't lie.'

'Is that straight into your bank account?'

'Yep. Straight in, no messing.'

'Fuck me,' Sally says, slowly as if thinking as she says it.

'So, what do you think now?' I ask.

'I'm in, fuck it, we have to be Anna, don't we? With money like that, we can't not be.'

'We could make £500 a day each ladies without trying. If we pushed it, we could make a grand a day each in the two hours we have allowed ourselves. Easy.'

'I don't think I could have that many orgasms in two hours,' Sally quips.

'You don't have to. You fake most of them.'

'Were you faking it there then?'

'No, that was real. My first of the day usually is, after that, I'll fake a couple and then finish off the day with another real one. Great work, you know if you can do it.'

'How often do you normally do this then?' I ask.

'Three times a week was my norm. How much do you want to make before you bugger off?'

'Twenty-five grand,' I say.

'We could do that in four months easily if we try hard enough. You could be out of here for May. You'll have to trust me, though, with the money side of it all unless you want to open a new account with all three of us as on the account.'

'There's no way I could get away with opening a new account. Jonathan would find out for sure. He mixes with all the bankers around here.'

'Same with Terry. We trust you, don't we, Anna?'

'Yep. We'll have to. We know where you live anyway,' I say sarcastically.

'Listen, I have my money. I could bugger off now, so I'm not in it for the money anymore. I'm in it for you guys and to see the look on Jonathan's face when you've buggered off. That'll be enough for me. Anyway, your turn, ladies. Who's going first with me?'

I look at Sally. I know she wants me to jump in here.

'Me,' I say.

'Right then, down to your undies and sit on the bed. I'll show you briefly what I want you to do, but only briefly as it needs to look natural, not staged, so you need to let your inhibitions run away with you once the camera rolls, ok?'

'OK!'

chapter nine

I'm standing in the middle of Rose's spare bedroom in just my bra and knickers. They're as sexy as it gets for me, and Rose remarks that they look nice. She tells me that I look good for my age and have a body that the guys will love. I'm not sure if she's just being nice and trying to install some confidence in me, but I take the compliments anyway. I look to Sally.

'What do you reckon?' I ask.

'You look great. I just wish I had your body.'

'Can you see any bruises?'

'Maybe one or two on your thigh, and there's one still visible on your left rib cage, but it's only because I know they are there. I don't think they'd be visible on camera, that's for sure. What do you think?' Sally looks to Rose for reassurance. She walks over to me and looks at the bruises.

'Falling downstairs?' she asks me as she raises her eyebrow to emphasise the sarcasm.

'Yes,' I say.

Rose shakes her head, 'Listen, you two, I could show you some right monsters who do this for a living and make a shed load of money, so believe me, you two have no worries. Don't get me wrong, you'll not be everyone's cup of tea, but then again, who is? Some men like big women, some like women who used to be men, some like women who look so false it's hard to tell if they are real or not, but a lot of men like fairly ordinary-looking beauties like you two and I say ordinary in the nicest possible way. Not that you are plain and boring but just that you look like many women that these men will fantasise about in their everyday lives. You, to them, are like the women at work that they can never get to shag. You are their fantasy for the few minutes they are wanking themselves silly over Brenda or Louise whom they desperately want to shag. Louise and Brenda will be ordinary women just like you two, so get ya'self up here on this bed, Anna, and I will give you a five-minute quick rundown on what to do.'

I get up on the bed. I'm shaking a little, but Rose puts her hand on my shoulder.

'Don't worry, the next twenty minutes or so will be the most nerve-racking it's ever going to be for you in this game, so get through this, and it'll be plain sailing afterwards. You can then enjoy watching Sally go through the same emotions.' She smiles, I smile. I look at Sally; she's not smiling. She looks traumatised. I look away. I feel ok.

'Right then, the camera is not yet on,' Rose tells me. 'So, watch me and do what I do but do it like you mean it. There's no second chance, Anna. You've got to take a deep breath; pretend you've got those big girl pants on and keep going and think of being free.' I take a deep breath.

'Ok, I'm ready,' I say.

'When you start to perform for real, and you hear a ping, that means that someone is watching and is paying with their card. It's game on. Sometimes I click to take me off camera and wait for another ping. That means multiple people are watching. Pings mean money.'

Rose then turns to face the cameras and provocatively talks into it. I do the same. She uses her tongue; I do the same. She takes off her bra and plays with her breasts. I pause, then I take another deep breath, and I do the same. She picks up her dildo. I look behind me and see mine that she's left for me. I do the same. She puts it between her breasts. I do the same. Whatever she does, I do. We end up sitting on the bed together. I'm playing with myself and am having to stop myself from enjoying it too much. I blank out everything around me as best I can. I dare not look at Sally, but despite everything, I cannot help but feel invigorated. Like I used to feel. I find it surprisingly easy to do what I'm doing in front of both Rose and Sally. In fact, for a brief moment, I have my eyes shut, and I forget where I am. I know I could easily continue and have a full-blown orgasm here and now. I hear a ping. I open my eyes; Rose has got off the bed and is out of shot of the camera. She has the mouse in her hand. I realise I am now on camera; men are watching me; they must be. That's what that ping means; Rose said so a while ago. I feel my heart racing. I feel adrenalin rush around my body. This is a fight or flight moment. I can either fight and carry on or jump off this bed and finish my porn career before it's even started. I think of Jonathan. I think of the 'fall' down the stairs. I think of the iron near my face. I think of how he makes out that I was the one who decided to abort our unborn child.

I decide to stay. I sit up and look at the camera. I pause for a moment. I'm on the verge of pausing for too long. I can see Rose in my wider vision.

'Come on, gentleman,' I say, 'you can see I'm a newbie. My name's Jenny, and if you want to see more, you'll have to give me more.'

Rose clicks the mouse. The screen goes off. I wait. Then I hear a ping, another ping, then another, then another. I'm excited. I turn into Jenny. Jenny is the one who can carry on and do this. I'm excited. Jenny is excited, and Anna is excited. I sit up and insert the dildo up as far as it can go. It feels great. I'm not faking this. Bloody hell, that feels good. I can hear more pings. I insert the dildo from behind. Then I feel a hand. I look round, and it's Rose. She takes over. She's naked. She's inserting the dildo into me. I'm screaming in ecstasy. I like it. I remember how I felt when I was at university. All I can hear are pings. I then cum and flop onto the bed. My breathing is so fast and heavy. I lie face down, my face buried in the duvet. I feel embarrassed all of a sudden. I want to look up, but I know I will be bright red. I can't believe what I've just done. My breathing starts to slow down. I lift my head and look around. The laptop screen is blank. I'm off camera. I look at Sally; I'm still breathing a little heavy. She bursts out laughing. She laughs so hard that I, too, burst out laughing. We laugh hard for what seems like an age. I haven't laughed so hard in so long. In fact, I don't think I've ever laughed this much with Jonathan. Ever. We both eventually stop. I sit there in bewilderment.

'Bloody hell Sally, I can't believe what I've just done.'

'Me neither, Anna, me neither. I was about to jump on too. You know what you said when Rose was doing her bit on her own, how you felt all horny and wanted to give yourself an orgasm? Well, that's how I feel right now.'

'Well, it'll be your turn soon, Sally, so hold that feeling. It'll feel ten times better if you hold off for a while. Anyway, ladies, £788 we made just then... look, here it is £788.'

'Fuck me,' Sally said again slowly, 'so what's that up to so far today?'

'£1105 so far,' Rose says, smiling.

'Fuck me,' Sally says yet again, very slowly. £1105, that's over £350 each today.'

'Yep, and there's still you to go, Sally. Shall we get a cup of tea, ladies, and have a rich tea with it? We will soon be rich after all?' Rose suggests. She looks at Sally and laughs.

'You make me laugh, Sally, you really do,' she says.

'Why, what do I do?'

'The way you swear. It's just so funny. I'd have never had you down as a swearer, but the way you say, 'Fuck me,' very slowly with your eyes so wide is really funny. I like you, Sally. You make me laugh.'

'She swears like a bloody trooper at times,' I say. Sally colours up a little. She knows what she's like. We all swear from time to time, but Sally, as Rose says, is just so funny.

'Well, if I make you laugh, then that's fine with me. It's how I am, and if anyone doesn't like it, then they can piss off,' she says mockingly. We all laugh. It feels good to laugh. Really good, in fact.

'I'll go and clean myself,' I say as I get off the bed. 'I'll be down in a sec.'

I go into the bathroom and start to have a wash. Rose comes in. She has her dressing gown on. I see her through the mirror on the wall.

'I hope you were ok with that?' she says. 'I just thought it would be a good earner, you know, after so many pings.'

I splash my face and dry it with the towel. 'I was a little taken by surprise, to be honest, but yeah, it was fine. I felt a little embarrassed afterwards when I was laying there, but that's the game, I suppose.'

'No, it's not, I should have checked with you first beforehand, but then you'd have run a mile.'

'Probably, but listen, no issue, I enjoyed it. It gave me a thrill, and that's the best orgasm I have ever had by a long way, so I'm happy.'

I turn back round to look at her through the mirror. 'Are you a lesbian then?' I ask. She laughs.

'No. I've dabbled a bit in the past, you know, tried it, but no, I wouldn't say I'm a lesbian, but then again, I do get a real thrill out of it. I certainly enjoyed that just then.'

She turns around and walks out of the bathroom, and I carry on getting washed. I finish and wrap a towel around me and think to myself how I enjoyed it too, even when I knew it was Rose doing it. Like Rose, I am not a lesbian, but again like her, I can sure as hell enjoy it when it happens. I go downstairs to have my tea and biscuit. I look at the clock on the wall. It's 10:55am. We've been here for an hour and 15 minutes, and in that time, I've watched Rose perform, performed myself, and had a bit of a lesbian romp live on camera for the whole of the internet to see. Do I feel alive? Fucking hell, I do.

chapter ten

I pull up outside my house. Neither me nor Sally has spoken a word since we left Lanercost. Sally did her bit, she did well, a little nervous, and to be honest, it showed in places, but we made just shy of £1500 today, a few coppers off £500 each in one day. Well, one morning, to be precise, in less than two hours. I cannot believe how easy it was to make that much money. It's just gone ten past twelve. I wanted to be back for midday, but ten past is not too bad considering what we've just been up to.

Me and Sally just sit there in the car, in silence. I think the enormity of what we have just done is dawning on us; it certainly is for me. I look at her, and she stares straight ahead.

'You ok?' I ask. Silence. 'Sally, are you ok?' She looks at me, expressionless. I'm anxious all of a sudden. She stares at me for around five seconds, but it seems like a lifetime.

'Say something, Sal,' I say without averting my gaze and without changing my expression. Sally just stares, and then I see the glimpse of a little smile. Sally then bursts out laughing, a big full-blown laugh. She has tears streaming down her face. She is laughing uncontrollably. I muster a little laugh, but I'm still anxious and quite nervous. I'm not sure what kind of laugh this is. Is it a real laugh because she's happy or finds something funny, or is it a sinister, sarcastic laugh where she cannot believe what she's just done and is going to finish it before it's really begun? I'm still laughing a little, but it's controlled.

'What's up?' I ask, 'Talk to me.'

'I can't,' she says in between laughing. 'It's just so bloody unreal.'

'I know it is, but what's so funny?'

'Us, bloody hell Anna, us. What we just did. Do you realise what we just did up there in that sleepy little hamlet, eh?... do you?'

'Well yeah, of course, I do, but I'm not sure what you are saying.'

Sally finally manages to stop laughing. She wipes the tears from her cheeks and smudges her lipstick. She looks like a clown with her bright red lipstick smudged across her face. She's breathing heavily.

'Wooh!' she says as she takes a deep breath in and exhales loudly and hard. 'Wooh,' she says again. She then looks at me and places her left hand on my cheek. 'Anna Fox,' she says. 'I am doing this for you. Yes, I want to get out of this shit life we lead as much as you do, but I would never do this without you. I would not do this for anyone else I know, but as I have said to you more than once, if you're going, then so am I, so I need you to promise me one thing.'

'What's that?' I ask.

'That now we are on this road, we can never get off it. I am not, even for you, going to proceed with this if we do not go all the way. I couldn't cope with doing all of this to back out further down the line, so promise me, promise me, Anna, that we will see it through if you continue to take me down this path. We will get away; we will get our freedom. Tell me we will do it, and it will be worth it. Just promise me that, Anna, just promise me that you will go the distance, 'cos if you do, then I'm with you. Just promise me you won't back out partway down that path.'

I have never seen Sally like this before, never heard her speak with such passion and assurance. Sally is, for the first time in our friendship, being assertive. She's making demands. She never does that, but I like it. As I sit here looking at her, feeling her palm on my face, I feel tears welling up in my eyes. I put my right hand over hers as it presses against my cheek.

'I promise,' I say, 'I promise.' Sally smiles as I say it. We then hold hands across the gear stick. I wipe the tears from my face and wonder if I, too, now look like a clown. We laugh and giggle.

'So, what were you laughing at?' I ask.

'At the fact that we will soon be free, but more so at how we are going to do it. It was a nervous laugh, but now you've promised me I'm no longer nervous. I need your strength Anna, I need it to get through this, but I know you'll be there with me at the end.' I look at my watch. It's twenty past twelve. Reality kicks in. 'Shit, come on, we need to go in. Look at the time.'

We both quickly undo our seatbelts and jump out of the car. We instantly and automatically check all around us. I have no idea what we are looking for, but I suppose it's because we know we're doing something we shouldn't, and that's not just having a bit of a lesbian romp for money, but more so because we are out of our houses without permission. I feel all nervous and anxious again. I want to get in the house. I need to get in.

'See you later,' I say as we turn on our heels.

'Yes, I'll be round in a bit, just as normal. I need to

be normal again,' Sally replies.

'Ok, see you in a bit,' I say as I walk towards the door.

I walk in. Silence. I don't know why but I just expected Jonathan to be here. He never is at this time, but that guilty feeling and paranoia just take over. I'm panting, more so, I think, than I was on that bed an hour ago. I feel like I'm hyperventilating. I look at myself in the hallway mirror. I laugh at myself as I do look like a clown, not as much as Sally did but bad enough.

I quickly gather myself and get on with finishing the remainder of the chores Jonathan has set for me. I only have the tiles in the bathroom to wipe down and the downstairs windows inside to clean. They do not need doing, but I cannot risk not doing them; he will know otherwise. I fill the bucket with warm soapy water and get a clean cloth and remember that today is Friday or, as Jonathan calls it, sometimes 'fun time Friday.'

He likes to watch a film on a Friday night, snuggled up with a glass of wine. It's just something we have always done. It used to be something I looked forward to, that I genuinely looked forward to, snuggling up next to Jonathan and watching a film together with a few nibbles on the table. That was a long time ago, though, or at least it seems a long time ago now. Friday nights are still generally just the same, but the genuine affection and loving aspect have gone, well, from me certainly. I play the game, of course, and snuggle into him, and sometimes I forget how things have changed and find myself enjoying the closeness of the moment. I can sometimes forget what he is like, and I am reminded of what I loved about him. Sometimes I reminisce about why I fell in love with him. It makes me happy for a brief moment, but then I remember what a bastard he is.

I still enjoy watching the films and enjoy a glass of wine, but it's not the same. It never will be. Well, tonight will be just the same, I suppose, but I think I'll struggle to concentrate on the film what with today's events running through my mind. *That won't be good,* I think to myself, as Jonathan will ask me about what is happening, just to make sure I'm concentrating on it and in his head to make sure I'm enjoying it. What he never realises is that I'd enjoy the films a lot better if I weren't anxious about getting something wrong. If I do, then he just turns it off and sulks. He says I mustn't be enjoying it.

I cannot think about that now; I have too much going around my mind. I'm nervous about him coming home tonight. I know it's just because I'm convinced that he'll suspect something or worse, that he'll know something. I tell myself that he can't unless Rose has tipped him off or if he came home when I was out and decided to go back to work and sort me out later tonight. I know that would not be the case, though. There is no way he would do that. He would never go back to work if he came home and I was unexpectedly out, so I know that would not have happened. I stop washing the tiles for a moment and think about Rose. *She wouldn't tell him, would she?* I say to myself as I stand there looking at myself in the mirror. 'Why would she?' I ask myself out loud. My reflection looking back at me is shaking her head *no way,* she says. That's right; I tell myself as I come back into the room and stop having a conversation with myself through the bathroom mirror. I tell myself the same thing as I carry on cleaning. Over and over again, I tell myself, *Rose would not betray us. She hates Jonathan.*

I finish my chores in between talking to myself. I put the kettle on and have a nice cup of tea as I wait for Sally to come over. I sit down at the kitchen table, slurp my tea, and think about the events earlier today... again. Wow, how I loved what I did. I know that I am running a very dangerous line and playing a very dangerous game, and I also know that I will have these bouts of self-doubt and doubts about Rose. I also know that if Jonathan finds out before me and Sally escape then he would probably kill me, but I above everything, above all that, I know that if I do not do this, I will regret it for the rest of my life. If Jonathan kills me, will I regret it? *No,* I tell myself, *I'll be dead, so how can I?* Will I regret it if he finds out and beats me to a pulp?... *maybe but only for a short while,* I remind myself, but I know I will regret it for the rest of my life if I don't do it as I would never get another chance. This is my only chance. My one chance to get money together and to be free of him forever.

Later that evening, Jonathan comes in from work. He seems ok, just the usual Jonathan. I have already laid his casual clothes out for him on the bed and put his deodorant and aftershave next to his clothes. He comes down from his shower and kisses me on the cheek.

'How was your day?' he asks. I tense up. I know why. I had prepared for that question for the last hour or so, preparing and practicing to stay unmoved by it, but as usual, human behaviour takes over, and I tense up. He doesn't seem to notice. He turns away as he says it.

'Oh, fine, just the usual,' I say.

'And what was that?' he asks. I turn around. He is

stood by the sink, leaning back into it slightly with his ankles crossed and his arms folded. He looks intrigued. I feel adrenalin shoot through my body. I try to look calm. I mean, why wouldn't I just be calm.

'Oh, just my chores, a cuppa with Sally as usual and then waiting for my lovely husband to come home. It's fun time Friday after all,' I say with a smile, trying my very best to look casual and as much like the loving wife as I can.

'Why is my checked grey suit still in my wardrobe?' he asks. I drop the wine glass I am holding. It drops to the floor and smashes. *Shit,* I think to myself, *shit, shit, shit.* I was supposed to take his suit to the dry cleaners today. He told me two days ago on Wednesday to take it on Friday. He does this on purpose, tells me in advance to do things on certain days. It had to be today, just like he asked, not yesterday, not tomorrow, but today. I look at the calendar on the wall. There it is, in my handwriting, *take grey checked suit to Dry Cleaners.*

'Well?' he asks again. His tone is sharp. I now know the reason for his frosty demeanour. It has nothing to do with him knowing anything about what I did today. It is solely because I have not taken his suit as he ordered me to do. Yes, as he ordered me. He didn't ask me like most husbands would. He ordered me. I haven't done it. I'm in trouble. My mind is racing, but I have to answer him.

'I, err, I...' I stutter. I cannot think of what to say. I cannot think of an excuse. 'I, err...' I stutter again. I'm now shaking. My hands are shaking. I cannot stop them. I can't think. My mind is a complete blank. He walks over to me. I'm still shaking. He stands in front of me and strokes my cheek, gently, downward strokes. I can hear the broken glass beneath his feet. I look down and see that he has no shoes on, just his socks. I feel a tear run down my face. He wipes it away.

'There there,' he says, 'don't cry, I don't like it when you cry. It makes me sad. You don't want me to be sad, do you?' he says whilst still stroking my face. I shake my head. He bends down and wipes the sole of his left foot. He has blood on his hands. He wipes it on my face.

'Look what you've done,' he says, shaking his head. 'My feet are bleeding. Why do you do this to me?' I don't know what to do. My breathing is heavy and fast. 'Answer me, you fucking bitch,' he shouts. 'Fucking answer me. Why do you do this to me?'

'I'm sorry,' I say in desperation. 'I think I must have just forgotten. I'm sorry, please forgive me?' I say in a rather pathetic way. He steps away from me. I hear the broken glass again. He then pushes the broken glass together so that it forms a small pile.

'Take off your tights,' he tells me, 'NOW!' I do as he asks. I take off my tights. I'm now standing there in my bare feet. 'Jump up and down on that broken glass,' he orders me.

'Jonathan, please?' I say, 'please don't do this?'

'Now,' he says... 'Jump up and down on the fucking spot on that broken glass. It's your own fault Anna,' he says. 'It was you who didn't go to the dry cleaners, not me. You only have yourself to blame. You have to learn, Anna. It's for your own good, now jump.'

The laughter of earlier has gone. I'm not Jenny anymore. I'm not Anna from university. I'm Anna, Jonathan's wife. Jonathan's pathetic wife. I think of what I did today and how I could not believe I did it. I stand here hating myself as I know I am going to do exactly what he asks. This is the real me. I'm not Jenny. I have the strength of character to fuck myself with a dildo on camera for the whole world to see, yet I do not have the confidence or the strength of character to tell Jonathan to go and fuck himself. Why is that, I ask myself? I wish I knew.

'NOW!' he shouts.

I jump up and down on the broken glass. Jonathan stands there, timing me with his watch. I jump for one minute. My feet are bleeding and are sore. I stand there looking at my feet. Jonathan walks over to me. He takes my face in his hands as if nothing has happened.

'Now go and have a shower, get cleaned up, and I'll choose a film. What do you fancy, a comedy?' He says lovingly.

I turn to walk away towards the stairs. I do not answer. This annoys him.

'Use the downstairs shower,' he shouts. 'I don't want any blood on the stairs.' I turn round and walk towards the downstairs bathroom, the bathroom I was in cleaning this afternoon. I do not say anything. I have a shower and wash my feet carefully. They stop bleeding. The bits of glass were fairly small, so after I have washed them, they do not look too bad. I open the door and find a pair of my socks outside on the floor. I assume these are to wear whilst I walk upstairs. I put them on and go up to my bedroom to get changed. I can hear the TV and assume Jonathan is choosing a film. I come back down and find he has cleaned up the glass and has poured me a glass of red wine.

He looks up and pats the sofa next to him like most loving husbands will do this very night. The difference is most loving husbands will not have made their wives jump up and down on broken glass.

'Come on, fun time Friday,' he says. I stand there and look at him and find that I am genuinely impressed at his ability to act as though nothing has happened. My feet are sore, it hurts to walk, I still have a bit of pain from when he pushed me down the stairs, but I walk over and sit on the sofa next to him. He puts his arm around me and pulls me in. He kisses the top of my head. 'You'll take my suit tomorrow, won't you darling?' he says.

'Yes, of course, I promise,' I say.

We watch the film. I cannot even tell you what it's called. It must be a comedy as Jonathan is laughing out loud. I take note, though, and I answer his one question. Only one question, he must feel a little guilty. I divide £25,000 by £500 many times in my head. The answer every time is fifty. That's roughly fifty mornings at Rose's, three times a week, approximately seventeen weeks, which is around four months. That's the middle of May. I tell myself I can wait that long. I'll have to. Four months for the rest of my life is nothing. As I sit here snuggled into my bastard of a husband, I think of Simon, the man of my dreams. How I wish I were snuggled into Simon, but I'm not; he is just a fantasy, someone I make up in my head, but as I put thoughts of Simon to one side, I'm more determined than ever. I will play the game; I will give the men who pay the money what they want, but if I've learned one lesson tonight, it's always to check the calendar. *Always check the calendar,* I tell myself.

chapter eleven

Monday 21st March 2016

I stand on the scales. 9st 6Ib. Perfect. Jonathan is standing over me as usual. I have this off to a fine art now, but that's because I'm in control of my life, I suppose. Jonathan has no idea at all what we do, me and Sally, and neither does Terry either. We play the game so well now that I cannot believe that I am so confident. I don't let it show, of course, as most of the time I am with Jonathan, I am still pathetic Anna who cowers at his every move. Yes, I still live the same controlled life, still the same pathetic life, but and this is a big but, over the past two months, Sally and I have gone up to Rose's every Monday, Wednesday, and Friday like clockwork and performed our stuff in her bedroom. We are making more money than we thought we would as we now do threesomes; yes, you've heard that right... we do threesomes, and you know what, the punters love it. They cannot get enough; we are a bloody internet sensation. We dress up in all sorts of disguises, even Rose, as I don't think she wants any more recognition than she has had previously, and the best bit is that I don't think anyone would recognise us.

I walk around Brampton doing my little shops and say hello to all the nice people, and I really cannot help but wonder if their husbands are watching us. I know that's naughty of me, but I cannot help it. We leave at 9:15 am on the three mornings, and we are back home for twelve o clock. We've been doing it for over two months now except for a week three weeks ago when me and Jonathan went away for five days on a Monday to Friday break. We debated whether Sally and Rose should do it on their own or whether we should have a break for the week, but Sally said without me, she couldn't do it, so we had the break. You should have seen the response on our first day back the week after. There were more pings on that first Monday morning back than there were at the National Ping Ping championships. It was quite unbelievable, but what a thrill it was, and even though I am a nervous wreck on the drive back home, every time, I would not change it for anything. This has really made my life worth living again. Don't get me wrong I want to get away just like we said once we have the money. I don't want to be doing this forever, but boy has it been enjoyable. I would never have imagined three months ago that I would be having sex with other women, and my best mate at that, all for money... never, but I am. I have found myself wondering if I am a lesbian because I do enjoy the sex with Sally and Rose, but the thought of once I get away being in a relationship with a woman full time doesn't quite sit comfortably with me. I think once it's over, I'll find my very own Simon and leave this all behind me. Will I tell my Simon about it all? I don't know we'll have to see.

'There you go, darling,' I say as I serve Jonathan his breakfast. He smiles and takes a slurp of his tea. Since the episodes of falling down the stairs and making me dance on broken glass, Jonathan has been quite aggressive towards me. I don't know why but I take it as I know I am in control. I know it will not be forever. I could go now, but the money would run out quickly, and to be honest, I want to stick to the plan. Twenty-five grand at least, if not more, and I think there will be quite a bit more, but as yet, me and Sally have not decided what we are going to do. We keep talking about it and coming up with plans, some of them safe plans like moving to the Shetland Isles and some of them ludicrous plans like moving to L.A. and making it big over there, but nothing has really struck the right chord. As I keep telling Sally, *we need a firm plan that suits us both,* but as yet, we haven't found it.

Jonathan finishes his breakfast, and I pass him his polished shoes. He slips them on and bends over to kiss me on the cheek. As he does, I glance at the clock; it's 7:48am. He turns and walks away without a word. He does this sometimes. Sometimes he says goodbye and makes a big thing of saying how he'll see me tonight, and other times he does this. It used to make me nervous, but now I am used to it. I still say goodbye to him, though. I have to. If I didn't, I'd be in trouble.

'Bye darling,' I say as he picks up his suit jacket. He stops and looks in the mirror and tilts his head to one side and then the other. He then stares at himself for a few seconds. He then turns to look at me. I know what to do. I get up and walk over and straighten his tie again for him. He rechecks in the mirror and then walks out of the door. I stand on the doorstep and watch him as he drives away—nothing, not a word, not a wave, nothing. I wait until he is out of sight and then stick two fingers up in his direction and turn to walk back inside. I now look at the list of chores I have been left today; it's the usual stuff with one notable exception. He wants me to go to the travel agent and get some holiday brochures on Croatia. 'Croatia!' I say to myself out loud. *Why Croatia?* I think to myself. I shrug my shoulders and go to make my breakfast before I quickly do some of the chores and before I go to Rose's. I decide that I will call at the travel agents in Brampton on my way back and pick it up. *No wait,* I think to myself, if I do that, then Sally will be with me, and that would be very out of the ordinary for me. I'll have to drop her back and then go.

I start the engine up and drive away from Rose's. Sally is doing her lipstick in the vanity mirror on the passenger's side of the car. 'Pretty good day again,' I say as I look over my shoulder for any oncoming traffic. I have no idea why I do that every time as there has never been one single car pass us either way on Rose's road out of Lanercost. It is such a quiet road that no one ever comes this way.

'Yeah, I'm jiggered,' Sally says as she shuts the mirror and smacks her lips before putting the lipstick in her handbag. 'How much have we got now then, between us?' she asks.

'We have around £15,400 each so far. I keep asking Rose if she wants anything for expenses, you know, for electricity and that, but she's adamant she's ok and doesn't want anything. She's been really good, you know.'

'She has, bless her. I really like her.' Sally quips.

'I know,' I say, laughing. 'A bit too much, I'd say.'

'Give over, will ya, any way you can talk, you are mesmerised by that bosom of hers sometimes, I can tell. Mind you, they are a good pair. I'll give you that.' I feel myself colouring up. 'Bloody hell, you've gone red Anna Fox, I'm right, aren't I?'

'Are you hell as like, I just get a bit embarrassed when we talk about what we do, not with the stuff for the camera, but you know with each other.' Sally smiles at me.

'It's a good way to make a living, though,' she says as she winks. I laugh.

'What you like, eh! I love it, how bubbly you are, you know. You really make me happy.' Sally pats my knee. She says nothing, but I know she feels the same.

'I've got to go and pick up a travel brochure, well a few actually from the travel agents in town on Croatia,' I say.

'Croatia?'

'I know that's what I thought. Never been, have you?'

'I have actually, went to Dubrovnik a few years ago. It's beautiful, really nice, very old city with loads of history and culture, very clean too.'

'Jonathan must be thinking of us going, mind you, if he doesn't hurry up, he'll be going on his own,' I say.

'Are we going now then?' Sally asks.

'Err...well, to be honest, I was going to drop you back first and then go.'

'Oh, come on, we can go now, can't we? It'll only take a minute or two, and we're practically passing the door. I can pick a couple up and look through them over our cuppa later. I can then drop a few subtle hints to Terry. I could do with a few days away. You had yours, didn't you a couple of weeks ago?'

'I did, only a break in the Lakes though, not exactly far away. Nice enough, though.' I turn off into the main street towards the travel agents.

'I knew you would,' Sally says. 'Makes sense,

doesn't it?'

'Don't hang about though Sally, things like this make me nervous. If we see anyone, we'll be in trouble.'

'Look, you can park right outside the door, there look. We've only got to walk in and straight out again. No one will see us. It's dead.' Sally looks around through the windscreen.

It is quiet today as it's a Monday. I look around, and there's only a guy walking his bulldog and a couple looking in a shop window. I get out, and Sally does the same. We go in and start to browse the shelves.

'Can I help you?' A young lady asks. She only looks around 20 years old, long blonde hair, fake tan, fake nails, and a top lip that has definitely had some work. She looks like the kind of young girl that would look so much better without all the fake stuff on her.

'Yes, I'm after some brochures on Croatia, please,' I say. The young girl gets up from behind her desk and walks over to me, and smiles.

'Looking to book soon, are you?' she asks, assuming I'm going to say yes.

'Not sure really, I'm just going to take them home to look through with my husband. We've not been before, but we've heard it's nice.' I say, smiling back at her. She stretches up and takes two brochures from the shelf, and hands them to me.

'These are both good, but if you are looking for something a little more exclusive, I have this one over here,' she says as she walks to the front of the shop. She looks through a few brochures and then says. 'I'll just pop into the back. I won't be a minute.' She walks away and through a door that is slightly ajar. Her perfume lingers in the air. I try and place it as I know I have smelt it before, but I cannot recall where.

It smells nice, though. I look to Sally, who has three brochures in her hand. 'What you got there?' I ask.

'Two on the Channel Islands and one on the Western Isles of Scotland,' she says. 'Always fancied Jersey, don't know why but just fancy going there.'

Another lady pops her head up. She is quite a bit older, early forties but very natural. Nothing fake about her at all. 'Jersey is lovely,' she says. 'Quiet but beautiful.'

'Thank you,' Sally says, looking quite nervous all of a sudden. I think it may be as she now knows that someone knows she's here even though I'm sure she doesn't know this lady. The young girl returns with another brochure and passes it to me.

'These are quite exclusive apartments and villas in here,' she says. 'Very modern and certainly a cut above.'

'Thank you, thank you very much,' I say as I turn to leave.

'That's no problem. If there's anything else we can help with, please do not hesitate to ask.' the young girl says with a lovely big smile as we walk towards the door.

We get outside, and I put my hand in my pocket to get my keys out. 'Anna,' I hear a voice say. I know instantly it is Mrs Simpson. 'Every bloody time,' I say under my breath as I look up at Sally. I unlock the car with the remote-control function on the key, and Sally gets in. I open my door, but at the same time, I turn around to smile and greet Mrs Simpson. 'Hi,' I say as I throw the brochures onto Sally's lap.

'Hello dear, how are you, keeping well, I hope?' she says with a smile and an underlying tone that reminds me again that she's no fool and probably knows more than I would care to admit.

'Fine thank you, are you? I reply.

'Ooh yes dear. I'm always fine, you know me?'

'I do Mrs Simpson yes, I do, so what are you up to today?' I ask, knowing that I need to be nice and calm and try and move this conversation on as quickly as I can. I am starting to get nervous, too now.

'Ooh nothing much, just having my walk out. I'm going to sit on my bench and watch the world go by, mind you there's not much world to watch today is there. It's very quiet, but then it's amazing what you can see,' she says with a little devilment in her voice. 'Mind you that's a rarity in itself,' she continues whilst pointing to something behind me. I look behind me to see to my horror a police car is pulling up beside my car and the policeman driving it is looks like he's going to speak to Sally. I can see from his lapel that he is a Chief Inspector. I know this from what Sally has told me. Her Terry has two stars on each lapel, but a Chief Inspector has three on each. I turn to Mrs Simpson.

'I've got to go, Mrs Simpson, err bye, good to talk to you.' I get in the car and slam the door. I can see Mrs Simpson has not walked away. I can hear the policeman talking to Sally.

'Holiday brochures, eh?' he says quite loudly. 'Hey Terry, your Sally has just been and got some holiday brochures, you taking her away then, eh?' he says laughing. I now realise why he is talking so loudly, and in that laddish kind of way, he has Terry on his phone in his car. I look at Sally. She just looks like she has frozen. I can hear Terry talking, but I cannot make out what he is saying. The copper continues. 'Ha ha, Terry says he'll sort it out when he gets home and that he's surprised you've got time to go looking for holiday brochures... oh just a minute, he also says he's skint, so it's you who'll be paying for it.'

With that, the copper drives off laughing, obviously not realising the implication of what was meant in that message *you'll be paying for it.*

Sally is still staring straight ahead. I don't know what he will have thought as I don't think she said a word. I start the car and drive off. I see in the rear-view mirror that Mrs Simpson is still standing in the same spot. She'll have loved that little episode.

'He'll kill me, Anna. He'll fucking kill me.' I can see that Sally is shaking. The brochures are resting on her knee, and her legs are shaking. I'm scared too. Terry will know she was with me as he's bound to find out, and then he'll tell Jonathan. *Fuck, why did I take her with me?* I think to myself.

'I'm done for Anna, he'll take this personally, that was his boss. Even though he will be totally oblivious to what goes on in our relationship, Terry will think I've tried to make him look a fool. That's it, Anna, this whole thing is off. I can't do it. We've got away with it for far too long, but it's over.'

I turn the car into my road and drive towards our two houses, side by side and try to think of what to do. I then slam on the brakes. There parked on the drive is Jonathan's car. He's home and I'm not and my chores are not finished. The chores have to be done before I leave the house even if it is to go to fetch something for him. I look at Sally, she looks at me. I don't know who is more scared now me or her. I take a second, then another, then another, as I think. I put the car into reverse.

'What are you doing?' Sally asks quite hysterical.

'We're going to Rose's,' I say.

'What, now, why, for fuck's sake,' Sally shouts.

I turn the car around. 'Why Anna, why are we going to Rose's?'

'Because after that we are getting on a train, or a bus or maybe even a plane, don't ask me where to Sally, but this is it, we go now, or we never leave.'

Sally stares at me in disbelief. 'What?' she says, 'Now, we can't go now, that's mad. We can't just leave now this instance.' I ignore Sally. I need to think, my mind is racing, my adrenalin is pumping so fast around my body that I feel like I can take on the world. The strange thing is I'm not scared, not nervous, not anxious, but excited. I know this is the right thing to do, just like I know that if Sally and I go home, we are done for. Jonathan would explode with rage if I walked in that house having dared leave it with the chores unfinished. That is a major no no and then if he ever found out, which he would, that I'd taken Sally with me, dared to see her before our scheduled allowed time of 3:00pm, he would explode all over again. For him to come home and me not be there would be too much for him to deal with. He would feel as though he had lost control, that he was being taken advantage of and being made to look a fool, that I could actually dare to think for myself, and that would just not do in Jonathan's world. He could not live with the shame. I turn out of Brampton onto Lanercost Road, that road where we never pass another car. I pull into the side and stop the car just as Sally again bursts into hysterics. 'What are we doing Anna, you're mad. I'm getting out. I need to get home,' she says. I grab her arm as she opens her door.

'Just listen, will you? Just listen to me.' I say.

'Remember what you said to me after our first time

when you were laughing hysterically?'

'What first time?' she replies.

'After our first session at Rose's, remember? You said to me that you were only doing this for me, that you wouldn't do it for anyone else, and that you asked me to make you a promise, remember?' Sally nods her head. 'You asked me to promise you that if I continued down this path that we had to go all the way because you said that you couldn't go through it all and not get to the end, remember?' Again, Sally nods. 'Well, this is the end, Sally, we are here, it's come sooner than we planned, but we are here, the end of that path. I kept my promise. Now you have to keep yours to me. You've said all along that you were with me, that if I was doing it, then so were you. Don't back out now, Sally. If you do, you know what's coming, you know what Terry will do, and after that, you may not have the courage to carry on with our plan, so we have to end it now. We have to go now. Where to, I have no idea, but I'm going Sal, and I want you to come with me. I can't make you any other promise other than wherever we end up. You will be free, no more beatings, no more control, just me and you, Sal. We can do this.'

Sally stares at me. She wipes the tears from her eyes and cups my hands in hers. 'Rose's it is,' she says.

chapter twelve

Rose opens the door. 'What have you forgot?' she says. We both barge in, nearly knocking her to the floor. 'Bloody hell, calm down, what's up?' she says as she steadies herself on the hall wall. 'We need to go, now,' I say.

'What? Go where?' she replies.

'We need our share of the money now, we need to go, we are going, but we need our money. We need to go today.'

'Whoa, calm down, I can't make head nor tail of this, so let's calm down, and I'll put the kettle on. Go and sit down at the table and take a breath.'

Sally and I sit at the table. I can see that I'm now shaking. The adrenalin has subsided. I can't stop my hands from trembling. Sally holds them. Rose makes a pot of tea and remains silent throughout. I sit there and watch her, admiring how calm she is. She hasn't said anything since she told us to take a seat. She has remained calm and hasn't added to the hysterics at all. I appreciate the calmness as I look at my hands. They are much steadier. Rose brings the pot of tea and three mugs over and sits down. She pours the tea, then gets a plate of biscuits before sitting back down. 'Now then, what's happened?' she says calmly.

We both tell her what has happened in detail, along with the consequences of today's events. She listens intently, and I'm amazed at how both me and Sally are needing her to take the lead, to tell us what to do, where to go. I have no idea why I think she should do this for us, but I know she will be able to help us and have some sort of plan. She sits back in her chair.

'Wow, that is serious. I see now why you were so hysterical. I mean, I agree if you were to both go home, you would both pay for it and some. Have they not tried to contact either of you?'

'No, we never bring our phones with us. We always leave them at home. That way, we can never be contacted by either of them because I know if I ever answered my phone whilst I was here, I'd give the game away straight away,' Sally says. 'My voice would give it away.' I interject,

'Plus, if they ever tracked our phones, which I'm sure they can and maybe do, they would know we'd been on the move.'

'I see,' Rose replies. 'Have they never tried to contact you whilst you've been here?'

'Yes, a couple of times, but saying we never heard it because we were busy doing our chores always seems to be ok. Having a vision of their wives at home doing as they are told seems to give them the power they need,' I say.

'Ok, so you need to move fast today... mmm. I've not got the money here. It's in the bank. I could go and get it, but to draw that amount out may need pre-ordering. We're talking about fifteen grand apiece, aren't we?'

'Give or take a few quid yes, shit, I never thought of that.' I get up and pace up and down. Rose speaks.

'Look, ladies, we trust each other, don't we, eh?'

'Yes,' I say. 'Yes, of course,' Sally replies.

'Well then, I could draw say, five grand out today.

I'm sure that amount would be ok, and then we could meet up in a few days, and I can give you the rest. Where are you planning to go?' Rose asks.

'No idea,' I say. I look at Sally, not wanting to see any apprehension in her face. There is some. I knew there would be. 'We're just gonna take off and see where life takes us, aren't we, Sal?' Sally looks at me and manages a smile.

'Yep, that's the plan, not a great one, but that's it.'

'Unless you can help us?' I say, looking at Rose. 'I was kinda hoping you'd... I don't know maybe know someone, or somewhere we could go from here, to start us off sort of thing.' Rose is deep in thought.

'Do you think they will look for you both?' she asks. 'Not just around here I mean, of course, they will look for you here in Brampton, but I mean if you two bugger off never to be seen again do you think they will report you missing, especially your Terry Sally, he's an Inspector ain't he?'

'He is,' Sally replies. 'And yes, I think he maybe will, I mean, he's got the resources, and I suppose if he does then, Jonathan will have to do the same, wouldn't he?'

'Fuck!' I say, 'that's something I hadn't thought of; we could be splashed across the front page of the papers this time tomorrow.'

'Fuck!' Sally says.

'Have you got your big girl pants on?' Rose asks. We all laugh. I mean, what else could we do. The seriousness of it is laughable all the same.

'But then again, what are you doing wrong?' Rose says. 'I mean, people can decide they want to disappear anytime they want. It's not as though you have broken the law or anything, so what if you are reported missing? That's your choice, isn't it? I mean, you don't have to be found because, in reality, you are not missing. You've both just decided to leave. You aren't running away from anything unless that's how you want to look at it. I'd say you were both just moving on to pastures new, as you can, and you just decided not to tell anyone. That's not illegal, surely?' I sit back down.

'That's it,' I say. 'That's so true. We aren't on the run Sal. We haven't done anything wrong. What were we thinking? Of course, I just want to move on with my life. I've earned a few quid and have decided to go and make a life elsewhere, and so have you, Sally. We don't have to explain ourselves to anyone.' Rose gets up and walks towards the hallway. 'What's up?' I ask.

'Just gonna make a call, wait here, I won't be long.'

As she walks out into the hallway, I take Sally's hand. 'You, ok?' I ask. Sally nods.

'I'm ok,' she says. She places her other hand over mine and continues. 'What Rose just said there is dead right, you know. When she said, you know about us not doing anything wrong, all made sense. It made me feel good about it all, 'cos she's right. We can just walk away. We never had the courage before, but we have now. I'm sorry I was hysterical in the car, sorry I had a wobble, and I'm glad you gave me that talking to. I'm glad I'm here with you.'

We hug each other, a real hug, one of those hugs that means something. We then sit in silence for a minute or so until Rose comes back in, just finishing a conversation on her phone.

'Right, she says, here's the plan, we go to Carlisle, and I'll draw five grand out of the bank. We then go to the station and get two train tickets to Manchester Piccadilly. When you get there two friends of mine,

Pam and Denis, will meet you and take you to their house. They live not far outside of Manchester in a place called Cheadle Hulme, a lovely couple they are. I met them on holiday in Greece, with another couple actually who live in Stafford. Great holiday that was, anyway, they will put you up for a few days, well as long as you need really until you decide what to do next. At least whilst you are there, you can see how the land lies and if you appear in any papers.'

'And they are ok with this, are they?' I ask.

'Yes, no problem. I've just spoken to them. Pam is lovely, and she's a great cook. You'll love it there and will certainly not go hungry. She'll mother you both, and let her, she loves to do that.' Just before I go to say anything, Rose quips in.

So, you up for that?' I look at Sally, who raises her eyebrows and then nods her head in approval.

'Looks like we're going to Manchester then,' I say. I then hear a knock at the door. All three of us immediately and instinctively look at each other with widened eyes and, for a moment, remain still and silent. 'Fuck who's that?' I say.

'Shit, Anna, how did they find us? Your car's outside, isn't it?'

'Bloody hell,' I say as I stand up.

'Look, you two stay here. I'll go. Just sit tight, keep calm. It might not be them.'

My heart is racing, the adrenalin's back but this time I feel scared. My hands are shaking again. I hold Sally's hand. She looks scared too. She is biting her bottom lip. I hear the front door close and hear two voices. One is Rose's, and the other one is also female. I recognise the voice. Rose then walks in, followed by Mrs Simpson. I stand up. Sally does the same.

'It's ok, dears. I'm not the enemy,' Mrs Simpson says.

I look at Rose, then at Sally.

'Let's take a seat, shall we?' Rose says as she pulls out a chair for Mrs Simpson. Me and Sally both sit down. Mrs Simpson smiles at me and then averts her gaze to Sally.

'I thought I'd find you two here,' she says.

'How did you know?' I ask.

'I know a lot of things, Anna, my dear,' she replies. 'I sit, I watch, and I sit some more,' she says.

'But I don't understand,' I say.

'I know what kind of life you two lead,' Mrs Simpson continues. 'I've seen the signs, I know the signs, you can't hide it from me. I've been there, you see. I've been where you are. Do you know why I walk into Brampton every day and sit on that bench near to the Moot Hall?' she asks. No one answers, it's one of those occasions where someone asks you a question, but you know not to answer it because the answer is coming anyway. 'Well, let me tell you. I walk and sit there every day because, for years, I was like you two. I was not allowed out unless it was with my husband, the successful author who everyone thought was wonderful. The man who used to control everything I did, and if I stepped out of line, I would get a backhander, just like you two, although I suspect you've had worse. I had that for years until he got dementia. I had years of control, years of manipulation, years of being told I was nothing and a nobody. That's why I became a school governor once he became forgetful. I wanted to be somebody. I wanted to be needed, to be wanted, to be known because for years, I was just Mrs Simpson. Do you know what? I bet you don't even know my first name, do you? I was just Mrs Simpson for that long that I will always be known as Mrs Simpson, but I am no longer Mrs Simpson, Patrick Simpson's wife. No, I am Mrs Simpson, school governor. Still Mrs Simpson but one who people now notice. Anyway, I digress. My point is, I saw your fear in town when that copper spoke to you and Sally. I saw you were petrified, and I saw how you never even looked at him as he spoke to you, never mind when he spoke to your husband on his phone. And Anna, I had already seen Jonathan go home before I saw you, so when I saw you two together, I knew that would be trouble for you too.'

'So how did you know we'd be here?' I ask, still quite mesmerised by her story. She smiles and nods her head.

'I've known about you two coming here for a while. As I say, I miss nothing. Sitting and watching does that, you know. Rose here announces at the school governors' meeting back in early January that she's leaving and going to Portugal, whilst making no apology for what she'd been doing.' Mrs Simpson looks at Rose. 'I really enjoyed that. It was very brave of you. The faces of your colleagues made me laugh and smile for weeks afterwards.' Rose smiles, obviously appreciating the vote of confidence from Mrs Simpson. She looks back at me and Sally, 'but then things change, she takes her house off the market, appears to be staying, tells the school that she's got unfinished business here, and then I see you two leave your house and head up towards Lanercost every Monday, Wednesday and Friday. I drive up one day, and I see your car on Rose's drive, partly hidden by her V.W. Beetle, of course, but for someone like me, I see it. I also notice the way Rose looks at Jonathan at the school meetings. She never liked him, that was obvious, but her looks towards him recently told me she knew things, things she hadn't previously known, so it doesn't take a maths genius to put that lot together and come up with 4... 2 & 2 always make 4, if you have the right numbers, of course. All those things gave me the right numbers, so I knew you three were up to something together. I have an idea what, but I do not wish to know those details, as I am sure you can imagine, but ladies, I can help, I want to help.'

The three of us sit there quite taken aback. I know I am, and by the look on Rose and Sally's faces, they are just as shocked.

'So, what is your first name?' I ask.

'Brenda, Brenda Simpson, but you can call me Mrs Simpson,' she says with a warm smile.

'So, what now?' I ask.

'Well, we may as well let Mrs Simpson in on the plan, hadn't we?' Rose says. I put my head in my hands and run them through my hair and then sit back in my chair.

'You can trust me, Anna, 100%. I want to help, anything I can do would be my pleasure, and my lips are sealed. I'll take whatever you tell me to my grave.'

I look at Mrs Simpson long and hard. It seems like an eternity, and then look at Sally. I don't need to ask anything; Sally's look tells me that she's comfortable with it all. I blow out my cheeks and exhale hard. 'Ok,' I Say, 'there's not much to tell other than I think you know what we've been doing, but as you say, you don't need to know the details but suffice to say we've made a few quid which Rose has, in her bank. The plan was for me and Sally to wait until we had enough money to just disappear, and we were on track for middle of May, but today's events have just brought things forward a couple of months. We now plan to go to the bank, draw some of it out and bugger off. Rose will meet us in a few days with the rest of our share. That's it, we have no idea what we are going to do, but Rose has fixed us up with a stay at some friends of hers until we decide what to do.'

'So now you know everything,' Rose says, 'and that I am heavily involved, so trust is the big thing here, Mrs Simpson.

'I know, my dear, but as you know, I've known about this set-up for a while and said nothing, so I'd like to think I've proved my trust.'

'Well, I trust you,' I say.

Mrs Simpson smiles at me. 'Thank you dear,' she says.

'I'm not sure where you can help, really,' I say.

'Well, I can get that car away from here for a start,' she says quite excitedly. 'Unless you are taking the car with you?'

'No, we were going on the train. Shit, I forgot about the car,' I say, holding my head in my hands again.

'We could take the car, I suppose,' Sally says.

'I wouldn't if I were you ladies. Jonathan is bound to report it missing, or if not, he's bound to cancel the insurance and tax and all that at the very least as he'll know that will shine a light on it,' Rose says.

'Mmm,' Mrs Simpson ponders, putting her index finger on her lips as she thinks. 'What about if I drop it at the end of your road, close enough so Jonathan will see it and close enough so as not to raise suspicion to anyone else. I could do that, and then I'll just walk back to get my car from here. I'd happily do that. I'd enjoy the walk back too.'

'Yeah, that would work, wouldn't it?' Sally says as she looks to me for assurance.

I nod my head.

'Yeah, I suppose it would, as long as Jonathan doesn't see you do it.'

'He won't, dear, I'm too careful for that and too smart for him. Trust me I'll be fine. I might be getting on a bit, but I'm still ok up here,' she says as she taps the side of her temple with her forefinger.

'Well, if that's the case, I want to leave a note in the car,' I say as I tap the table with some air of authority.

'What kind of note?' Sally asks.

I stare at the tabletop as I think. I want to leave a note that lets Jonathan know I have gone, that I have made my escape. I want him to know that I am not missing, that I have not been captured or abducted but that I have left him, that I am now free.

'I want to write a note that just says *FREEDOM*,' I say. 'Nothing else, just that. I want him to know that I am free. It can be from us both Sal,' I say as I look at Sally. She smiles and nods her head.

'Nice touch,' Rose says as she raises her hand and clenches her fist. 'Right, let's go. We need to move fast. I'll go and get those wigs and glasses that we have, and you can wear those. We will go in my car, and Mrs Simpson, you can do your thing with Anna's car.'

'What's your plan now then?' I ask Rose.

'My plan?' she says as she walks out of the kitchen into the hallway, 'Just what it always was. This house will be back on the market, and I am off to sunny Portugal, as quick as I can,' she shouts as she walks up the stairs. As I get up, Mrs Simpson takes my arm.

'Here,' she says, 'take this. It has my home number on it. You can ring me anytime you like, and I will keep you updated of any developments or news from this end. You know I will find out everything that is going on so I can tell you both what those husband's of yours are doing. I'll keep close tabs on them.' I look down and in her hand is a business card. All it says is her full name, address, and telephone number on it. I take it and smile at her. I then give her a big hug. She hugs me back. She feels so frail and old, bony, and quite fragile, but I can feel her strength in her hug. It has real feeling. As I pull away, I wipe a tear from my cheek. 'Don't cry dear, everything will be fine, now go and write that note and give me the car keys. I won't let you down,' she says in assurance. Sally hugs her too. 'Look after each other,' Mrs Simpson says. Rose comes down with the wigs and glasses, and I write my note. I pass it to Mrs Simpson and give her the keys. 'Is there anything in the car you want?' she asks.

'Nothing,' I say, 'that car and anything in it is staying the other side of the line.' Rose walks back in with the wigs and glasses, a handbag, and a small suitcase. One of those small carry-on ones that the budget airlines allow you to take on board.

'I've brought you a handbag with a mobile phone in it. It's an old one, not a smartphone or anything, I've had it a few years, but it's working, look.' She shows me the screen. 'I can't remember the phone number but ring my phone, and it will bring up the number. I've also brought you this suitcase. You can put the money from the bank in there and keep a few quid in the handbag. I'll get you a spare purse of mine in a sec,' she disappears again. I can't remember her number, so I wait until she comes back in with the purse. I then ring it, it rings. We are all good. We have a mobile, a purse, a handbag, and a small suitcase, all the things a lady needs when she's running away or starting a new life, as I tell myself.

chapter thirteen

Sally and I are waiting in Rose's VW beetle on Cecil Street in Carlisle. She has gone to the bank. As we sit here, I am getting nervous. I am in the passenger seat, and Sally is in the back. I am struggling to keep the enormity of what we are doing from my mind. After seeing Jonathan's car in the driveway, I had not had time to let thoughts creep into my mind, but as we sit here, nerves are creeping in. I'm scared all of a sudden. Scared that Jonathan knows something, scared that he'll knock on the window any second and drag me from the car.

I can sense Sally's trepidation too. It's quite tangible. I need Rose to appear soon and just get us on our way as I know once we are on that train to Manchester, there's no going back. At the moment, I could go back home and take what comes, but once I get on that train, that will be the point of no return. *Come on, Anna*, I say to myself. I am trying my hardest not to appear scared or nervous for Sally. I know she needs my strength. I wish I had someone to draw from, too, but I haven't. I am the one who needs to be strong.

I tell myself again and again that I am worth more than what I have been used to in recent years. I remind myself of that as I sit here waiting to see Rose appear. I think of Simon and wonder if I will meet my Simon somewhere, sometime soon. I wonder what he will look like. I wonder if he will be tall, handsome, strong, caring, yes caring, and loving. That's all I want, I tell myself, someone who is caring and loving and who loves me unconditionally, and who will treat me right. Maybe I won't ever find him. Maybe I should stay single, and maybe I should find a woman. These thoughts have passed some time as I wait, but I tell myself I will find my Simon, that's my dream, and all of this must be for something, and that something is for me to find my Simon, or whatever his name will be. I sit forward as I see Rose come round the corner. She is holding a large brown envelope.

'She's here, Sal,' I say.

'Bout bloody time,' Sally replies. 'I couldn't have sat here much longer. Here look at my hands,' she says, as she puts them out in front of her. I look behind me. They are shaking.

'Well, she's here now, so not long and we'll be on that train,' I watch as Rose gets closer. She opens the driver's side door and gets in. 'I got ten grand,' she says quite excitedly. 'I didn't think they'd let me draw that much out, but they did.' She passes me the money. I look in the envelope, and there is what I assume will be ten bundles of cash, with a strip around each bundle, each with a stamp on it, and a squiggle which I assume is the cashier's initials. 'So that's twenty grand to come,' says Rose. 'I'm not worried about a few coppers either way,' she continues. She looks at me. 'So, we'll just call it thirty grand, yeah?'

'Fine with me, that ok with you, Sally?'

'Yep, no problem with me.'

Rose starts the car. 'I've also put the contact details in there for Denis and Pam. Ring them when you get to Manchester station, and they'll come and fetch you.'

'Ok,' I say as I look at the piece of paper in the envelope with their details on it.

'I'm not sure how much credit you have on there, so top it up as soon as you can?'

Rose is just about to pull off as I grab her arm.

'Thank you, thank you for all you have done. We could not have done this without you.' I lean over and give her a hug and a kiss. She hugs me back. I then feel another pair of arms and know it's Sally. Rose says nothing as she pulls away, and then as she looks in her rear-view mirror, she says, 'it's been a pleasure.'

We pull into Carlisle train station car park, but there are no parking spaces. Rose goes round again, but nothing. She pulls up.

'You two gonna be ok on your own?' I nod and then look at Sally.

'We'll be fine. We are capable of getting two one-way tickets to Manchester, you know.' We have another hug standing next to Rose's car. She then gets in and drives off, giving us a wave and blowing us a kiss. We both do the same. We then walk into the station and stand in the ticket queue. I look at the monitor. The next train to Manchester Piccadilly is 3:40pm on platform one. The time now is 3:12pm.

'Not long to wait, look.' I say to Sally as I point towards the monitor.

'Well, I need a pee,' Sally says as she looks around for the toilets. 'I'll nip for a pee, and then I'll see you on platform one.'

'Ok, but here, get us some sweets too and a drink,' I say as I give her a crisp twenty-pound note. I love the feeling of having my own money. I haven't had my own money for so long now I've forgotten how it feels. Sally takes the note and smiles.

'Hardboiled? She asks.

'Of course,' I say. I love boiled fruit sweets. It always reminds me of car journeys as a child going on holiday or days out. My mum always had some hardboiled sweets for the journey. I stand there and think about my parents. Neither of them are alive. Both died of cancer. My dad when I was still a teenager and my mum around five years ago. I miss them terribly, and I know had they still been alive, I would be on my way there now.

'How can I help you?'

I snap out of my trance and look up at the lady behind the counter. She's heavily made-up but very pretty all the same.

'Er, two tickets please, one way to Manchester. I'm not sure when we'll be coming back, if ever.'

The lady behind the counter smiles. A smile that says she knows what was behind that implicit comment. Maybe she does, maybe she doesn't, but I'm on my way. I grab the tickets from her and make my way to platform one to join Sally, who is waiting for me.

'Thank you,' I say as I bend down and pick up my suitcase full of money. Carlisle railway station is busy, which is surprising as it's a Monday afternoon. I walk out of the ticket office to join Sally on platform One.

'I walk towards the platform and look for Sally. She's not there. I stand next to a bench and look around. I can't see her. I walk towards the toilet. I'm sure she'll come out to meet me. I go into the toilets. She's not there. I come back out and walk towards platform one. She's not there. I walk back to the ticket office and then outside. She's not there. I walk back inside and sit on the bench. She's not there. I start to panic. Has

Terry seen her? Has he got her? Is Jonathan here? My breathing is heavy. I'm starting to panic. I stand up and look around, nothing. I sit back down. I look at my watch. It's 3:29pm. A man sits down next to me. I look up.

'I was asked to give this to you,' he says as he hands me a piece of paper. I look at it, and it just says; *Good luck, I'm sorry, love you, Sally.*

I stare at the piece of paper. I start to cry. I realise that Sally is not coming. I'm on my own. I sniffle as I try to stem the tears, aware that this man is still sitting next to me. I wipe my eyes and tell myself that if I can find a quiet spot and a seat on my own that I can cry on the train. I need to stay strong. This cannot change anything. I grab my suitcase. I don't know why. Maybe it's because I am mindful it has nearly ten grand in it.

'Are you ok?' the man says to me. 'You're obviously upset.'

'Who gave you this note?' I ask.

'A lady outside. Dark hair, red lipstick, wearing glasses. She just stopped me and asked if I'd do her a favour and come to platform one and give this to a lady of your description who had a small green cabin-sized suitcase and a black handbag. I was coming to platform one anyway as I'm catching the next train to Manchester, so it was no problem for me. Are you ok though?' he asks again. I sniffle again and wipe my eyes.

'Yes, I'm fine, thank you, and thank you for doing that.'

He smiles and gets up and walks away. I wonder who he is and think he's maybe someone who is just pleased that they've done their good deed for the day. I'm so sad that Sally is not coming. After all we have been through and the promises, she made me. I really did think we were in it together and that we would see it through to the end. We nearly made it, I suppose, I mean Sally did get this far, and she could see the finish line. It was so close for her. All she needed was one last little leap of faith, one last piece of courage, and she would have made it. Once we were on the train, we would have never turned back. I wonder where she is now, probably in a taxi or at the bus station waiting for a bus back to Brampton. I wonder if she would still be here if I had not given her that £20 note to go and get some sweets with because without that, I doubt she would have had a penny on her. She could still have got a taxi, I suppose, and maybe paid with money she has in the house, but then again, maybe she doesn't have any money in the house, that wouldn't surprise me.

I wonder what she will tell Terry, how will she explain her actions today, will she tell Terry about the last few weeks and all about me?... will she betray me?... I look up to the roof of the train station. I'm looking for some divine intervention, I suppose, some strength and courage from somewhere. I'm sure I'm going to need it as this journey just got all that much harder. It's going to be hard on my own. It would have been hard enough with Sally, but at least I would have had some support, someone to lean on, but as I lean back on the bench and check my watch, I tell myself that this is it, this is what I've been waiting for. So, what if it is just me, so what if I have to do it alone?... I can do it, and I will do it. Jonathan will never control me again. He will never again tell me what to do. I am free. I can do as I please. I imagine what he will be doing right now. I cannot even imagine. As much as I know him and know him very well, I cannot even imagine what he will be doing right now. This will be uncharted territory for him. He will never have experienced anything like this before. He may crumble, he may become a shadow of his former self, he may never recover from this, from the knowledge that I left him. Then again, he may try and find me. He may come after me; he may actually find me. So, what, I tell myself, what if he does? I would not swap the time I am going to have as a free person for anything. Not even if that means that I will suffer or even die as a result of him ever finding me, no fuck that I say to myself, I'm worth more than that.

As I look around the station at the people milling about, all going about their daily business. I feel so alive, ready for this adventure, for this next chapter in my life. I then hear the announcer telling everyone that the next train due on platform one is the 3:40 to Manchester. I look at the tickets, both of them, and put Sally's in my pocket. I want to keep it to remind me that she very nearly made it. I just pray to myself that she is ok and that she will survive whatever Terry has in store for her, and I hope again that she does not betray me.

I stand just behind the line and watch as the train comes in. It's quite a long train, I'm not sure what I expected, but I just thought it would be smaller with a lot fewer carriages. I wonder where it has come from and think maybe Edinburgh or Glasgow. I walk down one carriage into the next and manage to get a seat by the window. I opt for a seat without a table as I do not want to have to engage too much with anyone, plus I put my suitcase on the seat next to me. I need to keep my eyes on that at all times. I need time to think too, but I tell myself that I cannot think negatively and must remain positive. I see the guy who gave me the piece of paper get on. I look out of the window, hoping that he will not see me and so not sit next to me and try to chat. I don't mean to sound awful, as I appreciate what he did, but I just want to be on my own as I need to process what has happened today. I mean, four hours ago, I was leaving Rose's as usual, just under four hours ago I was going to the travel agents. Then my life changed for good, for the better, I tell myself. It just brought forward this momentous day, that's all. I mean, so what if I do not have as much money as planned. I will just have to make what I have work for me. I then realise that I have Sally's share of the £10k, minus £20, of course. I wonder if when I meet Rose in a few days if she will just bring me another £5k to make it up to my fifteen grand share or whether she will bring me Sally's share too as she may be unaware that Sally is not here. I ponder this hard, and I want Sally to have her fifteen grand but then wonder how on earth she will spend it, or moreso how on earth will she explain the money to Terry. I tell myself that I will just leave it to the powers that be, and I'll see what happens. If that extra fifteen grand lands in my lap, then I shall gratefully accept it and will make sure I do good with it, Sally would want that, but if I only get another five grand from Rose that that is ok too, and I will just do good with that. I need to ring Rose when I get to Pam and Denis's house to let her know I am here safely, so I will let her know about Sally then.... if she doesn't already, of course.

I look out of the window for the whole journey, only looking up to show the guard my ticket. By the time I reach Manchester Piccadilly, I am feeling very positive. It is amazing how the further I got from

Carlisle train station, the more confident and positive
I feel. The feeling of anxiousness and fear that was in
my stomach like a brick, no matter how many times I
told myself to be positive, was going, slowly but surely
as the train passed Kendal, Lancaster, and then
Preston. The feelings were going. I just felt the further
I travelled; the less chance Jonathan has of finding
me. He seems such a long way away now as I get off
the train. He cannot have any idea where I am unless
Sally has told him, of course, but the more I processed
those thoughts, the more I was convinced that Sally
would not do that. I know that even though people's
personalities can change, and people's characteristics
can alter, that the core values we all have remain the
same, and Sally would not do that to me. As she told
me many times, she may not value herself very much,
but she would rather die than do someone a wrong
turn when it comes to other people, those she cares
about.

I step off the train and look for two people who could
be Denis and Pam. Rose told me what they looked like,
so I scan the faces looking for who I think might be
them. I then catch sight of someone waving to me. I
look behind me to see if there is anyone behind me
who they could be waving at, but I decide it can only
be me, and I wave back at who I assume must be Pam.

'Anna?' the lady asks.

'Yes, are you Pam?'

'Yes, that's right, how are you? Was the journey,
ok?'

'Yes, thank you, and yes, I'm fine.'

'Where's Sally? Pam asks.

'She couldn't do it.' I tell her. 'She made it to Carlisle
station with me but then just gave me this note.' I take

the note out of my pocket and show it to Pam, who reads it and looks at me with a sad face.

'Oh dear,' she says. 'I hope she's ok.'

'Me too. I couldn't believe it, I was so sad when I read the note, but she must think it's the right thing for her.'

'Yes, that's right,' Pam agrees. 'It had to be her decision. Anyway, come on, Denis has just gone to the toilet. It's an age thing. He can't hold it, you see, comes to us all, I think.' Pam says as she ushers me towards the exit. We then hang about for a minute for Denis, who comes out of the gents and stands looking for us. Pam shouts. 'Denis,' he looks around and walks our way. 'This is Anna,' Pam says as she gestures towards me with her open palm.

'Hi, I'm Denis, you ok?' he asks.

'Yes, thank you. It's very nice of you to do this for me. I hope I'm not causing you any trouble.'

'Don't be silly,' Denis says. 'We're happy to help. Anyway, where's your friend?'

'She didn't come with me, last-minute thing,' I say.

'Oh, err ok, no problem as I say we are happy to do what we can. We love Rose and will do anything we can to help her. Here let me take that,' he says as he takes hold of my suitcase handle. 'We don't want this going astray, do we?' he says as he strides away. I assume by that comment that he knows what is in there. I just follow behind him with Pam like a lost puppy. I have no idea where I am going. I cannot even remember where Rose said they lived. 'Where is it you live Pam?' I ask.

'Cheadle Hulme,' she says. 'We live in a bungalow, lived on the same street for years. We used to live further along the close but then bought where we live now quite a few years ago. We love it there. Lovely and quiet it is. No one will know you are there, trust me,' she says with a warm smile. Pam looks around 60 with short grey hair, around 5'5', and has a very warm and caring face. Rose said she would want to mother me, and I can already see that in her. She is warm in her mannerisms and has a lovely smile, one that tells you she is trustworthy. Denis is slightly taller, probably around 5'8', and looks around the same age. He dresses well for a man of his age. He is in trainers and jeans and a hooded top that you would normally see on a younger man. He has a very good complexion for his age. They both wear glasses.

'We would normally get the train in,' Pam tells me as Denis waits to pay for the parking. 'But we brought the car today, seeing as we were picking you up. The train is free for pensioners you see so we can come here for free anytime we want from our local station. It's really good, isn't it, Denis?'

'Yeah, we often get the train in, have a look round Manchester, have a coffee or something, and then get the train back. Helps to fill your day sometimes,' he says, nodding.

We get up to level three and get into Denis's car and take the drive to wherever it is they live. I still cannot remember it and don't want to ask again. After about twenty minutes, I see a sign that says Cheadle Hulme. *That's it,* I say to myself. *Cheadle Hulme.* I know it is on the piece of paper Rose gave me, but that is in the envelope in the suitcase. I must make sure I do not lose it. We pull into an Estate and follow a longish road through until we come to a bungalow right in the corner. Once inside, Denis puts my suitcase into a bedroom immediately on the right as you walk into the hallway.

'I'll just leave that there for you Anna,' he says.

'Thank you,' I reply as I take a deep breath in through my nostrils. 'That smells nice,' I say.

'I made some chicken stew earlier, fancy some?' Pam asks.

'That would be lovely. I'm starving,' I say.

'We thought you would be. Did you not have anything on the way down?'

'No, I just needed to think, you know to get things right in my head.'

Pam puts both arms out, inviting me for a hug. She must know that I need one. I wrap my arms around her and stay there for a good while. I can feel myself filling up, but I stifle the tears. As I pull away, Pam gets a piece of kitchen roll and blows her nose.

'Rose didn't tell us much, you know, all she said was you needed a place to stay for a few days, perhaps longer because you were getting away from an abusive husband, that's all she said, but if you need to talk, we've got a very nice bottle of vodka that we could put a dent in, and we've got all night too. We're both retired.' Denis says as he points to himself and then Pam.

'Thank you,' I say. 'I might take you up on that. Only thing is I hate vodka, love gin, though.'

'And tonic?' Denis asks.

'Yes, and tonic.'

With that, he picks up his car keys.

'Not be long, love,' he says to Pam, who is checking the taste of the stew. 'Any particular brand of gin?' he asks.

'Any,' I say. 'Do you want some money?'

'Don't be daft,' he says as he walks out of the kitchen door. He then pops his head back in, 'she also told us about the bundles of money you'll have with you too, so fifty quid a night, ok including breakfast,' he says, laughing as he walks out again.

'Ignore him. He's only joking,' Pam says, shaking her head.

'I'm just going to ring Rose if that's ok, Pam.'

'Yes, of course, listen if you want some privacy go through to the lounge.' Pam takes me through into another room. It is quite a large room with a cream carpet, two cream sofas, and an armchair. It is very clean and tidy with everything in its place. I sit on one of the sofas and dial Rose's number on the phone she gave me. I just hope that there's enough credit.

'Hi, it's me,' I say as Rose answers.

'I'm so glad you've rung Anna. I've not been able to rest. I've been pacing up and down constantly. How was the journey down? Are you at Pam and Denis's house?'

'Yes, I am. The journey was fine but listen, Sally didn't come.'

'What?'

'She didn't come,' I say. I can hear the genuine shock and surprise in her voice.

'Fucking hell, I'm speechless, why?'

'I don't know for sure. She went to the toilet and never came back. This guy gave me a note that she'd gave him to pass to me. A total stranger he was. All it said was *good luck, sorry. Love you, Sally'*, that was it. I assume she must have just decided she couldn't do it after all.'

'So, you went on your own then?'

'Yep. I left the total stranger on the platform, mind you. He did get on the same train. I saw him but yep, just me.'

'How are you feeling?' Rose asks.

'Surprisingly upbeat, to be honest. The further I got from Carlisle, the better I felt. All those feelings of fear and dread just left me. It was as if the further I got, the safer I felt. I feel safe here.'

'You will do. They are lovely people. Listen, I know things have changed, but I just want you to know I think you are so brave. To just carry on knowing it was just you was fucking brave girl, I take my hat off to you.'

'Thank you,' I say.

'Listen, I can get the rest of the money tomorrow, so I will come to Manchester and bring it to Pam and Denis's house. I may as well. It'd be good to see them. I'll come down on Wednesday, tell Pam for me, will you? I'll aim to be there about lunchtime. Tell them I'll make my own way to their house. I'll go straight down to Mrs Simpson's house now and tell her about Sally. She'll need to know, especially as she's gonna be keeping an eye on Jonathan for you. She might also find something out about Sally. You know what she's like, a real amateur sleuth she is.'

'Ok, listen, tell her if she does see Sally to tell her from me that I understand. No hard feelings... and tell her that I love her, she was my best friend, my only friend.'

'I will, I promise, now get some rest, think about what you are going to do. You need a plan.'

chapter fourteen

I wake the following day having slept quite well. I did lie awake thinking about the day's events... wow, what a day yesterday was, but I fell asleep, I think just after midnight. I told Pam and Denis most of what had led up to me arriving here yesterday, I hadn't planned on telling them as much as I did, but a couple of gins does that to you, well, especially Denis's measures. I told them all about my life with Jonathan, the control, the abuse, the beatings, and I told them about what me and Sally did to get away. A watered-down version anyway. I didn't go into too much detail. Denis nearly dropped his vodka when I told him that I'd stripped for the camera, so telling him I'd had lesbian threesomes would have really shocked him. They were very sympathetic, though, and very understanding. They both just listened to me as I poured my heart out. I didn't get upset though, I just talked and talked until there was no more to say. Pam just gave me a hug and told me I'd be ok now and that I could stay as long as I wanted. Denis told me that if Jonathan ever came knocking on his door that he'd punch his lights out. He was so sweet.

I do feel safe here, though. I also thought a lot last night about Pam and Denis and how they are with each other. I watched them as they were just themselves. They were just so natural with each other. They didn't seem to be on eggshells. No one was watching what they said or was on edge. I thought about how they joked with each other and how when Denis asked Pam if the kettle had broken, she told him it would when she cracked him over the head with it. All in good fun, though, and we all laughed as she said it. It was so nice to see, and it just reinforced what a sham my relationship was with Jonathan. That natural element of our relationship went a long time ago. In fact, it was only ever-present for such a short time. I thought back to how I have been controlled by Jonathan for so long and could have easily got annoyed with myself and beat myself up for being so weak, but then I thought how that would do no good. I can't change the past; it is what it is, and I can only affect my future. Regrets are nothing to dwell on, I told myself.

I have a shower, get dressed, and go into the kitchen to put the kettle on. I haven't heard any noise, so I am unsure if either Pam or Denis are awake. I walk into the kitchen. Denis is sat at the table reading a paper.

'Morning,' he says as he looks up. 'Wow, you look different, really different with blonde hair. I thought that was a wig yesterday but didn't like to ask.'

I laugh as I run my fingers through my hair. I'd forgotten all about the wig yesterday and had not thought about it until I went to bed. I just put it in my suitcase along with the glasses. I did consider keeping the wig on as I lay in bed last night, but in the end, I just thought *no, why should I? I'm not on the run. I don't need to hide who I am. Jonathan has no idea where I am.*

'Natural blonde me Denis, and yes, they do have more fun,' I joked.

'Yes, last night's stories confirmed that,' he says

with a wink. I have to stop myself colouring up slightly.

'Tea?' I ask him as I fill the kettle with water. I realise what I am doing. Here I am in a couple's house that I only met yesterday, and I am treating it as if it is my own, just filling the kettle to make myself a cup of tea without even asking. I love it here. I feel so at ease and so at home. I do not have to make anyone's breakfast. I do not have to get anyone's clothes ready, and I can do as I please, something I couldn't even do in my own house.

'Aye, go on then,' he says. 'I'll have another cup. What you got planned today, anything?'

'Well, I just thought I'd have a walk around Cheadle Hulme, go for a coffee, sit, and people watch, that sort of thing for an hour or so, I haven't been able to do that for so long, and then I need to get a few bits, clothes and that sort of thing.'

'Well, there are some lovely coffee shops just a few minutes walk from here, and there are a couple of Bistros too on the same stretch if you fancied something a little stronger, and there are some little boutiques too, it's a great little area.'

'Great, I'll have a walk out there if that's ok?'

'Of course, do as you please here Anna, its no issue to us.'

'I'll definitely need some new clothes as all I have is what I came in yesterday. I'll need a toothbrush too and that sort of thing. I did use some of the deodorant in the ensuite in my room and the shampoo and shower gel. I hope that was ok, but I will get my own today?'

'As I say, make yourself at home, use anything you want. I'm sure Pam will have a spare toothbrush somewhere, she's bound to, she's got everything and anything, I'll be amazed if she hasn't, I'll go and check with her, she'll be out of the shower by now.'

I put his mug of tea on the table as he goes out of the room and sit down with mine. It would be nice to brush my teeth before I go out. I decide that I will go for that coffee, have a mooch about and see if I can get some clothes. I'm not sure about boutiques, though, as they'll probably be a bit pricey. I need something high street, something a bit cheaper to get a few different outfits to start with. I decide that I will go to Manchester later if Pam will come with me. I'm sure she will.

Pam comes into the kitchen with a new toothbrush still in its packet and a tube of what looks like travel-size toothpaste. I brush my teeth and feel instantly better, although drinking my tea straight after does make the tea taste a little strange. I ask Pam about Manchester, and she's delighted. I'm so excited to be going shopping with Pam. Simple things like this have been lost on me for so long. We agree to go at lunchtime, so I can wander along the shops and coffee bars of Cheadle Hulme for an hour or two this morning. I want to do this, this simple thing, without worrying about the time or who is watching me. I feel great.

As I wander along the stretch of bars, boutiques, and coffee shops, I marvel at the freedom of it all. Jonathan keeps popping into my mind, but I am determined not to give him any headspace. He's had enough of my headspace for far too long. I see a coffee shop that, for some reason, appeals to me, and I walk inside. It has that lovely aroma of fresh coffee that says I must have a slice of cake too, so I sit in the corner near the window and sip my filter coffee as I slowly eat my slice of coffee cake. The stretch is quite busy. Well-dressed ladies wander along, browsing in the shops, and groups of young girls heavily made up walk along on their mobile phones. I also see a few well-dressed men in suits with long overcoats, some with umbrellas just in case it rains, but all walking at speed totally oblivious to their surroundings. They must all be in work mode as they all walk looking as though they are in some sort of trance, some on their phones but others deep in thought, possibly about that big deal they are working on.

I realise that most of these people I see are controlled, just like I was but just in a different way. The ladies all seem to be controlled about looking good, looking their best, maybe trying to make sure their husbands or boyfriends do not stray, the young girls are certainly controlled by their mobiles, and the men all seem to be controlled by work, by that need to achieve and be important. They all look important in their suits and with their umbrellas but are any of these people really free? Are they really happy? Could they all give it up tomorrow and walk away, like I did yesterday? I smile at myself as I realise that I doubt any of them could and realise that as I sit here, sipping my coffee and eating my cake, I am probably freer than any of them. I realise that I now have the choices and the options to do whatever I want to do, go wherever I want to go, and be whoever I want to be... and I want to be me, just me. I don't care where that is or what I do, but I just want to be me. I raise my cup of coffee to the window and nod my head, not at anyone in particular but just to the world and also to me, Anna Fox, and say to myself under my breath, *'Here's to you Anna, here's to the rest of my life and here's to freedom.'*

I finish my coffee and walk out into the fresh air; it's cool but bright, a normal day for early spring. I check my watch. It's 11:10am, and I decide to wander back to Pam and Denis's house so that me and Pam can go to Manchester. I then see a music shop across the road and cross over to have a look. I miss my guitar. I love playing it, or moreover, I used to. I loved to sing too. I can sing, not great, but I can certainly hold a tune. As I reach the shop window, I see a range of musical instruments on display. I peer inside and can see a wall full of guitars. I walk inside and instantly feel the warmth again. The left-hand side wall is full of guitars, mainly acoustic, and they appear to be in price order from the cheapest nearest the window along to what is evidently more expensive. I stand and look and feel how I would love to play again.

'Hi, are you ok?' a voice says to me from the back of the shop.

'Yes, thanks, I'm just looking.'

'No problem, give me a shout if you need anything.' I smile and wander slowly along the line.

'If you want to try any of them just let me know. I'll be happy to get one down for you.'

'Thank you, can I try this one?' I point to a guitar about four up from the cheapest. It's £140.

'No problem, do you play?'

'Used to, not played much though in recent years, just at get-togethers and parties, you know.'

I sit down on a chair and play a song that I used to love playing years ago. It's a song that everyone knows, and with a couple of drinks inside you at a party really gets everyone singing. It brings back some great memories.

'Not bad, sounded really good,' the man says.

Again, I smile, appreciating the comment. I know that if I had my own place, I would have bought it. I have the money on me as I brought some out with me in case, I saw any clothes I wanted to buy, but as I am at Pam and Denis's house, I resist the temptation.

I spent about £300 on some new clothes, just fairly cheap ones from the high street but enough so that I can mix and match and make quite a few outfits. I loved my time with Pam in Manchester. I didn't have to worry about the time, didn't have to clock watch, didn't have to think about anything really other than having a good time shopping, something I haven't done in ages. We had a sandwich in a nice bistro-type place in the centre, and I told Pam some more about my life with Jonathan. It made me think of what he will be doing, about how he will be dealing with it all. Will he be planning to track me down, or will he just accept that he's been a bastard over the years and just let me go. I know deep down that he will do whatever he can to track me down. He has Terry at the end of the day, who I am sure will help him with his connections in the force.

That then made me think about Sally. I thought about how she was and what she'll have had to endure from Terry when she got back. I spoke to Pam about it, and Pam raised a very good point in that Sally could have got back home before Terry had got back from work and could if she timed it right and kept her nerve have kept the fact that she made it to Carlisle railway station from him. She could if she wanted to have played dumb and just made out that after the travel agents, I'd dropped her back, and she could make out she knows nothing about anything to do with me vanishing. The more I thought about it, the more I realised that neither Terry nor Jonathan know anything of our trips to Rose's or anything to do with that, and unless Sally told them, they would remain oblivious to it. All Jonathan has to go on is my note. He knows nothing else. I hope and pray that this remains the case and that Sally was able to get away with keeping her mouth shut about anything other than a short trip out to a travel agents. I fold my clothes up and hang a couple of pieces in the wardrobe in my bedroom just as I hear Denis shout that my G'nT is ready for me. *I like it here.* I think to myself as I close the wardrobe door. I then walk through to the lounge and sit down and take a sip of my drink.

'Can I ask you something?' Denis says. He looks a little serious and a little concerned. I can see it in his expression.

'Yes, of course,' I reply. I'm suddenly a little nervous.

'When Rose comes tomorrow with the rest of your money, where are you planning to keep it all, long term, I mean. Have you got a bank account of your own?' I take a second to think before I answer. Denis continues before I have a chance to reply. 'Don't think we are poking our noses in Anna. It's not our concern, but I did just wonder if you'd considered where you are going to put it. I mean you can keep it here; it will be safe unless we get burgled, of course, but longer-term it won't be sensible to keep carting that suitcase round full of money, that's all I'm thinking, but tell me to mind my own business if you want. It's no problem.'

I'd not given this a thought. I mean, I'd not really had a chance to sit and think about things like this, but Denis was right. I'd need a safe place to put it, a bank account ideally, but that is something I'd not had for a long time now. Any account was always in Jonathan's name.

'I'd not thought of that,' I say. I take another sip of my drink. I try and think of what to do. Rose is coming down tomorrow with at least another five grand, maybe more. 'I've not had my own bank account for a good while.'

'We suspected that,' Denis says. 'And to open a bank account, you'll need ID and a registered address too, I'd say.'

I pick up my phone and ring Rose. She answers on the third ring. 'Hi, it's me, how's things?' I ask. She tells me that she's heard nothing, which I find quite reassuring. She tells me that Mrs Simpson had been up to her house today and again had nothing to report. Jonathan was still going to work, and there was as yet no gossip in the town. It was as if I was still up there, locked away in that house. I mean, if no one saw me for weeks, they'd suspect nothing as I was rarely out except to buy groceries, except for going to Rose's, of course, in recent times, but other than Mrs Simpson no one knew.

'What about Sally?' I ask. 'Has anyone seen her?'

'No,' Rose replies. 'Mrs Simpson has not seen anything at all at Sally's house. She's not even seen Terry come and go, so no, sorry, I have no news on Sally.' I get a bad feeling in my stomach as she is telling me this.

'Are you still coming tomorrow?' I ask.

'Yes, and I'm bringing you Sally's money too. I've thought long and hard about it, and to be honest, Anna, I can't see how I can get it to Sally or even if I did how she could spend it or hide it if she wanted to. It would probably just make things worse for her.

What do you think?'

'I know what you are saying, yes.' I say. I then tell her about my thoughts that Terry may not be aware of anything other than a trip out to the travel agents.

'Hopefully, you are right,' Rose says.

'Well, look, that makes my little issue a bit bigger,' I tell her. 'I cannot keep that amount of money in my suitcase forever. It's just not practical. I need a bank account, but without ID and proof of address, I cannot open an account. I need to ask a huge favour.'

'I thought you were leading up to that. Come on, what is it?' Rose asks, sounding as though she will be up for anything.

'Well, can we put you bringing the money down on hold for a few days?'

'Yes, I can do that, is that it?' she asks. I laugh out loud, 'No, there's more' I say. 'Thought so, come on spit it out.'

'Well, if I post you my door key up tomorrow first class recorded delivery, can you get into my house and get my passport and driving licence?'

'Break in, bloody hell, of course I can. In fact, put me a note in with the key in your own handwriting that says, 'Where were you ya bastard?' in big capital letters. I'll leave it on the kitchen table for him. He'll be bloody seething,' she says, laughing loudly. 'He'll think you've been in the house; he'll bloody well hate it.'

I put my hand over my mouth and widen my eyes and look at Pam. I can tell she's itching to know what's being said. 'I will' I say, 'Nice one. I'll definitely do that.' I clench my fist as I say it.

'I'll get Mrs Simpson in on it with me. She can watch the house, she's good at that, and she can tell me when he's gone. So where do I need to look?' she asks?

'In the dining room, there's a set of drawers under the big clock on the wall. Inside the left-hand cupboard drawer, there's a black file. It's not a lever arch file or anything, but it's like a, ooh what are they called?' I say as I struggle to remember the name. 'You know it's like a box, erm....'

'A foolscap box file?' Rose says.

'That's it, one of them, black. My passport and driving licence are in there. There's lots of paperwork on pensions and council tax, all that sort of thing, but they should be in there too. If you see Jonathan's bring them too, I don't know why but just bring his as well, so he hasn't got them.'

'Will do. Once I have them, I'll be in touch, and I'll bring them down with the money.'

'Great.'

'But you still can't open an account as you have no proof of address other than your address up here.'

'I know, but at least I'll have those documents for when I do, one step closer at least.'

Rose doesn't reply. There's a silence. 'You still there?' I ask.

'Yeah, I'm just thinking. I have more than one account. I tell you what I'll do as well as getting these bits for you. I'll transfer the money into my other account. It only has a few quid in it, less than £100 for sure, and I'll bring you the debit card and my PIN. That way, you can use it as your own to draw money out or use my card to buy things. Just treat it as your account until you are able to open one of your own. I'll even put that ten grand in you have for you if you give it to me when I bring you the card and your bits down. How's that?' I'm speechless. I put my hand over my mouth again and start to cry.

'That's so nice of you, Rose,' I say.

'Stop blubbering, it's a pleasure but listen, if I EVER need a favour, you best get ready 'cos you'll be the first person I ring.'

'Anything,' I say, 'Anything at all, I'll post the key first thing tomorrow. Make sure you are in on Thursday 'cos you'll need to sign for it.'

chapter fifteen

I told Pam and Denis what Rose had said, and they loved it, especially Pam. It must be a woman thing; you know, supporting a fellow female. Denis was excited too, don't get me wrong, but Pam was that giddy I thought she was going to drive up to Brampton and put it on the table herself.

The queue in the post office is moving nicely. I have my key and my note, written just as Rose said, 'WHERE WERE YOU YA BASTARD?' I know that this will wind him up, but when I think of the years of abuse I suffered from him, I'm more than ok with it all. I get to the front of the queue and post the key and note. I send it special delivery before 1pm. I need to know it makes it there. It's the only key I have. If it gets lost in the post, then I have no way of getting my passport and driving licence. Then I would be in the shit because I'd have to reapply for them, and I do not want to have to go through all of that. I'd have to prove my previous address probably, and that would be hard to do without Jonathan getting wind of it somehow.

I walk out of the post office and head back to the music shop. We had somehow got onto the subject of music last night as we were chatting. One of Pam and Denis's friends they were telling me about plays the guitar, so I said that I used to play, I then told them about being in the music shop, and they both said straight away that I should go and buy the guitar. I wasn't sure as after a while it may get on their nerves, but they said that I cannot be as bad as their friend from Mansfield who plays. I really want to get it as I have not played properly for so long, and it was a real passion of mine. I walk in, and the guy recognises me instantly.

'Hi, you back to buy one then?' he asks as he looks up from behind the counter. I smile at him and nod my head.

'Yes, couldn't resist.'

'You're not local, are you?' he says obviously noticing my accent.

'No,' I say, not wanting to give anything away.

'Where you from, Cumbria?' he asks. I must admit I'm impressed. Not many people can pick out a Cumbrian accent.

'Yes, that's right.'

'Where abouts? I lived up there for a while at Silloth, just on the West Coast, do you know it?'

'Yes, it's quite a nice place, Silloth.'

'I loved it. I was only there about three years. Moved back here for work, but I do miss it, the peace and quiet, you know, just the slower pace of life.'

'I'll have that one.' I say, pointing to the same guitar that I tried yesterday. I want to move the conversation on as I do not want any more questions about where I am from. He gets it down and strums it with his thumb.

'I'll just tune it for you,' he says and sits down on a stool. I slowly wander around the shop as he tunes the guitar, and I get the money out of my pocket.

'So how long you here for?' he asks. I do not want to appear rude, but I just wish that he would stop asking questions.

'Just a few days,' I say. 'I'm staying with my auntie and uncle, but I'll be gone soon.'

I didn't know what else to say, and making Pam and Denis, my auntie and uncle, seemed a good way to explain my reasons for being here and would hopefully pacify him.

He stands up and passes me the guitar. 'That's a shame,' he says. 'I was hoping we could go for a drink.'

That's the last thing I need. I think to myself, but I smile automatically and think instantly how long it is since anyone asked me out.

'But then I assume that ring means it's out of the question,' he says as he nods to my left hand. I look down and see my wedding ring on my finger and realise that I hadn't even given it a thought. I had not, at any time since, given any thought to my wedding ring. *Why did I not think to take it off?* I think to myself as I subconsciously hold my hand up in front of me and look at it.

'That's very sweet of you, but I won't be here long, and well, let's just say it's complicated.' I cringe at how corny that sounds, but it could not be truer, and I want to say to him, *don't even consider it. You'd run a mile if you knew.*

'It often is,' he says as he smiles at me. 'If it ever gets uncomplicated and you're, well, back round this way, the offer of a drink will remain.'

I smile at him again and genuinely like his warm smile as he smiles back at me.

'£140?' I ask him.

'That's right. Do you need a case for it?'

'No, just the bag it comes in will be fine, thanks.' I pass him the money and take the receipt.

'So, where abouts in Cumbria did you say you were from?' he asks.

'I didn't,' I say as I turn and walk towards the door. 'Oh, I need a plectrum and a Capo.' I turn on my heels as I put the guitar down.

'Take your pick,' he says as he opens a case on the counter that displays an array of plectrums. He then turns round and takes a capo off a small upstanding rack behind him. 'This one, ok?'

'How much?'

'Twenty quid for the capo, and you can have the plectrum for free.'

'Wow, thanks, a whole pound free of charge, you are too generous,' I say, teasing him.

'That sounded like flirting,' he says, raising his eyebrows as he looks at me.

I smile and laugh a little. 'No, just teasing, not flirting.' I pay for the capo and take it and the plectrum and pick up my guitar.

'See you again then, I hope,' he says a little louder as I walk away.

'Maybe,' I say without looking round.

'What did you say your name was?' he shouts. I stand in the doorway with the door half open and turn back to look at him.

'I didn't. I never tell anyone my name on the first date.' With that, I close the door and walk away, smiling to myself. I feel really good inside. I remember these feelings, these feelings of butterflies, these feelings of excitement when someone takes an interest in you. It's been a long time since that happened, and as I walk along the street, I hear him shout, 'my name's Tony.'

Tony, I say to myself. I'll remember that name. I used to know a Tony at school, and he was one of those guys who all the girls fancied. You know one of those lads that all the lads liked and wanted to be his friend and that all the girls liked too. Good at sport, good looking, good at everything really, so yes, I'll remember that name, plus I tell myself I'm bound to need another plectrum soon. I was always losing them when I was younger. I again look at my ring. I cannot believe I still have it on my finger. I wish I had realised before I sent my key and the note to Rose as I would have put my ring in there. That would have been good to have left it on *the kitchen table*. I say the kitchen table as I cannot bring myself to say *our kitchen table*. I do not see any of it as ours anymore. None of the possessions in that house or the house itself can ever be ours again. The only way it can be in any way mine is if Jonathan were dead.

I take my ring off and consider throwing it down the drain as I stand on the pavement. I can just about hear the water below ground running through the drainage system below my feet. I wonder where it will end up. *Do I care?* I ask myself. 'Do I fuck!' I say out loud and throw it down the drain. It feels good. I feel good. I still feel good about the attention I got from Tony in the music shop. I ask myself as I walk along the road towards Denis and Pam's housing estate why I turned the offer down of a drink. I am free at the end of the day. I can see whoever I please. There was nothing to stop me from going for a drink with him, only myself. Is it too early? Am I falling into the stereotype of thinking that within two days of running from my abusive husband, I could not possibly go for a drink with a handsome stranger?

He is handsome, about 6'2' or so, and fair mousy hair cut short and looked quite lean and toned in his jeans and jumper, but what would people think? That's the real reason, I know it. I am wondering what people would think. They would think that I was in the wrong somehow, think that I cannot possibly be a victim if I am having a drink with someone I have only just met so soon after running from my marriage. *Why else did I turn that offer down?* I ask myself, *come on,* I say to myself, be honest, why? Is it because I do not want to get involved with anyone else so soon after? No, it's not? That would be so if I had been hurt by Jonathan, if he had cheated on me and if I were distraught, but I am not hurt, I am not distraught, I am free, I am happy, so why not?... and who the hell is going to think anything of it? Certainly not Rose. She'd tell me to go for it. I won't probably ever get to tell Sally, and Mrs Simpson would just say, *you do whatever you feel is right for you dear.*

I then think of Pam and Denis. I am living in their house after all, what would they think? I don't know them very well, but from what I have seen of them up to now, I'm sure they would not care less, as long as I was doing something that made me happy. They seem very easy-going people. They have opened up their house to me and seem very genuine. I feel as though I could tell them anything, but I still don't know them that well, so I decide I will tell them of the drink offer tonight, and I'll see what their reaction is as I do not want to offend them or for them to think that I am taking advantage of their hospitality. I also think of Sally. Oh, how I wish I could see her, to see how she is. When Rose told me of the fact that Mrs Simpson had not seen Terry or Sally, it did make me think that he has beat her badly and is staying in until the bruises disappear. I cannot wait to hear how she is; I pray that she's ok. I look at my left hand and see the white mark where my wedding ring was. It looks funny without a ring on my finger. I cannot understand how there is a white mark there as I am pale as it is, so it baffles me how on earth my skin can be a different shade of white where my ring was. I merrily walk back to Pam and Denis's house, so happy that I am here. I still cannot believe that I did it. *'Yes!'* I shout out loud as I turn into the estate. A man who is pruning his hedge looks up at me. I smile and laugh to myself inside. He just turns his head back and carries on pruning.

chapter sixteen

I check my watch. It's 11:15am. Rose will be here soon. She was driving down. She was going to catch the train but decided to drive down instead. It's a beautiful drive through the lakes on the M6. When you go past the Shap turn off, and through to the Kendal junction, it is breath-taking. I remember that drive when Jonathan used to go to South Cumbria. His firm of solicitors had another office down there somewhere, so he would often go there, and on occasion, he would take me with him. Not many times but on a few occasions. Mainly after he'd hit me and was either feeling bad about it or wanted to keep me close to him, I could never work out which, but the scenery was spectacular, and I enjoyed the drives out just the same. She said she was leaving at 9:30, so it shouldn't be too long now.

'She'll not be long,' Denis says. I smile at him, but he can see I'm nervous. I don't know why because I know she has got my passport and driving licence. She said it was easy. Mrs Simpson watched the house, inconspicuous as usual, and just rang her when it was clear. She said she'd been nervous in case Terry came out of his house, but she said she'd seen no activity there, nothing. I do worry about Sally. I make a cup of tea for the three of us. Pam is excited to see Rose. She's not seen her for around four months, she told me.

'I wonder if she's got her house back on the market?'

Pam asks.

'She told me she was going to do it straight away, so knowing Rose, she'll be on with it, I'm sure,' I say. 'I bet she'll be over in Portugal soon, and why not?'

'Why not indeed, just do what's right for you, that's what I say,' Denis says, looking straight at me. I know what he's saying, just with that look he has on his face. They were fine with me going for a drink with Tony from the music shop.

'Yes, yes, I know,' I say, smiling at him. 'Yes, dad,' I say, teasing him.

'No too late though, mind,' he replies, pointing his finger at me. 'Front door is locked at 11, lights out at 11:30.'

'Ok, dad,' I say. I feel so relaxed here it's quite remarkable. I am amazed at how quickly I have settled in. Pam is exactly like Rose says she would be. She mothers me, which I revel in. My mum was just the same, that was until Jonathan made her feel so unwelcome that my relationship with her had deteriorated somewhat by the time she died. It still makes me sad to think that I allowed that to happen. I know I was powerless to stop him. I was so controlled by him and under his spell that I just did not have the strength to go against him, even though I could see it hurt my own mother so much. That is a regret I will take with me to the grave. I know she won't have blamed me, though. She was always the kind of person that saw good in people, and I know she will have known deep down that I was just not in a place where I could challenge him.

I did ring her twice a week whilst Jonathan was at work. He knew I did and used to scoff at it, but even he wasn't cruel enough to make me sever all contact. He just never wanted her round, never wanted to share me with her. He just wanted me all to himself, all of the time. That's why he had the snip; he couldn't even bear to share me with our own children. I do wonder if I will ever have children. I want to have a family now more than ever. I want to find my Simon, maybe not now, Tony will do for now. Maybe he will be my Simon, that I don't know, but I will go back to the music store, maybe tomorrow, and see if that drink is still on offer. I hear a car pull up on the drive. It must be Rose. I put my mug of tea down and run to the door. I'm like a child who is waiting for their grandma to arrive. I remember as a child whenever Grandma and Grandad would visit. I would be just the same. I would run to the door to greet them, not wanting to wait another second. This is different, though. I'm not waiting for Grandma to arrive, but I am so pleased to be seeing Rose again. Maybe it's because she is a reminder of what I have achieved, and she is a little bit of confirmation that I need to remind me that this is all real. I open the door just as Rose gets out. She opens her boot and gets a little suitcase out. I run and fling my arms around her.

'Woah, give me a chance to get my case out, girl,' she says before letting go of the case handle and returning the hug. I squeeze her tight. I'm so pleased to see her. 'How are you?' she says.

'I'm fine, just fine. So glad to see you.' Rose then turns and hugs Denis.

'Good to see you,' he says. 'Come on, let's get inside.' He takes her case, and we walk to the door where Pam is waiting with a huge smile on her face.

'Ooh,' she says as she hugs Rose tight in the doorway. 'It's great to see you. Come on, I'll boil the kettle again.'

We sit at the table in the dining kitchen and talk about Rose's trip down. She sips her tea.

'I saw Jonathan the other night,' she says.

'What, where?' I ask.

'At the governor's meeting. I thought you'd forgotten as you never mentioned when you rang me to ask me to get these for you.' She bends down, takes a large brown envelope out of her handbag, and passes it to me.

'Bloody hell, yes. I forgot all about those meetings. What did he say? How did he look?' I say as I look inside and see two passports and two driving licences.

'Well, he looked perfectly fine. His usual smug self, to be honest, that was until we broke for coffee, and I asked him in front of everyone, and so that they could all hear how you were.'

'What did he say?' I ask as I lean forward on the table and rest both my elbows on the envelope.

'He just said you were fine, that was it, nothing else, and then Mrs Simpson told him that she'd bumped into you that very morning in Brampton near the Moot Hall and that she thought you looked a bit peaky. You should have seen his face. I thought he was going to explode. His face was about as red as that passport cover in that envelope. Honestly, I don't know how I stopped myself from laughing.'

I bite my bottom lip a little and widen my eyes as I say, 'bloody hell, she's a bugger, isn't she?'

'Who's Mrs Simpson?' Denis asks.

'A very sweet lady who lives locally. A lovely lady too who doesn't suffer fools and doesn't take any crap off anyone,' Rose says.

'She's the other lady I was telling you about. You know who took my car back and said she'd keep an eye on any developments or gossip for me.'

'Oh yes, I remember. Wow, she's got some bottle by the sounds of it.'

'She has, she's one of those people who have a real presence you know and real respect from people, mind you she did tell us that her life was very similar to mine and Sally's once upon a time, hence why she is so keen to help' I say.

'Anyway', Rose continues, 'He was seething for the rest of the night and couldn't stop looking at me and Mrs Simpson, he must suspect something, I'm sure. If I'm honest, I wish she'd kept her mouth shut 'cos he's bound to be curious now, but hey I can handle him, and I'm bloody sure Mrs Simpson can. Anyway, I'm off to Portugal as soon as I can.'

'When are you going?' Pam asks.

'Two weeks, three tops. My house is back on the market, but I'm going once I've tied up a few loose ends here. I'm renting a place first while I look for somewhere. The last place I was looking at has been sold,' she says as she glares at me, teasingly, of course. I stick my bottom lip out, looking for sympathy as I know what she means by that comment, even though it was light-hearted because she lost the last villa because of Sally and me. 'I'm only teasing,' she says as she takes my hand. I feel better immediately.

'So, what did Jonathan say then when Mrs Simpson said she'd seen Anna Tuesday morning when she couldn't have done as she was here?' Denis asks.

'He just smiled nervously and just said that she was feeling better but had been a little under the weather lately. It was a classic, but I just hope it doesn't have any repercussions.'

'Anything on Sally?' I ask.

'Nothing,' Rose says, shaking her head. 'No sign of any life at all. I tried to have a look when I was in your house but nothing. Mrs Simpson is driving past daily and will let me know, and you too, I'd assume if she ever sees anything.'

'I have thought about ringing her, but I daren't until I know Terry is going to work. If he answered, I don't know what I'd do, plus I don't want to make it worse for Sally. I pray she's ok.'

'I'm sure she is. She's probably taken some sort of beating, but until we know otherwise, we have to just pray she's ok. She's a big girl Anna. She made the decision not to come, so don't beat yourself up over it. It might sound harsh, but that's just life, I'm afraid.'

I know Rose is right, but the mood has dipped slightly in the room. We sit in silence for a few seconds, all just sort of processing those thoughts until Rose asks, 'anyway, have you looked in that envelope yet?'

I had, and I'd seen the two passports in there and the driving licences too, but I realised I'd not even thanked Rose yet.

'I'm sorry, I was just caught up in what you were telling me.' I take the passports and licenses out and check them. They are mine and Jonathan's. 'Thank you,' I say and get up and put my arm around her as she stays in her seat. 'I don't know what I'd have done without you.'

'It was easy, I was a bit nervous, of course, but with Mrs Simpson watching the outside, I knew I'd be ok. Anyway, they were exactly where you said they'd be, and I put the note on the table. I wish I could have stayed to see his face.'

'Me too.'

'Anyway, here's your key.' Rose takes it out of her

purse, and here's the bank card. The PIN is on the post-it note, look.' I take the card and see the 4-digit PIN on a yellow post-it stuck onto the front.

'I've put the rest of your share and all of Sally's in that account, so if you want me to put that ten grand or at least some of it in too, just let me have it before I go back tomorrow.'

****

We are all stood in the doorway. Rose stayed overnight but is leaving this morning to go back to Cumbria. We had a great night last night, a few too many drinks, but we all enjoyed it. Rose can be a right laugh, and Pam and Denis certainly like a few drinks when the mood takes them. They love their vodka, both of them, and are really genuine people.

We wave Rose off. She has seven grand of the money I brought with me to take back with her to put in the bank for me. I cannot believe that I will have twenty-seven grand in the bank and a few quid in my underwear draw. That is more money than I have ever known. Jonathan looked after the finances in our relationship. I was only allowed the money that he gave me or rather that he controlled. I've never known so much money myself. We had money alright, I knew that. I mean Jonathan is a solicitor, and that's not a bad earner, so we must have been ok for money, but it's just that I never saw any of it. We always had nice things in the house, and I was allowed to buy nice clothes to wear. Plus, whenever we went anywhere, it was always to nice places, places that were frequented by people who just liked a few nice things in their lives. Some people would say snobby, but to be fair, I always found the people in those restaurants or in the hotels we stayed in to be just ordinary people who like to look nice and smell nice. I was never impressed by any of it, far from it, I'd be just as happy eating anywhere or staying at any hotel as long as it was clean, but I did always find the people friendly. Maybe they were just all controlled, a bit like me. The women would most probably have been controlled to varying degrees by their husbands. The men controlled to varying degrees by their wives, so no one ever really let their hair down or did anything too adventurous. The people I came across, I suppose, as I think back, were fairly boring and well, just ordinary.

I plan to go back to the music shop today. I want to see if the guy there, Tony asks me out again. If he does, I'm going to go for a drink with him. No one seems to have any issue with it... only me. I do think *ooh, should I?* but I know it's only because I am worried what people will think. I'm even worried what I think to be honest, as I have tried to convince myself that it's too soon, but I know that is just my conscious mind replaying the old behavioural traits that we've been shown since our childhood. In the cold light of day, and if I step back and think about it rationally, there is no reason in the world why I shouldn't go out for a drink with him, so I am.

It's a warm spring day today, so I sit in the garden with Pam and Denis and have a cup of tea and a biscuit. We chat about all sorts of things and nothing in particular, just as people do when they are killing time.

'Right then, I'm off for a stroll,' I say.

'Music shop?' Denis asks with a wry smile on his face.

'Maybe, detective Denis,' I say to him as I touch my nose with my finger, indicating he should mind his own business.

'Leave the poor girl alone,' Pam says teasingly as she pats his knee playfully. 'You'll embarrass her.'

'What, after what she told us about that stuff with the camera, I don't think so.'

Denis laughs as he throws his head back on his chair. Pam bites her lip as she looks at me as if to say *ooh, I'm not sure he should have said that.*

'Well don't worry,' I say. 'I won't give you any of the details of what happens on my date. Don't want to embarrass you.' I say this mockingly, but inside I'm colouring up. I hope it doesn't show on my face, as I'd hate for Denis to think that he's embarrassed me.

'Good, I don't think my ticker could take it. I've only just got over what you told us the other day. I've not been able to sleep, what with the images in my head.'

'Just ignore him Anna, and you...' she says, pointing to Denis, 'you, stop being vulgar, it doesn't impress anyone, you're not at the match now you know.'

Denis sheepishly looks at me and bites his bottom lip. 'That's me told... anyway, have a nice stroll, and we'll see you later.'

I slip on my jacket. Even though it's mild, there's still a slight nip in the air if the wind blows. As I walk to the music shop, I start to get butterflies in my stomach. I wonder if he was joking the other day, and maybe he won't ask me out again. I tell myself that if he doesn't, then so be it. I stop at a cash machine and put in the card Rose has given me. I want to see the money in the account. I think the most I've ever seen on the display screen before in my life was around £2000 when I was still at university. My mum had transferred me some to get me started. That didn't last long as money never does at that age. If it came easy, then it went easy so that money never looked back at me for very long on the display screen. I have the PIN in my phone. I type in the number and wait to see the screen. It should say twenty thousand pounds. It asks me what I want, and I click *on screen balance.* I look around to make sure no one is stood behind me and then look back. Something must be wrong, I should have twenty thousand pounds in the account, the fifteen grand that is Sally's and five grand left of my fifteen, but as I look at the screen, I see it says thirty-five grand. That is fifteen grand more than I should have. I take my card back and ring Rose.

'Hi it's me,' I say.

'Hi, listen if I lose you, it's because I'm going past the lakes, so the signals not great. You ok?' she replies.

'Yes, but I have just checked the bank balance, and it says thirty-five grand rather than twenty.'

'That's because I have given you my share too Anna, I don't need it. I made my money. I was doing it for a long time, don't forget, and I only stayed to help you and Sally out.'

'But that's your money.'

'Not now. It's yours. I don't want it, and I don't need it. I will have the proceeds of my house sale too, and that's mortgage-free, so I'm ok. Please don't worry about me. Take it as a gift and accept it gracefully.'

'I don't know what to say. You are being too kind to me. I don't deserve this,' I say as I struggle again to stem the flow of tears.

'Now don't start blubbering again, bloody hell, you don't half cry a lot you do... listen I want you to have it. You need it more than me. It would make me happy to think you can use it to start again. Honestly, Anna, take it, well it's in the account, so you're stuck with it, I suppose.'

'I will pay you back, you know, one day I will.'

'Well, that's up to you, but there is no need; it's a gift.'

'Thanks Rose, you have no idea how much that means to me.... hello, are you there? can you hear me?'

I look at my phone. I have three dashes, so Rose must have lost her connection. I disconnect my phone and stand outside of the music shop. I hadn't realised I had walked so fast. I wipe my eyes and just hope that I do not look a sight. As I straighten my jacket and take a breath, the music shop door opens and Tony stands in the doorway, arms folded.

'Couldn't resist me, eh?'

'Err, I've lost my plectrum, actually,' I say quite sharply, a little too sharply really. I don't mean to sound so sharp.

'Oh, ok, come in, I was only messing.'

'Sorry,' I say as I close the door, 'I was just on the phone and... well... the conversation just took me by surprise, can we start again?'

He gestures with his hands for me to go outside again. I open the door and stand back on the pavement. He shuts the door for a couple of seconds and then opens it again. 'Couldn't resist me, eh?' he says again in the same cheeky tone.

'I've lost my plectrum, actually,' I reply in a far more pleasant manner.

'That's better, now come on in,' he says as he steps aside for me to walk in.

'How did you lose that so quickly?'

'I don't know. I was always losing them when I played before.'

'It's well known in the music shop world that whenever someone says that they've lost their plectrum when they obviously haven't, that what they really mean is *I regret not accepting your kind offer of a drink the other day and would actually like to now take you up on it.*'

I smile more at the cheesiness of the line than anything else. 'Does it really?'

'Well known... ask any music shop in the world, and they will confirm I am telling you the truth, been known for centuries apparently.'

'Well, must be true then,' I say. I know I am flirting with him, he knows it too, but I am loving every second of it. The freedom I feel right now is fantastic. This time last week, I could only speak when spoken to out in public with Jonathan, but here I am flirting openly with a guy I have known for no more than five minutes. This is what it is like to be alive.

'So, tonight, 7:00... that's if your auntie and uncle will allow it, of course.'

'Confident of yourself, aren't you?'

'I knew the other day when you walked out of here that I'd take you out. I just didn't think it would be so soon. I'd love to take you for a drink, though. I'd love to get to know you a bit better.'

'Where shall I meet you?' I ask as he walks towards the window.

'See that bar over the road next to the zebra crossing, the one with that couple walking in?'

'Yes.'

'In there around 7:00?'

'Don't be late,' I say, trying my very best to remain cool. I have no idea why. I'm acting as if I'm a seventeen-year-old, smitten by some good-looking local guy in a band, whereas in reality, I'm a thirty-three-year-old flirting with a guy who works in a music shop. He is good-looking though I remind myself and tall. I like tall guys; they make me feel safe. I've never really been into small, scrawny guys.

'I won't,' he says, 'always on time me.'

'Ok then, well, I'll see you later,' I say and smile as I turn around, aware of the sudden awkwardness in my composure.

'No plectrum then?' he says. I turn back around, fully aware my cover has been blown.

'Oh yes, the plectrum, of course, erm. I'll have the same one as last time.' Tony picks one out of the display and passes it to me.

'That's £1, please.'

I smile at him, knowing that he is referring to the last one which he gave me free of charge. I pay him the pound.

'Thank you, so I'll see you later, Tony.'

'You will. You still haven't told me your name.'

'Anna, my name's Anna.'

'I see you ditched the ring, Anna,' he says, pointing to my left hand. 'Uncomplicated?' he asks, raising his eyebrows. I had forgotten about the ring; it had totally slipped my mind. I now, all of a sudden, feel as though I needed to explain in great detail why I had taken off the ring. I feel that he can sense the uneasiness. 'Hey, listen, none of my business, no need to explain. I just don't fancy an irate husband spoiling the drinks tonight, that's all. It's not what I had in mind.'

'There'll be no irate husband. It's not uncomplicated. It's over, it's still very complicated actually, very complicated indeed, but over.'

'See you at seven.'

chapter seventeen

I'm quite nervous as I walk to meet Tony. I haven't dated in so long I am unsure now how I should behave tonight. Should I be reserved and quiet, or should I be confident? I then tell myself that I should just be me. That makes me smile. Who is me? I am unsure. I used to be confident and the life and soul of any party and used to be bubbly, but that was back as a teenager and at Uni, but was that the real me or was that just an extroverted image of the real me?... was I just overcooking my natural character to fit in back then or to be noticed, or is that who I am?

One thing I do know is that the submissive, pathetic Anna I have been for so many years with Jonathan is definitely not the real me. I am not that person. Ok, I was for a long time, but that was someone that I was forced to be, someone who I was moulded into, forced into, beaten into even, and that is not me and never will be again. I then think once more of where I am right now, walking to meet a guy called Tony when less than a week ago I was still living at Brampton, that small little town East of Carlisle with a monster who controlled everything I did.

I can't believe that was less than a week ago... wow, I cannot believe what I have done in a week. Monday, me and Sally make our bid to escape on the spur of the moment, Sally backs out, I decide to make a break for it with ten grand on me, I get to Pam and Denis's house Monday evening, Tuesday I meet Tony, Wednesday, I post the key to Rose, Thursday she gets into our house, I mean my house, I cannot call it our house, it will be my house once again, I just know it, anyway Thursday she gets my passport and driving licence, along with Jonathan's, that I still have incidentally. Friday, she brings me my key back, the documents, and a bank card and pin number, today, which is Saturday, I check the bank account and find that I have thirty-five grand in it, a couple of grand in my knicker draw, and another seven grand which Rose will likely deposit on Monday for me so by then, a week after I made my escape, I will have forty-two grand in the bank... *forty-two fucking grand* I whisper as I smile to myself.

I want to jump up and down on the spot. I am so excited I feel like I could burst. I never, not in my wildest dreams, not in all my time with Jonathan, ever thought I would be in this position five days after getting free from him. What a week it has been, and it's not finished yet. The night is young, as they say, well it's 6:45pm actually. I decided earlier today that unless I needed to spend Sally's money to survive or something like that, that I would keep it for her. I want to one day give her the fifteen grand that is hers. I know she will want me to have it, she would not give it another thought, but I want to give it to her one day. That would make me really happy.

I can see the bar up the road. The street is busy with early evening drinkers, either having a sneaky one on the way home from shopping or working or, like me just venturing out for the night. I haven't ventured out for the night since before I met Jonathan. Right from the off, we only ever went out as a couple and only when he wanted to and only where he wanted to go. It was never my decision, and I never went out on my own, ever from the first date I had with him. I never saw the controlling aspects of his character at first. I just thought he was being protective and that he just wanted to spend time with me. I thought it was sweet. I can't believe how naive I was, but I tell myself once more as I get nearer to the bar *that was then, a long time ago, this is now.*

I'm not sure how the conversation will go tonight, but I don't want to divulge anything of Jonathan to Tony, so I hope he does not press it. He knows I'm married, or maybe he thinks I was married. I'm not sure exactly what he thinks on that score, but if he asks, I will just tell him that I am married but am now separated and leave it at that. I don't want him to know much about my past, especially not about Jonathan and how he treated me... oh, and definitely not about my little crack at being a lesbian online porn star. Mind you, he might find that a turn on. I need to get that thought out of my mind as I enter the bar. Then I think to myself as I catch his eye, *I hope he's not seen me on the internet...* now that would be interesting, I tell myself as I walk towards him.

'Hi,' I say.

'Hi, you look beautiful,' he tells me as he leans in to kiss my cheek.

How sweet, I think to myself. 'What would you like to drink?'

'Ooh, a nice gin and tonic would be good, thank you.'

'Any particular one?'

'You choose.' Tony turns to the man behind the bar. 'I'll have a gin and tonic, that one there in the tall bottle, the pink one, and an orange juice, please.'

'You not drinking?' I ask.

'No, I have an ear infection, so I'm on penicillin. It's the second lot I've had. I'm hoping it clears it up this time for good. I thought it had, but it came back after a few weeks, so I've got a stronger dose this time, so don't want to risk it. Don't worry, it's not contagious.'

Tony must have seen my reaction when he said penicillin. It sends a shudder down my spine. Both me and Jonathan are allergic to it. I only know because my mum told me as a child that I had it once as a baby, and it brought me out in a rash, so it's on my medical notes, but Jonathan was apparently severely allergic to it. I never quite understood how someone could be severely allergic to something and someone else not be. I always told him that he was no more allergic to it than I was, but he was quite paranoid about it, told me it could kill him if he ever took it. He wouldn't go into the office once for over a week just because one of the office staff was taking it for an infection of some sort. I always just thought he was overreacting, but if I ever tried to tell him not to be so paranoid, he'd tell me I was thick and stupid, and just because I would only get a rash, that didn't mean that's all that would happen to him.

'It's ok. It's just that I'm allergic to penicillin, that's all, so as long as you don't spike my drink with it, we'll have a good night.'

'I won't, I promise.'

We get the drinks and sit down on some nice sofas. I like bars like this that have sofas to sit on and are more like your living room with a bar in it. It makes it so much nicer to sit and have a drink.

Tony tells me that he is originally from Nottingham,

has one brother, three years older, who lives in London and works in the city, and that his parents are both still alive and still live just outside of Nottingham in a little village called Oxton.

'So, what took you to Silloth then?' I ask.

'I just wanted to go and live on the coast, near a beach, you know, near the sea. It was just something that I always wanted to do. I'd moved to Manchester in my early twenties with a girlfriend I'd met on holiday as she was from here, but when that fizzled out, I just wanted to get away, you know have some space and all that and I just got a map out and decided I'd go to Silloth as it looked ideal, you know on the coast and just a stone's throw from the lakes. That was it, no other reason really, just on impulse, but I was there for about three years, worked in bars mainly and a hotel, plus I bought my first guitar whilst I was there and spent hours learning myself to play, and that's when I fell in love with music. enjoyed it while it lasted but moved back here to try and make some decent money and then I opened the music shop that you walked into the other day.'

'Oh, is it your shop?'

'Yep, well I rent the premises, of course, but yes, the business is mine. Just me and a part-timer called Lesley. She works three afternoons a week and all-day Saturday, but she was off today, or else you'd have met her. She's a natural talent; she can play just about any musical instrument and can play a tune after just listening to it. She's wasted really in my shop, but she loves it. She has a toddler, so the hours suit her, but she really could achieve so much more.'

'Maybe she will one day. You never know what's around the corner, and you can do anything you want if you put your mind to it.'

'So, what's your story? Why are you here in Manchester?'

I knew this was coming. I could tell. Sometimes you just know where the conversation is going. I could tell that he was leading up to it. I suppose it was inevitable really, I mean, how can any man go for a drink with a woman who three days ago was still wearing her wedding ring and not be inquisitive. I feel relaxed, though, and I feel easy in Tony's company. I wonder as I sit here sipping my drink to buy a few seconds whether I should tell him anything. I decide against it.

'I'm just visiting my auntie and uncle. You know, just getting away from it all, finding some space, finding time to play my guitar.'

'So, Manchester is your Silloth?'

'Maybe, maybe, who knows. I'm just going to see what happens and where life takes me.'

'Sounds like a good plan to me. Shall we have a walk and a drink somewhere else?' Tony asks as he drinks the last of his orange juice.

'Lead on. I don't know any of the bars around here, so we can go wherever you want to go.'

We have a couple of drinks in another trendy bar further up the road. This one was a bit livelier with a live band on who were very good. They knew Tony, due to the music shop and I think he liked the fact that he was well known in front of me. We then come out and walk along the street, passing the many bars and bistros that line the road. It has a nice feel to it, and I feel happy, maybe due in some small part to the three gin and tonics I've had, but happy all the same. I am linking arms with Tony. I don't recall when I did that;

it just seems to have happened.

'You hungry?' he asks.

'I am actually, well, a little peckish. I just fancy a bit of something, are you?'

'Yeah, same, just could do with something, but not too much.'

'You must know somewhere around here. What do you fancy?' I ask him. He stops and turns square on to face me.

'I know this may sound a little presumptuous, and well maybe a little forward, but I only live around the corner, and I make a great little tuna and pasta dish, you know a bit of gnocchi and some tuna with a few tomatoes and mushrooms. Only takes ten minutes to do and is very light.' I smile at him and chuckle a little.

'You knew what you were doing didn't you, eh with those three gins?' He holds his hands up as if to say, *what me guv?* and then nods his head.

'No flies on you, Anna, is there? Ok, so you sussed me out, but honestly, you'll love the tuna and pasta.'

'How far is it?'

'Two minutes walk. Just to the lights, turn right, and there's an apartment block. I live just there.'

'Come on then, but it better be tasty.' I say as I link arms with him again. As I walk with him to the lights before turning right, I remind myself once again how different this Saturday night is from how my life was just a mere seven days ago, well five days actually, but so different all the same. I feel like a normal woman, walking with her date, linking arms, looking forward to a bit of something to eat and hopefully a glass of wine to go with it in front of a fire of some sort. It sounds idyllic, and as I turn the corner, I hope I'm not disappointed.

Tony opens the front door to his apartment, and I'm quite surprised at how nice it is. I'm not sure why but I just expected something rather scruffy and typical of a man living on his own. I know how that may sound, and maybe I'm doing him and other single men a real disservice, but the flat, or apartment, should I say, looks very clean and very well presented. The hallway is very bright with flooring that I've not seen before with a door off to the kitchen, a door off to the bedroom and at the end a very nicely appointed lounge which is quite large and quite deceiving. We walk into the kitchen, and Tony immediately puts the kettle on. 'Tea or Coffee?' he asks, 'Or something stronger?' I know I did say that I was looking forward to a glass of wine, but I like the sound of a coffee.

'Coffee please, milk and half a sugar please.'

'Half a sugar, I wouldn't bother. Let me guess. You used to take two sugars, then one and now it's down to half a teaspoon full?' he says as he gets the cups from the cupboard.

'Spot on,' I say. 'How did you know?'

'I did the same, well I tried to, but I'm back up to two sugars now. I just don't think it tastes the same without a good bit of sugar in it. Anyway, you go and make yourself comfortable, and I'll make the drinks and the food. I'll bring you your coffee in a mo.'

I walk through to the lounge and take a seat on the white leather sofa. It's very soft and obviously very good quality.

'What's the flooring in the hallway? I thought it was wood or laminate when I first walked in but it's not, is it?' I shout, hoping he can hear me. He walks through from the hallway.

'No idea, it was down before I moved in. It's not hard

like wood or laminate, so doesn't make a noise, and it's not cold on your feet like tiles are. I really like it. I'm hoping to do this room with it soon.'

He goes back into the kitchen. I get up and look closer at the flooring. It does look really good. The lounge is carpeted, and I think how lovely it would look with that flooring down. He has a large television on the wall, central and sunk into it so that it is flush with the wall itself and a lovely marble design coffee table in the middle of the room. I look out of the window at the view of the night sky. There is little cloud, but I cannot see many stars as the streetlights and lights from the many bars and restaurants that I can see from the window make it hard to see anything at all in the night sky. I think about how different it is in Brampton, where light pollution is very low, especially when you get out of the town itself. The night sky looks amazing. I used to love seeing it, looking at all the stars glistening away, sparkling away to themselves, and I would wonder at the fact that the light I was looking at was thousands of years old.

'Here's your coffee.' I turn around and see Tony placing my mug of coffee on the coaster on the coffee table as he takes a seat on the sofa. I wonder whether to sit on the armchair but opted for a seat next to Tony. He has his tablets in his hand. 'Last one before bed,' he says as he pops one on his tongue and places the part open packet on the coffee table. 'Will you be ok sat so close to me as I take this?' he says, swallowing at the same time. 'I don't want you to keel over or anything.'

'Yes, I'll be fine, thank you,' I say mockingly. 'How many you got left to take?'

'Just the rest of that strip there, then that's it done, hopefully!' He says as he gets up to go and check on the gnocchi.

I check my watch; it's 9:50pm. I'm amazed at how time flies. I can't believe it took me two and a half hours to drink three gin and tonics, but then again, we were talking a lot. He did ask again about Jonathan, well about *my husband,* but I just told him that I was still married but that it was over, and I was never going back. I then told him that I might tell him all about it one day but that right now, that was the last thing I wanted to speak about. He said he understood, and that was that. Other than that, we just talked about everything and nothing, just as you do when you are comfortable with someone.

'Here you go, the best tuna and gnocchi you will ever taste.' Tony gives me a bowl of gnocchi, mixed in with tomatoes, onion, mushroom, and a chilli sauce with a few pieces of tuna steak neatly placed on the top. I must admit it does look very nice and very neatly presented.

'That looks very nice actually. Who taught you to cook?' I ask, genuinely intrigued as to how he can present such a lovely-looking dish in such a short space of time.

'No one really,' he says, having already started to tuck into his bowl. He waits until he finishes his mouthful before continuing to talk. I'm rather pleased about that as for a second, I thought he was going to share with me the contents of his mouth, and that is something that I hate to see. 'I just kinda taught myself, just simple bits like this, nothing too special, but it's tasty, try it.'

I start to eat my food and really enjoy it. Tony, in between mouthfuls, continues to tell me what else he likes to cook, and it all sounds very healthy and very tasty. He obviously likes rice, pasta, fish, and poultry, and mind you looking at his body, I can see why. Whilst he is tall and quite slender, he is rather firm and looks quite athletic. As he tells me about the benefits of spinach and how he likes to eat it most days, I cannot help but undress him with my eyes. I am feeling rather sexy as I sit here imagining what he looks like with his top off. I have that feeling in my undies again that I used to get when I was stripping for the camera, the feeling that I need to be satisfied, that I need to orgasm. It's just come over me all of a sudden. I can feel myself getting wet inside my knickers, and as I sit there trying my level best to show even the slightest bit of interest in spinach, all I want to do is unzip his flies. I recall the times that me, Rose and Sally got it together on Rose's bed for the camera, and I remember how I enjoyed it, but I cannot ever see myself having a full-on relationship with another woman. The thrill of doing that on the bed for the camera was very sexy and satisfying, but that was Jenny, not Anna, that was an alter ego, a character that I played, like an actress but in reality, as I sit here all I want is Tony.

I decide to just go for it. Why not? I'm a free woman who has not been able to do as she pleases for so long. I have no reason not to do as I please, and right now, I want pleasing. So I get down on my knees just as he puts his bowl down on the coffee table and position myself between his legs. I look at him, straight in the eye. He looks back at me but says nothing. I unzip his flies as I hold his gaze. His look says to me I am free to carry on, and he then lies back to enjoy the moment. I wonder if I am going to stay the night. I guess I am. I did tell Pam and Denis that I may be home late, but Denis just said, *well, if you don't make it home tonight, we'll see you in the morning.* So I know that they will not be too worried if I am not back until tomorrow.

I lift my head and stand up to take off my top. Tony gets up and helps me, and as he does so, I remove the rest of his clothes. We then fall onto the carpet. He takes my breasts in his hands and kisses them tenderly. He seems so gentle, so different from what I am used to. He then goes down on me and shows me that Jonathan knew nothing. Tony does things to me down there that I have never experienced before. He makes me want to explode as he kisses and caresses, and plays with me. I have at least two orgasms as he licks me like I've never been licked in my life. He then gets up and goes into the bedroom, telling me he'll just be a second. He returns, putting on a condom and turns me over, and enters me from behind. I want to turn over and get on top, but I also do not want to stop as the feeling is fantastic. I then feel him cum. I can tell from the feeling of his penis that he has cum. I put my right hand behind me and hold his thigh to keep him inside of me as I orgasm once again. I then flop into the carpet, exhausted and out of breath. Tony takes his condom off and takes it through to the kitchen. I hear the pedal bin lid flip up and down. He then comes back in and lies beside me. I lie on his chest and stroke his stomach.

We do not speak. There is no need to. We both just lie there and enjoy the aftermath of what has just happened. I feel appreciated, something I have not felt for such a long time. Did I just make love? It's so long since I made love I've forgotten, but whatever it was, seems so different from sex with Jonathan. This is what love-making must be like. I then fall asleep. Tony wakes me sometime later, and we go into his bedroom. I think we may have sex again, but Tony just pulls me to him, and again we lie there until I once again fall asleep. I wake up the next morning at just after 7:30am. Tony is already up, and I can hear him singing to the radio. I pull the covers up to my chin and take a deep breath in. I think of Simon, my imaginary guy who I hope one day to meet, my Mr Perfect, and wonder if Tony could be my Simon. I wonder.

I have breakfast with Tony, and we chat about music mainly and our love for it. Tony reckons that I should do some busking in Manchester city centre. He used to do it apparently and made some good money some days, he told me. I give him a rendition of my voice, and he reckons I could do well. I'm not so sure. I can hold a tune, but I'm no showstopper. He said he would go with me if I wanted to just until I gained my confidence. I told him I'd think about it. He then told me how he wants to open a second shop in a place called Wilmslow. He says that's his dream, to have a chain of music shops. I told him it was good to have dreams, and maybe one day it would happen.

On my way back to Pam and Denis's my phone rings. It's Mrs Simpson.

'Hi, Mrs Simpson, how are you today?' I say all bright and cheerful.

'Good morning, my dear. You sound chirpy this morning.'

'Why thank you,' I say. 'Today's a good day.'

'It certainly is. The sun is shining up here, and it's a beautiful morning. I've just seen Sally.' I stop in my tracks.

'When, just now?' I ask.

'Yes, I've just come away from her. I finally saw

Terry's car drive away about half an hour ago. You would not believe the hours I have sat watching the house, waiting for him to leave. I was beginning to think he'd retired or something. This is the first day he's left the house, to my knowledge. I even saw them having supermarket deliveries a couple of times.'

'How is she?' I ask... 'Is she ok, what did she say? Did he beat her?'

'One question at a time dear,' Mrs Simpson tells me. I realise that I'm bombarding her. 'Yes, she's fine,' she tells me, 'She certainly took a beating for what she did, but that was only for going out with you that day to the travel agents. Terry knows nothing about your visits to Rose's or from what she tells me that she was a cat's whisker away from getting on that train with you. He knows nothing about that. He did try and beat it out of her as to where you were, but she's said nothing. She's just told him and that husband of yours that she has no idea where you are, that you said nothing to her, and she's as gobsmacked as anyone as to where you are. She's a good friend you have there, Anna.' I can feel tears trickling down my face.

'Does she know why I've not rung her? Did you tell her that I would have but that I couldn't until we knew Terry was out of the way?'

'Yes, of course, she knows that, my dear. I made sure I told her. She knew that anyway, though.'

'How is she though in herself? Is she looking ok?'

'Not too bad, the bruises have subsided somewhat, and of course, they are not visible. She did show me a few, though. They are bastards the both of them but listen; your Jonathan will not rest until he finds you, apparently. He is still telling people that you are at home if anyone asks, so other than Sally, me, and

Rose, no one knows you are not just sat at home, cleaning away, looking after your husband. You know what he said at the governor's meeting last week, don't you? Well, he's also told the lady in the butchers too apparently as she was asking after you, according to Sally. She heard him tell Terry yesterday.'

'I need to ring her,' I say. 'Is it safe now?'

'Yes, Terry is back at work today. He just took some leave he was due apparently but he's on until 4:00 this afternoon, Sally told me. She'd love to hear your voice. She feels so bad for letting you down. I don't think she felt any of the blows she's taken. I think she's just so sad at all this because of how she feels she's let you down. She'd rather die than tell them anything, Anna. Be gentle with her, dear.'

'I will, of course I will. I love her. She's my best friend in the whole world... but, Mrs Simpson...'

'Yes dear?'

'Thank you for all you have done. You have no idea how much that means to me. I will never forget it.'

'It's a pleasure, my dear. I will still keep you informed of any developments. I'm not stopping now, but listen to me, watch out for Jonathan. He's got Terry on his side you know, and Terry has access to all sorts in his job. Just be careful and be on your guard.'

'I will, I promise and thank you again Mrs Simpson, take care.'

I disconnect the call and sit down on a bench outside Tony's music shop. I am so pleased that Sally is ok. I know what kind of beating she will have taken, but I also know that she'll recover from it. We always do, it's just how we are programmed. I dial her number and nervously wait for her to answer. I have no idea why I am nervous. I have no reason to be, but I am—a voice answers.

'Hello?'

'Sally, it's me.'

'Oh, Anna thank goodness, how are you? I miss you so much.'

'I miss you too, but never mind me, how are you? Mrs Simpson told me he beat you, are you ok?'

'I am sweetheart. I am, they are only bruises. The pain has just about gone. I'm a tough old bird; you know that. I'm just so pleased to hear your voice. I am so sorry Anna that I left you; please forgive me, please tell me you forgive me.'

'Of course I do. I understand. Look, you mean the world to me, and I know you must have had good reason, so please do not worry about it. I am fine. I'm with Pam and Denis, the couple that Rose put me in touch with, and I'm happy. I wish you'd have come with me, of course I do but I know you couldn't do it, it's fine honestly.' I can tell in Sally's voice how upset she is. I know it must have been so heart-wrenching for her to leave me at Carlisle station like that, but I forgive her, of course I do. I love her.

'I just couldn't do it Anna, when it came to it, I just didn't have the bottle. I knew when we were sat on Cecil Street waiting for Anna to come from the bank that I wouldn't go but I just could not tell you. I couldn't look you in the eye and tell you. I'm a coward, I know I am, but I'm sorry.'

'Don't be, listen there's no need,' I assure her.

'When you asked me to get some sweets, I couldn't believe that I had my chance to go. I was just going to say I was going to the toilet and then I was going to go, but I didn't have a penny on me to get home, but when you gave me that twenty-pound note to get some sweets, I knew then that I might make it back before Terry and he'd know nothing of the fact that I was in Carlisle. That way, I could say nothing and just make out you'd dropped me back off after the travel agents, and that was the last I saw of you. It worked out, too. They know nothing. I swear it; you're free girl, don't ever come back here 'cos he'll never let you go again. He'd kill you. But I won't ever tell them anything. I'd rather die.'

We talk some more, and I so enjoyed catching up with her. I told her about Tony and last night, which she found hilarious, by the way, and how I am playing my guitar again. She agreed that I should go busking. I told her I might do it if I can find the confidence. Again, she laughed out loud at that remark, not understanding how I can be short on confidence when I've taken part in a three-way lesbian romp on the internet. I told her that was a fair point, and I tell myself that she is right. What the hell am I waiting for? Busking should be a doddle after what I've done. It's amazing how quickly you forget lesbian romps in front of the whole world within a week or so when your life changes so much so quickly. I should not have baulked at busking at all, given what I have done. Confidence just should not be a problem for me, especially when it only involves playing a guitar, which I am fairly good at in front of maybe a handful of people. I should be able to do that without a second's thought. After all, I am used to performing for an audience, the difference being that the audience before was one that I could not see, and I was Jenny, not Anna.

Maybe that makes a difference, who knows, but as I turn the corner into the estate, I decide that I will go busking and decide I will do it today. Why the bloody hell not! Ooh, and before I forget, me and Sally have agreed to speak twice a week if we can. She will give me three rings on my phone, and I will ring her back. She'll just have to ring her mum afterwards, each time we speak. I can't wait to speak to her again.

chapter eighteen

It's been three weeks since I first spoke to Sally. We have spoken twice a week since then, every Tuesday and Thursday. We will keep it on these days unless Terry is off work, but he normally works normal office hours now, so we will hopefully be ok. I have to keep remembering to top my phone up. I just know one of these days it will run out of credit mid-sentence as we can talk for ages about nothing like we used to do every afternoon when we used to pop round to each other's houses.

I really enjoy our chats. If we can, we like to make them around two or there in the afternoon so we can pretend we are just like we used to be. Jonathan is still keeping up the pretence that I am just at home. Not many people will be asking him, of course, as I hardly ever went out other than to get food and a few bits now and again, so me not being around is not that unusual. I do wonder how long he can keep it up, though. Sally is fine, which I am so pleased about. I am missing her terribly still, as she is me, but our chats keep us together. If we ever had to stop doing that, I would find it so hard. I try not to think about that and am just grateful that we can still chat.

Pam and Dennis have gone to Dusseldorf for a few days with some friends and are due back tomorrow night. Their two sets of friends stayed overnight before they went. A couple from Stafford and a couple from Mansfield. The guy who also plays the guitar was there. He was pretty good and had written a song about them all going away. It was very funny, and we had a good night. I am their niece, so no one asked any questions. When they get back tomorrow night, they are going on a three-week cruise the very next day around the Mediterranean and the Canaries. Well, a two-week cruise and then a week's holiday in Malta, but they will be away for three weeks altogether. They love their cruises and tell me I should go on one. I'm not sure I'm old enough yet, but I'm sure I will one day.

I have seen Tony quite a lot. In fact, this last week and a half every night except one. I really enjoy his company. He is so laid back and expects nothing from me. That is the best bit. I do not have to try with him, and I feel so comfortable. We are already at the stage where we do not have to be doing anything when we meet, you know we do not have to be going out for a drink or a meal or anything, we can just go for a stroll or watch a bit of telly, or sometimes we just play guitar. He's so good, much better than me. He can play anything without having to practice it. I have to practice; that's the difference, I think, and I've also done quite a bit of busking. Tony did come with me that first time on that Sunday after I'd stayed over that first night, just to show me where the good pitches were, and we did a bit of a duet for an hour or so, but since then I've been about seven or eight times during the day and love it. I can be myself and just get lost in my music. I have a kind of regular pitch now, and I see the same people most times. They now smile and say hello, and a lot of them give me their loose change. The other buskers are great too. We meet up and have a coffee sometimes. Tony introduced me to one of the regulars who sort of took me under his wing, and then I got introduced to some of the others. I did think initially that I would not be made welcome with being an outsider, but they have all been great.

I still haven't told Tony about Jonathan, and to be fair, he hasn't asked. I have thought about it, but it's never come up in conversation, so I don't want to spoil things. I like things just as they are. I am happy; my life is good. Compared to a lot of people, my life would look shit. I mean, I'm living with a couple I only know through a friend; I'm busking for a living, and I'm a married woman who I suppose is having an affair with a guy who owns a little music shop and by the sounds of it doesn't make much of a living but in all fairness is someone who does have dreams. But I'm happy. Happier than I have been for such a long time, years in fact. I'm paying my way. I pay Pam and Denis a bit each week to cover my groceries and a bit towards the bills, and I'm not touching my money in the bank. I am saving that for another day. Pam and Denis didn't want to take any money off me, but I insisted, especially once I started busking. So, I am one happy woman.

I am sat in a coffee shop just along from Tony's shop as I am meeting him. He is taking me to look at a little shop he has found in Wilmslow. He says it would make a great second shop and says that I could run it for him if I want to. A proper job and something I would love to do too, and the best bit is that it has a one-bedroom flat above it that he says I could live in. I'm really excited and can't wait to see it.

I feel someone behind me and feel a kiss on the back of my neck. I turn my head and instantly smell the aftershave. I know it's Tony. 'Another coffee?' he asks.

'Ooh. Go on then, a latte, please,' I say as I take in his aroma. I love the smell of him. He reminds me nothing of Jonathan. Don't get me wrong, Jonathan always smelt nice too, but Tony just smells different, and even though Jonathan did use to smell nice, I could never really enjoy his smell because of who he was and what he was, and I am just so thankful that Tony smells nothing like him.

We have our coffee, and then we make our way to Wilmslow. It's only about five miles away, but we take the bus and enjoy the scenery. This is a lovely part of Cheshire, and I sit and look at some of the houses and wonder if I will ever live in something similar, but then I remind myself that my home in Brampton will one day be mine again. I just know it. I'm entitled to half of it anyway if I wanted to push that route, but never seeing Jonathan again is a small price to pay for not getting half of the house. I will bide my time, I tell myself, and wait until I can call it my home again. I have no idea when that will be but, call it whatever you like, intuition, sixth sense, or just a knowing, but I just know I will be able to again one day.

We get off the bus and walk a few hundred yards to a small but very neat and nice row of shops on Knutsford Road. There are only five shops in the row, next to a couple of wine bars and a small development of apartments. It looks very nice. The shops are small, but all seem to have an apartment or flat of some sort above them and seem to be brand new. Three of them are occupied, one being a florist, one being a hairdressers, and one being what looks like a shabby chic type of shop selling candles, mirrors, and little ornaments that people buy these days.

'It looks very nice around here,' I say as I look

around at the area.

'I know, I thought this would be ideal for a little music shop. The clientele around here will be ideal. There'll be a lot of sons and daughters who will be into their music, you know having music lessons and that. I can see it being a real destination type shop. What d'ya reckon?' Tony asks.

'I agree, I think it would do well. Is there any other music shops locally?'

'No... mine at Cheadle Hulme is the nearest, so I think it could be a winner.'

'Won't it compete with your other one, though?' I ask, thinking that it would seem silly to take business from one shop only to direct it to another.

'No, not at all. Nearly all of my customers are local, from Cheadle Hulme. This is what this area needs, a music shop of it's own. I'm telling you; this could be me on the road to global success,' he says as he pretends to toast the sky with an imaginary glass of bubbly.

We walk to the shop and knock on the door, and a man in a grey striped suit holding a brown leather briefcase comes to let us in. He looks very important and also wealthy. He might not be either, but he looks it and is well-groomed.

'Mr Walker?' he asks as he opens the door.

'Yes, hi, I'm Tony, and this is Anna.'

'Hi Anna,' the man says as he shakes Tony's hand. 'I'm Mr Newey, please come in and have a look around. I'm sure you will like what you see.'

The shop is just really an empty room, but as it's new, it looks very nice even if it is empty. We walk upstairs and look at the one-bedroom flat. It is very well appointed with a wooden floor in the hallway and a lovely cream carpet in the living room and bedroom.

It smells new, and the kitchen is very well appointed. I do like it, and as I take in the smell and look out of the living room window, I can certainly see myself living here. Tony is talking with Mr Newey about the costs and things, but I am more interested in visualising myself living here. I can see myself with my wine glass sat looking out of the window, and as I survey the area, I can certainly see myself wandering around here. It does all look very nice. I hear Tony tell Mr Newey that he'll get back to him soon, and I also hear Mr Newey tell Tony that there's been a lot of interest, and it will be snapped up quickly. As we walk outside, I shake Mr Newey's hand and then stand there with Tony, who has his hands on his hips looking back at the shop. 'Nice innit?' he says.

'It's lovely, everything about it is, but it's your decision,' I tell him.

'Yes, but you would be living here and running the shop, so it's your decision too. I want us to do this together,' he says as he takes my hand. I don't say anything as I hold his hand. I'm not sure if I want to do this thing together, so soon after escaping Jonathan. Don't get me wrong, Tony is nothing like Jonathan, the total opposite in fact, but what he said just now did seem a little serious, and whilst I am truly enjoying my time with him, I'm not sure that I want to do anything like this together with anyone. I would really like to work in the shop for him, to run it even. I've never had a job like that before, with responsibility and being my own little boss, making decisions and such, and I would respond well to it, I am sure, and I would love the flat upstairs, but I'm just not sure that doing it *together* is what I want. That sounds a little too much like a partnership to me, you know, as a couple, and as I walk away from the shop hand in hand with Tony, I ponder whether I want that sort of relationship, that sort of commitment even. I would much prefer to be an employee, on the books, doing my job and being paid for it as an employee. I would much prefer to be in the flat upstairs as a tenant, paying my rent and having a proper tenancy that is totally separate from the shop. That way, I think as I walk with Tony, I would still have the flat even if the job didn't work out, or at least that is how I understand a tenancy agreement works, but then what do I know? I've had no experience of this type of thing, but I'm sure I've picked up that information somewhere off the T.V, maybe on one of those tenant-landlord-type reality shows that are on from time to time. I need to think about this properly. Something is just telling me to keep that side of things strictly business-like and not let it interfere with our personal relationship, which is going really well.

I like Tony; I like him a lot. He is kind to me, puts no pressure on me, is laid back, and just goes with the flow. I like the freedom we have in our relationship; that's if we have a relationship, that is. I am so out of practice on these things that I don't know how it works these days. Are we an item? I have no idea. We seem to be, but then again, is what we are doing how things pan out these days? Do men no longer ask the ladies in their lives to be their girlfriend? Am I too old for that question? Is that only when you are at school or college? I don't recall Jonathan ever making anything official in the early days of our relationship as I come to think about it. It just sort of happened, you know, over time, we became an item, so I suppose me, and Tony may well be, even after only around three weeks.

'Are you ok? You're a bit quiet?' Tony asks me as we

sit in a coffee shop a few hundred yards from the shop we have just viewed. 'Did you not like it?'

'Yes, it was lovely. I think it would be ideal for what you want.'

'I just need to convince the bank now for my loan. I have an appointment tomorrow, remember,' he says, crossing his fingers on both hands.

'What time?' I ask, trying to remember the time.

'10:30am, I told you the other night when we had our pizza.'

'Oh yes,' I say, trying my best not to let on that I'd forgotten. I know how important this is to him. I think I got away with it. We were watching a great film at the time, in between talking about the shop, so I tell myself I have an excuse.

'I'm sure it will be fine. They'll see what a great idea it is, and anyway, you have your business account with them now, so they know how you run a business.'

'Yeah, but that doesn't always count for much. I don't make a lot of money, but I manage the money well, so they should at least see that I'm able to manage my money ok. Anyway, all I can do is try. If it's meant to be, it's meant to be. Are you sure you are ok? You look as though your mind is elsewhere?'

I can tell that he wants to know what is bothering me, and I am thinking that I should get this out in the open, at least put my cards on the table. I just hope that it doesn't spoil our relationship. I am just about to tell him how I feel when my phone rings. I look at the number. It's Rose.

'Hi,' I say. 'Are you still in the U.K.? I thought you might have buggered off by now.'

'Yes, I'm still here, listen, can you talk?'

I look at Tony. He smiles at me and leans back in

his chair, sipping his coffee. I want to say *'no, I'll ring you back later,'* but that would look suspicious and strange in front of Tony, so I say, 'yes, what's up are you ok?'

'Terry's been stabbed. He's in a bad way apparently, got stabbed whilst on duty earlier today.'

'What?' I say as I sit up straight in my chair. This has certainly caught me off guard. 'How do you know? Is Sally ok?' I ask.

'Mrs Simpson's here. She was just walking down your and Sally's road, as she does regularly, and saw Sally come out of her house with a taxi waiting outside. She shouted to her and just managed to get some sense out of her before she shot off to the hospital. That's all I know, but Sally did say that she was told by whoever rung her that it doesn't look good. Just thought you should know.'

'FUCK,' I mouth to myself. Tony frowns and mouths, 'what's up?' as I say to Rose 'right, well, I'll try her later. I don't suppose from what you say Terry will be coming home today, so I should be ok to ring her. If she's not in, I'll keep trying, but if you hear anything else, will you let me know?'

'Of course I will, no problem, Mrs Simpson will know before Sally does,' she says laughing. I laugh too. I know I shouldn't as Terry sounds in a bad way, but then I remind myself what a bastard he is and say, 'well, it couldn't have happened to a nicer guy.'

I finish my call and sit there wide-eyed, looking at Tony. 'One of my friend's husband has been stabbed. Quite bad, apparently.'

'Bloody hell, how bad is quite bad?'

'Don't know but bad, I suppose. He's a ...' I look

around before I say the word and then whisper the word, 'bastard.'

'Why, what's he done?' Tony asks.

'Lot's of things. Beats her up, you know, things like that. I know you shouldn't wish anyone dead, but I'd happily celebrate if he cops it,' I then laugh.

'What's funny?'

'Cops it,' I say... 'He's a copper. Got stabbed on duty. Just thought that was funny.'

Tony smiles. 'Well, let's hope your friend is ok.'

'I hope so. I'll try her later.'

'Ring her now. She'll have a mobile, won't she?'

'It's ok,' I say as I shake my head. 'I'll try her at home later. She'll have enough on.' Tony stares at me. He then curls one side of his lip up as he continues to smile at me. 'You still haven't told me your story; you know why you are here. I don't mean to pry, but I'd like to know one day.' I suppose this was bound to come up again sometime soon, and me taking a call from my past was bound to stir up the thoughts in Tony's head. I'm still not ready and certainly not in a coffee shop just outside Wilmslow.

'And one day you will,' I say. He nods his head.

'Ok, whenever you are ready. I'm a good listener.'

I decide that telling Tony about my thoughts on the shop can wait. Nothing is spoiling. The call from Rose has kind of put things into perspective a little bit, and after Tony mentioning my past himself, I don't want to tell him my thoughts now as it may look as though his question has me running scared or something, or that I've got something to hide. I suppose I have, in a sense but not how it may come across, so I decide to leave it for another day. It will keep.

I try Sally later that afternoon whilst I am sat at Pam and Denis's and again early evening. No answer from her phone. I assume she still must be at the hospital. I also try Mrs Simpson and Rose, who have both heard nothing. Mrs Simpson told me that she had walked past Sally's twice but no sign of her. I hope Terry dies. I really do. Sally would be free then. That would make me so happy.

I miss Pam and Denis and look forward to them coming home tomorrow night. I miss Pam's cooking that's for sure. Tony is due around 7:30pm. We are just having a night in, in front of the T.V., I have told him that he cannot stay over though whilst they are away as that would not sit right with me. I'm sure they would be ok with it, but I wouldn't be, not in someone else's house while they are away, and I told them I would look after the house, so I am not sleeping at Tony's either. Thankfully, Denis said there was no need for me to stay at night because they are used to leaving the house empty when they go away, but I promised, so I am... I'm glad he said what he did, though, because when they go on their three-week cruise, I want to be able to stay at Tony's some nights. A girl has her needs!

I'm struggling to sleep tonight. I have been tossing and turning for hours, thinking about Sally mainly but also thinking about Tony and his shop. I know that he has the meeting with the bank in the morning. I wished him good luck as he went home earlier, and I hope he gets the money he needs. He has dreams, and I want him to realise them. People should have dreams. I remember my dreams when I was younger before I met Jonathan. I would dream of being a star, an actress, or something. My mum used to tell me I would. I know it was her dream for me, too, but as I got older, I wanted to put on those large events and be a major player in the corporate eventing world. I would have been good at it. I often wonder what if... what if I hadn't met Jonathan, where would I be now, probably not sleeping in someone's spare room, that's for sure. I look at my phone. It's 1:37am. I'm sure I haven't been asleep. I put my phone down and decide to get up to make a cup of tea. That always works. A nice cup of tea can sort anything. I just walk out of my bedroom door when my phone rings. I rush to pick it up. It's Sally. I wait for her to ring off. She doesn't. It keeps ringing. I tell myself how strange that is, but on the sixth ring, I answer it, not expecting it to be Sally on the other end. My breathing quickens. 'Hello,' I say.

'Anna?' Sally asks.

'Yes, it's me, Sally, how are you? I heard what happened.'

'He's dead. Terry's dead,' she says, sounding quite upset.

I don't know what to say. I don't answer straight away. I want to say, *'thank fuck for that,'* but stop myself as I am unsure what Sally would say to that. He is her husband at the end of the day.

'Are you still there Anna, did you hear me?' she still sounds upset. I'm slightly annoyed.

'Yes, I'm here. How are you feeling?' I ask.

'He's dead, Anna, he's fucking dead. The bastard is fucking dead, and I should be elated, but I'm sad. I'm upset. I shouldn't be.' Sally then screams before continuing, 'I hated the fucker. I loved him too in a strange way, fuck knows why but I did, but I'm free, he's gone, and I'm upset. Why am I upset, Anna? I don't want to be upset. I want to be happy; I should be happy. I want to feel happy and relieved. Do you understand, do you know what I mean? Please say you do.'

I don't. I don't bloody understand. She should be jumping for joy, she should be dancing around that lounge of hers with a very large glass of very expensive champagne planning a very expensive foreign holiday, but she's not. She's upset, and for the life of me, I do not know why but I say, 'of course I do, he was your husband at the end of the day, and despite whatever he was Sally, he was still your husband, so yes I do understand.' I don't, not at all. I'm confused, but that's not what she wants me to say.

'He got stabbed multiple times,' she continues, 'he got called out to a serious incident on the Botcherby Estate. That's all they told me. Some family dispute that escalated, and he just got caught in the middle of it. I'll be fine in a day or so. I know I will. I did hate the bastard, and I'm sure I'll be glad he's gone soon enough, but when you've been married and together for as long as we have, it's just not normal that he's not around. I nearly only gave you three rings, you know, but then I thought, *what you doing Sal, he's dead, he can't hurt you anymore,* but I still nearly cut off after three rings, though. It'll take some time to get used to. You know, not having to think about everything I do for fear of upsetting him. I so wish you were here, Anna; it's going to be so hard on my own.'

I feel a real pang of guilt. I know she needs me, but there is no way I can go up there. I just couldn't risk it. I'd be potentially undoing all I've done to get this far, so I say, 'I know Sal, I wish I could be there with you too. Maybe you could come down here for a few days, you know, just to have some time out, some time to think. I'm sure Pam and Denis would not mind, in fact, I'm certain they wouldn't. What do you think?'

'I can't mate, too much to do up here. I've got to organise everything, funeral, and things, you know all of that. There'll be so much to sort out. I'm not looking forward to it. I'm no good with things like that. Terry sorted everything out. I don't even know how to pay a bloody phone bill.'

I think for a moment. Maybe I could go up, just for a couple of days. I could go in disguise. I still have the wig and the glasses that I wore on my way down here. Jonathan would be at work all day anyway, and if I just stayed in the house with Sally, I could at least support her for a day or two. She is my best mate, after all. I bite my lip as I think. 'I could come up for a day or two and stay at yours, just to be there for you whilst you get your head around things, and I could help you sort things out.'

'Would you, Anna? ... would you really?'

'I will, yes. You mustn't breathe a word of it thought to anyone. Not anyone, Sally. My life could depend on it, and I'm not joking.'

'I won't breathe a word of it, I promise, not to anyone. Are you sure you want to do this? I'll be ok, you know; I'll get through it.'

'It's ok. You're my best friend in the whole world, Sal. I want to be there for you. I can wear the wig and glasses I have and can just stay at your house. I won't be able to go out though, not even on your driveway, or on your garden for that matter, and I daren't risk it for more than two or three days, but at least I can help you sort a few things out and... well, just be there for you.'

'I feel much better already. It will be just like old times, only this time we can be together all day. Good riddance to that nasty bastard... I FUCKING HATE YOU, TERRY, GOOD FUCKING RIDDANCE!' Sally shouts. Then she laughs out loud. 'There, I feel happy already. When are you coming up?'

'In a couple of days. Pam and Denis are back tomorrow, well tonight actually,' I say as I remember what time it is. 'So, I want to see them first, plus they go on a cruise the day after tomorrow ... err, no, they go tomorrow. Bloody hell, I can't think what day it is.' I say out of frustration as I again remember it's the early hours of the morning. 'So let me see them off. I'll be up in a couple of days. Just hang fire but remember, say nothing to anyone, not even Mrs Simpson or Rose ... nobody.'

'Promise?... Ooh, I'm so excited to be seeing you. You won't believe how different I'll be in a couple of days. I'm free, Anna. I'm bloody well free at last.'

'It will also give me time to get you your fifteen grand. You can have it now Terry's gone. You earned it after all.' I tell her.

'I Don't want it,' she says quickly.

'What, why?' I ask, quite surprised.

I want you to have it, Anna. I'll be ok. Terry's boss told me that I would be fine financially. I'll get a pay-out or something, he said, you know for Terry being killed in the line of duty and all that, plus he had life insurance of his own, so that will pay out too, so I'll be fine. Honestly, I want you to have it, so please do not bring it.'

'Are you sure? I ask, really quite taken aback that I have been given a fair chunk of money for the second time in a few weeks.

'100% Anna, you're my friend, and like you want to help me now, I want to help you too, but the only way I can do that at the moment is financially, so keep it, use it for something, something good.'

I wait for the kettle to boil. It's now ten past two in the morning. I'm looking forward to seeing Sally, I really am, but I do have this little knot in my stomach that I can't shake off. I'm not sure if I am just nervous about going up there and being next door to Jonathan or if I'm nervous about how unpredictable I suddenly feel Sally is going to be now that she's on such a high. She went from being sad and upset to happy and elated in the space of less than ten minutes.

I just hope above all else that she keeps my impending visit to herself. I sit down and hold my mug of tea close to my chest as I look out of the patio window into the garden and wonder if I will live to regret my decision to go up to see her. I tell myself not to allow these negative thoughts into my head and that I will be fine. Jonathan has no reason to think I will be up there. He has no idea where I am, and as far as he is aware, Sally doesn't either, so I tell myself to stop being silly and finally go back to bed. I fall asleep and sleep quite well.

chapter nineteen

Even though the house is immaculate, I dust, polish, and hoover throughout just to make sure it is nice for when Pam and Denis get back. I have been to the shop and bought three nice pieces of steak to do for us all for tea. It's the first piece of steak I have bought since I left Brampton, and for the first time in my life, I have been able to buy steak without any thought as to what size or weight they were. I love it.

Sally rang me again, just to talk. I get the feeling she'll be on the phone to me quite regularly. I told her about Tony. She couldn't believe it, so soon, but was happy for me. In fact, she told me to get all the sex I could and to bloody well enjoy it. She also told me to be careful and to make sure he always treated me well. I told her he did. She's so different from how she was when I answered the phone to her last night. She's so happy and full of it you'd never think she'd just lost her husband. She told me she'd play the game of the grieving widow though to anyone other than myself, Mrs Simpson, and Rose. She told me Mrs Simpson dropped by early this morning. She knocked Sally up out of bed apparently, couldn't wait to find out the gossip. Sally assures me she didn't say a word to her about me going up. Rose rang her also and was calling round later. I asked Sally to try and be discreet where Rose and Mrs Simpson were concerned because if Jonathan sees them going round, it will look peculiar to him. I do not want him to have any suspicions whatsoever about anything at all that may be connected to me. She assured me she would be, but I still cannot shake the feeling that Sally just needs to calm down a little bit. She needs to play the game but also needs to understand there are other players other than herself, and one of them is me.

I rang Tony first thing to wish him good luck and also told him about me going up to Brampton. He knows nothing about Jonathan, so I just said it was to go and support my friend Sally. He said I should go and support her; it's what friends do. That's another thing I like about him. He never has an issue with what I want to do. I said I would meet him at the shop after lunch as he needs to get straight back there as Lesley is covering for him this morning whilst he is at the bank. I've still never actually met Lesley; I just never seem to be at the shop when she's there. Mind you, when she is there, Tony normally isn't so it's no real surprise. I hope he has good news to tell me. It will set me up for my afternoon busking. If he has bad news, it will be harder for me to put on a smiley face for the passers-by, who always prefer a smiling face to which to give their hard-earned change to. I make myself a cup of tea before I decide to sit down and play a few tunes on my guitar. I have a busy day ahead.

I walk into Tony's shop. 'Well, how did it go?' I ask.

He shakes his head. 'Knocked back, I'm afraid. They said that because I have no collateral, it's a no-go in the current economic climate,' he uses his fingers as speech marks to emphasise 'the current economic climate' bit. 'He can't have been more than 20 years old the guy who seen me. Knew fuck all, but he has the power to give it to me or to turn me down, so to speak, and turn me down he did.'

I put my arms around him and cuddle him close. 'I'm so sorry,' I say. 'I really thought they'd help you.'

'Me too, but as I don't own the building to this place, and I only rent my apartment, I have nothing to put down. I told him that I had nowt to put down last time, but they still leant me money to start this place.' He looks around the room and throws his arms in the air in a show of despair.

'What did he say when you told him that?' I ask.

'Just said things have changed, different times, the bank has changed their lending criteria, all that shit.' He looks dejected.

'It's not like I wanted a fortune. Only needed about fifteen grand, that's all, fifteen poxy grand, and they couldn't even lend me that.'

'What will you do?' I ask.

'Just have to put that dream on hold, I suppose. I really wanted that shop. I know it can be a great success. I'll just have to try and find someone with a spare fifteen grand that wants to come into the business with me, you know, like a partner who can share in the profits and get their money back that way. I'll find someone, or something will turn up. I've just got to be...'

'I'll lend it to you,' I say, interrupting him mid-sentence.

'What, you? How?' he says, looking genuinely puzzled.

'Never mind how. I have a few quid, and I can lend you the fifteen grand in return for a share of your little empire,' I say. I cannot believe I've said it, but what he said about having a share of the business really excites me. I know what I thought yesterday about not wanting to do this together and just being an employee, and all that will now sound strange, but this is different. I'll have a stake in the business, a real share, and can make the decisions with him. Yesterday, when I was having my wobble, and he was talking about doing it together, he was still the boss. I was not part of it. I did not have any 'collateral' as he put it earlier, within the business, but this way, I would, I would have a share of the profits, for years hopefully. I think how I can use Sally's fifteen grand, well the fifteen grand that she gave me really, so I tell myself I am not spending any of my money. Sally said she wanted me to do some good with it and helping Tony out and buying a stake in his business is good for the two of us. I'll tell her when I go up; she'll be thrilled to bits.

'Will you really, but how, when?' he asks rather excitedly. I can see the excitement in his eyes.

'I can give it you whenever you need, but what stake would I have?'

'Bloody hell, all business-like all of a sudden,' he says mockingly.

'Yes, well. Old Anna Fox here can be business-like too, you know, so what stake?'

'Mmm,' he says, narrowing his eyes, 'How about twenty percent?' I am unsure if he is asking me if I would accept twenty percent or if he is putting that down as a marker. I decide to play hardball.

'Twenty percent? No way Mr Walker, thirty-three percent at least. I want a third of your business I say pretending to be a real businesswoman and trying to look serious in the process.

He smiles at me. 'Thirty-three percent, bloody hell,

that's more than I had bargained for.' I wonder whether to come back with a lower offer as I do not want to miss the chance. I'm not sure if he is serious or playing with me. We look at each other in some sort of stand off. 'I'd need it asap so as not to miss it,' he says.

'You can have the money tonight. I can get it this afternoon,' I say, again trying my very best to be professional and assertive. He hugs me.

'A third it is Mrs Fox, welcome to the board,' he squeezes me tight. 'But listen, seriously, is there any chance I can have it before you go to Cumbria? I just want to tell Mr Newey I want the shop, and I want to be able to leave him a decent deposit on the first three months' rent to show I am serious and to make sure it's mine.'

'If that's what we need to do, then yes, I'll see if I can get it out of the bank this afternoon whilst I am in town. I'm sure I'll be able to.'

'You can just transfer it to me, can't you? No need to draw out in cash,' he says.

Shit, I think to myself. I wasn't expecting that, and I need to think on my feet. I don't want to do that as I don't have online banking or anything like that. It's not even my account, so I'm a strictly cash kind of girl these days. I pause a second.

'I don't have any access to the internet, so I'll just draw it out for you.'

'Ok great, as long as I have it before you go to Cumbria, that's fine.'

'We never even shook hands,' I say as I hold out my hand to shake and he does the same. We shake on the deal.

'I can't believe this Anna. You are the best thing to ever happen to me. You really are. This is the start of things to come.'

I go into town with my guitar, and I stand in my now usual spot. The city centre is busy as usual. It amazes me how busy Manchester is. Coming from Brampton near Carlisle really does shelter you from the masses; even Carlisle, which is a city, after all, is only really a town, but it does have city status, maybe because of the cathedral I think, but it's nothing like this in terms of people. I do like Carlisle though; it is a very historic city and has lots to offer. I just wish I'd been able to enjoy it more when I was there. I do an hour or so and make a few quid, and then I head to the bank to draw out the money for Tony. I'm so excited to be doing this. I never thought in my wildest dreams I would be a partner of sorts in a business, a real business.

Tony said I would need to be registered as a director for the company. I don't really know how to go about doing that, but he said he would sort it for me. He's good like that. He knows the ins and outs of that side of things. He also said that he will get his accountant to draw up a document for my shares. Again, I don't really understand it all, but he said that he would need to sell me thirty-three percent of the shares so that I will then own that part of the business. It all sounds very real and very professional. I just hope that I can draw the money out today. I've never drawn that much out of a bank before, and as it's not really my account, I'm a little bit nervous. I'd not considered that when I said I would draw it out for him as I've gotten so used to it being my account, but I'm sure that if I have my bank card, it should be fine. I've never had to do this kind of thing before as Jonathan dealt with it all.

I wait in the queue and look around at the people.

They are mostly men in suits and women in their office wear, although I listen to an irate lady at one of the counters arguing with the young girl behind the counter because her benefits have not yet been paid in, and she's got bills to pay. I feel sorry for the young girl who is doing her best to remain calm and professional, but I also feel sorry for the lady who is in obvious distress and is struggling to hold it all together. Her toddler sits in his pushchair wide-eyed, looking around him totally oblivious to the stress and worry his mum is feeling right now. I look at some of the other people in the bank and realise that hardly any of them have actually noticed the lady who is now wiping tears away from her face as she gathers her papers and stuffs them into her handbag. No one really cares. They are totally unaware of her stress and anxiety. I catch her gaze, and I smile at her, trying to give her a little bit of reassurance. She looks right through me, and I'm unsure if she has actually noticed me. I guess not. I feel so sorry for her. I have no idea what her circumstances are or what life she has back home. Maybe she's a single parent on her own just trying her best to make ends meet, maybe she has a partner or husband back home who will give her the support she needs and a cuddle, or maybe she has her own Jonathan back home waiting to tell her how stupid she is and how she's useless and maybe she'll get a backhander or two.

I'm making my own story up; I know, but as I watch her walk out, she stops and bends down in front of the pushchair just at the side of the front door of the bank and gets a lollypop out of her handbag and gives it to her little boy. He pops it straight into his mouth and sucks on it without a care in the world. She strokes his hair, kisses her forefinger, and plants her finger on his forehead. I notice that she is wearing cheap clothes. They are clean, and so is her little boy, but he too is dressed in rather cheap clothes and has a hole in one of his knees. Her hair is scraped back and looks as though it hasn't been washed in quite a few days. She's just a young girl really, and as I study her closer is no more than 25-years-old. She just needs a bit of help. I hear someone say, 'Can I help?' and look around to see a lady from behind the counter looking at me. It's my turn. I take a second and look around at the young girl. She is walking out of the door. I turn to the lady behind the counter, a middle-aged woman who has eaten a few too many cakes in her life and say, 'It's ok, I'm sorry,' and I turn to walk out of the door. I walk onto the street and look for the young girl. I can see her about 20 yards away. I catch her up and tap her on the shoulder.

'Excuse me,' I say as she turns around. 'I'm sorry to bother you, but I couldn't help overhearing your conversation in there, in the bank. I was in the queue. Are you ok?'

She looks behind her, over her shoulder, and then back at me. 'Who me?' she asks. 'Yes, I just wanted to make sure you were ok. You looked a bit stressed in there.' I tell her, softening my voice to try and make me sound as friendly as possible.

'Erm, yes, erm, who are you? Are you the police?' she asks. I shake my head.

'No, nothing like that. I'm called Anna, I'm just someone who plays the guitar, over there,' I say as I point to where my spot usually is. 'I just wanted to make sure you were ok, that's all.'

'I'm fine, thanks,' she says in a soft voice. 'I'd have been better though if my benefits had come through like they said they would. It's a nightmare, a bloody nightmare sometimes. All I want is what I'm entitled to, you know to feed this little one. They should have been in at the end of last week but still nothing. I've filled in all the forms and everything,' she says, sounding very dejected.

'What's your name?' I ask her.

'Sam,' she says, 'short for Samantha, but I prefer Sam.'

'And who's this little one?' I say as I kneel down and smile at the little boy in the pushchair who is still sucking on his lollypop.

'Harry, he's my hero, aren't you Harry?' She crouches down next to me and squeezes his cheeks.

'Do you fancy a coffee and a piece of cake, Sam? My treat, just over there in that cafe. Harry can have something to eat too if he likes.'

'Really, are you sure? That's very kind of you.'

'No problem, come on.' I indicate with my head that we should walk on over to the cafe. Sam and Harry walk with me. We go inside, and I order two lattes, two slices of cake, and an egg and cress sandwich for Harry with a carton of orange juice and a straw. Harry eats his sandwich and drinks his juice as though he's not had anything to eat or drink in days. I'm sure he has, but he really does enjoy his little treat. I can tell that Sam is a little awkward. She struggles to make eye contact with me and eats her cake slowly as if she is uncomfortable. I understand how she will be feeling, she doesn't know me after all and has probably never had anyone do this for her before.

'Are you going to be ok?' I ask her, 'You know with money and that sort of thing.' She shrugs her shoulders.

'Who knows?' she says.

'Is there anyone in your life that can help you?' I ask, trying to find out if there is a boyfriend of any sort. She shakes her head. 'No, his dad disappeared a few weeks after he was born. Said he wasn't cut out for this life, so he just left me to it. I have my own flat, well a council flat but it's just me and Harry, isn't it sweetheart?' she says as she smiles and rubs the top of his head. I feel so sorry for her. She looks dejected but also comes across as though she will always be there for her son and will keep fighting on to try and make something of her life. I like how she doesn't swear and also how she obviously dotes on her son. I then think about the money that I was going to get out of the bank for Tony and the shares and the business and all that and think about what a whirlwind few weeks I have had, and I suddenly want to stop the bus and get off.

In the moment, as I sit here and think of what I was about to do I realise that I don't want to do it, not any of it. I don't want to get the fifteen grand, and I don't want to go into the business with Tony. I don't want to keep going on this treadmill that I suddenly find myself on. I want to stop it and get off, and I want to go back to just taking my time with my life. I want just to be me, Anna Fox, and only have me to worry about. What was I thinking? I ask myself as I sit and look at Sam and realise that I have only known Tony for a few weeks and that yesterday I was ready to tell him that I do not want to do any of the stuff with the new shop 'together,' that I just wanted to have a job and somewhere to live. To have no stress in my life and then all of a sudden, I got swept away by a dream of having part of a business, because I saw that as a mark of success, but as I put the last bit of cake in my mouth, I ask myself who was I doing that for? What was I trying to prove and to whom?

I look at Sam and think how meeting her may have just been the best thing that's happened to me today. Had it not been for her, I'd have been on my way home with fifteen grand in my pocket in cash to hand it over to someone who I hardly know. I shake my head as reality sets in. I know for sure now that I do not want that. I don't want to be in partnership with Tony, or anyone for that matter. I'll just have to tell him later tonight. I'll be seeing him after I've had an hour or so with Pam and Denis, so I'll tell him then. If he is the man I think he is, then he'll understand; he'll be fine.

'Can I get you another coffee?' Sam asks me.

'No, don't be silly, I'll get them, same again?'

'I'd like to at least buy you a coffee. I can afford two cups of coffee, you know, only just mind, but I can get these.'

'Sam, please put your money away. Keep it for you and Harry.' I get up and walk to the counter, and order two more coffees. I look round and see that Sam has taken Harry out of his pushchair, and she is sat with him on her knee. He looks tired. She is wiping his mouth and face with a baby wipe she has in a carrier bag on the back of the pushchair. I wonder how much she needs to tide her over. I'd love to help her. If I knew her better, I'd suggest we get a laptop with an inbuilt camera, but I smile to myself as I know that would not be a good idea, well not right now anyway. So, I walk back over and sit back down with the coffees.

'How much do you need to tide you over?' I ask.

'Depends on how quickly my benefits come through. I had a job, you see, but it got finished two weeks ago. It was only a temp job, but I'd been there nearly a year, so I kind of got used to it, so when they finished me, it came as a shock.'

'So, what would get you through?' I ask.

'£300 or so would be a lifeline for me. I had enough put by to pay the rent, so I know that's all up to speed, but I need to pay the gas and leccy bill, and well,' she looks down at Harry. 'As you can see, a new pair of trousers and that would not go amiss; then I just need some food. I'm sure my benefits will be through soon. They'll have to,' she says.

'Sup up and I'll go to the cashpoint, and I'll get you the £300, you can have it as a gift from me.' She shakes her head.

'I can't, really, that's so nice of you, but I couldn't, I don't know you.'

'That doesn't matter, look I know you don't know me, but I want to help, honestly. Someone helped me recently, well, more than one person, to be honest, and I know how much a leg up can really help, so please let me do this. I don't want it back. I'll probably never see you again. All I ask is that you don't waste it and that you spend it on the things you've just told me about. That's all.'

She looks at me and wipes a tear from her face. Then wipes another one. 'Thank you,' she says, 'Thank you so much.' I take her hand and place it between mine.

'You'll be ok, Sam, and listen, see over there,' I point out of the window across the square to my usual busking pitch. 'That's where I do my busking. Two or three times a week or so, so if you ever need to find me, I'll be there at some point.'

I go to the cashpoint and give Sam £300. I feel great; helping someone is so good, much better than handing over fifteen grand for a share in a business that I now know I do not want to be part of. I know Tony will understand.

I go home and get there before Pam and Denis get back. I cook the steaks, and we have a nice early evening tea. They tell me about Dusseldorf, saying it was lovely. It sounds like a good place to go. I met their friends again, but they only stayed for a quick cuppa, then they got themselves off home. They all seem to get on well. As soon as we finish our tea, Pam and I do the dishes while Denis unpacks. Pam then says she needs to do a load of washing and packing again as they are off on their cruise tomorrow. They don't leave until late morning. They are catching a coach down to Southampton, so I will see them before they go. I imagine I will be stopping at Tony's tonight as we've not been together for the last three nights as I've stayed here. That's unless he falls out with me about the money. I know he won't; I know he'll understand.

chapter twenty

'Come in, partner,' Tony says as he kisses me on the cheek as I walk into his apartment. 'How did it go? Did you get the money ok?' he asks. He stands there with is hands on my shoulders from behind as we walk along the hallway into the lounge.

'I didn't get it,' I say. 'Look, sit down; I want to talk to you.'

'Err, ok,' he says as he sits on the couch and crosses his legs. 'Everything alright?' he asks.

'Well, yes, everything's fine, but I had a think about what we said and what we spoke about and all that, and well, I've had second thoughts, and I don't want to go into any partnership or anything in the business. It's just not me. You know all that running a business and that. I'm happy as I am, and I think I just got a bit carried away with it all. I'm sorry, Tony, but you understand, don't you?'

He says nothing but leans forward and puts his head in his hands, and then runs them through his hair.

'So, what are you saying?' he asks, putting his arms out with his palms facing upwards.

'Just that I don't want to come into the business, that's all. I'm happy as I am, and if you still get the shop, I'd love to work in it for you, like we said, you know, like we talked about initially.'

'So, what about the fifteen grand?'

'Well...,' I say, as I'm starting to feel a little uneasy. Tony's body language says he's not too pleased. 'Well, I didn't get it 'cos like I say I had second thoughts about it all.'

'So, you aren't giving me the money?' he asks. His face looks angry. I feel nervous. I've seen that look before many times, not with Tony, but many times with Jonathan, especially when he was trying to make out something was my fault when it wasn't at all.

'Err, no, like I say, I just want to stay as we are.'

He stands up. 'Stay as we are? Why would I want to stay as we are? Why the fuck would I want to stay as we are, with you?' He grabs my hair from behind and pulls my head back. It hurts.

'Ouch, Tony, you're hurting me.' Images flash through my mind as I am taken back to Brampton in my head. I see Jonathan in my mind's eye. I hear Jonathan in my head. I cannot believe what is happening to me.

'I want that money, you bitch. I owe people. Did you really think that I wanted to go into business with you?' He laughs. 'I don't even have a business. I don't own that music shop, you stupid cow. You just believed I did. I want that money, and I want it quick, tomorrow, or else they'll kill me. Are you hearing me, you bitch? I want that money.' He throws my head forward, and I land face down on the floor. He grabs my head from behind and grinds my face into the carpet. I scream out as best I can. He lets go. I stand up. My face hurts.

'What do you mean you don't own the music shop? What about the shop we looked at?' He spits at me as he speaks.

'I just arranged that viewing to make it look

convincing. I knew you must have had a few quid, coming down here from Cumbria, all smoke, and daggers, telling me nothing, stringing me along, none of that added up, so you must be running from someone or something and that, in my experience usually means a few quid is involved. I knew if I shagged you enough times and played the nice guy that I'd get you to give me some money somehow. Lesley owns the shop. I just work there part-time,' he laughs, 'Ha, you really fell for it, didn't you? How fucking stupid can you get?' He walks over to me and grabs my chin with one hand and strokes my hair with the other. 'Now I don't know your story, and to be honest, I don't care, but I want that money you promised me, and I want it tomorrow. I owe some nasty people, and I ain't getting bumped off, you hear me?' I lift my knee and knee him in the balls as hard as I can. He groans loudly and immediately lets go of me as he crouches down in pain. I step to the side.

'Bitch,' he shouts out as he makes a lunge for me. I step back out of his grasp. He is still crouched down. He falls on one knee. I want to kick him in the head as hard as I can, but I cannot bring myself to do it. I turn and run. I can hear him trying to run after me, but I get his door open and run down the stairs. I do not stop until I am outside on the street at least a good fifty yards from the apartment block on the corner of the traffic lights. My heart is racing. I am breathing so heavily. My adrenalin is pumping so fast. I burst out laughing. I don't know where that comes from. Wow, that felt good. When I kneed him in his bollocks, it felt so good. I never fought back with Jonathan. I would always freeze in fear, and for a moment, up there in that flat, I could feel myself going to freeze, and then

I told myself, *no way, not again, no man is going to do this to me again.* That was when I brought my knee up into his groin.

I take deep breaths. I can't see him. He has not come out of the apartment block. The street is busy. I feel safe. I turn and walk towards home, towards Pam and Denis's house. I look into a shop window at my reflection. I look ok; there's no sign of blood on me. My head hurts where he pulled my hair, and my face feels a bit sore from where he pressed it into the carpet, but that will subside soon. I realise as I keep on walking that I need a drink. I walk into a bar and order a glass of wine and sit down on my own and think about what just happened. The bar is fairly quiet, with only a handful of couples having a drink, and a couple of guys at the bar sat on bar stools. I see them look over in my direction, probably wondering why I am sitting on my own, but I do not even catch their gaze. I cannot believe what has just happened.

What is wrong with men? Why do they treat women like they do? I really thought Tony was different. I really thought he was a nice guy. He'd been kind, attentive, understanding, sensitive, but it seems it was all just a ploy to see if he could get any money out of me. I wonder if that was his motive right from the beginning or whether he really did like me that first day I walked into his shop. Ha, that's funny. It's not his shop, after all. That was not real either. He must have had ulterior motives right from the off because he told me it was his shop on our first date if I remember correctly. The bastard. Why Tony, why? I am proud of myself, though; I really did kick him in the goolies. I smile to myself as I recall my actions and in my head.

I raise my glass to myself. I do not really do that,

of course, as I would look rather silly sat in this bar raising a glass to myself. I am proud of myself, yes, but I am also sad. Sad, because once again, men like Jonathan and Tony think they can just treat women like shit. Women like me, and probably like a lot of women who just for some reason seem to attract the wrong kind of guy. *What is it about me?* I ask myself, what do I give out to attract arseholes like I do? I also realise though, that I've just had such a lucky escape. I could have got drawn into all sorts with Tony. I do not even know who he owes money to or what he owes it for. It's probably drugs or something sinister like that, and I could have been caught up in it, plus I doubt I would have ever seen my fifteen grand again, well Sally's fifteen grand. I know she's told me I can keep it, but I really do one day want to give it her back.

I can accept Rose's share that she gave me, and I can accept that in the good faith it was given to me but with Sally, for some reason, I just want her to have it. I was happy to let Tony have it as I thought I would get it back in time, and in my head, I would still one day be able to give it to Sally. At least now I still have it sat in the bank. Yes, I have had a lucky escape, and this time I do raise my glass to myself, and in my head, I say, *you did good girl, you did good.* I then wonder what Tony will do. Will he get the money to pay off the guys he owes money to? Will he come looking for me? Maybe he's watching me now, waiting to get me when I leave. I ask the barman for a number for a taxi. I order one for fifteen minutes time. As I wait and finish my drink, I think about Simon. Why can I not find Simon? That's all I want, just a man like Simon. I wonder if Simon actually exists, and will I ever find him? Is it really too much to ask, just to have a man who loves me for who

I am and who treats me like I deserve to be treated?

My taxi arrives, and I go back to Pam and Denis's house. They are surprised to see me. They assumed I'd be staying out all night. I did too, but I don't tell them anything. I just tell them that I wanted to see them before they go on their cruise tomorrow. I have not told them about Terry or Sally or my decision to go to Cumbria tomorrow. I do not want them worrying when they are on their cruise. If they knew I was going up to see Sally who lives next door to Jonathan, they would only worry. I will see them off, and then I will go to the station to get a train to Carlisle. I will wear my wig and glasses just in case. I'm nervous but excited too. I can't wait to see Sally, but I'll be on edge as Jonathan will be only a few feet away.

chapter twenty-one

I hear the station announcer call that the next train on platform four is the 12:47pm to Glasgow. This is my train; it will be in Carlisle in around two hours. I should, therefore, get to Sally's at Brampton before Jonathan gets home from work. I really hope that his car is not in the driveway as I have to walk past our house, or rather my house, to get to Sally's next door. I get on the train and find a seat with a table. I remember when I came down that I got a seat without a table so as not to have to speak to anyone, but today I am not that same person. On that day, I was a wreck. Today, I am nervous, yes, but no more so than anyone who is going for that big interview.

If anyone strikes up a conversation, I will speak to them. I put my handbag on the floor under my feet and my little suitcase in the overhead luggage rack. A middle-aged lady sits opposite me. We exchange smiles, and I say hello, and she replies the same back. She has long blonde hair and big blue eyes. She is dressed casually and looks like she's going on a little break of some sort.

'Well, next stop Kendal,' she says as she gets a book out of her handbag to read.

'You going for a holiday or something?' I ask.

'Three-day spa break with the girls. Can't wait, I can taste the prosecco, it's calling me, it really is,' she says quite excitedly. She looks in her early forties, and I'd guess from the lack of a ring on her finger that she's divorced and ready for a good three days on the prosecco with her girlfriends. I imagine how wild they will be.

'I bet it is,' I say. 'How many of you are going?'

'Five of us, all divorcees, the latest one just got her decree absolute through three weeks ago, which is why we booked this. Should be a real blast. Where are you off to?'

'Carlisle to see a friend, just a bit of a catch-up. Not as wild as your few days though,' I tell her. We have a nice chat for a good 20 minutes or so before we run out of things to say. She told me a lot more than I told her. It's amazing what people will tell you about themselves, most of it unnecessary and most of it without any prompting. Her name is Helen. She's got two children, a boy and a girl who are both at their dad's for a few days, who incidentally, she found shagging her best friend's daughter at the daughter's eighteenth birthday party. It was at her friend's house; Helen went to the bathroom upstairs because the two downstairs ones were both being used and walked in to find her friend's daughter bent over the sink and her husband shagging her from behind. She told me it was an image she will not get out of her head for as long as she lives. As much as I felt sorry for her for having to see that when she walked into the bathroom, I could not help but feel a little bit of comfort and satisfaction that it isn't just me who seems to find arseholes in her life.

I told her next to nothing about me other than my name was Jenny, didn't want to tell her my real name for some reason, and that I'd never been married. I saw her glance at my ring finger when I said that, and I could see the pity she felt for me as she assumed that I'd never had a man in my life, and to be honest with my track record, I wish I hadn't. She got off at Kendal, and we wished each other all the best, and she left with that old favourite *I might see you again sometime, but if you fancy a good time, come over to Kendal...* I smiled but doubted very much that I would see her again and could not see myself skipping my few days with Sally to go to Kendal for a few days of whatever Helen will be getting up to.

I close my eyes and think about last night. I still cannot believe what happened with Tony. I just didn't see that coming. I wonder how he is and what he did once I left. I haven't had a call from him, I thought I might have done by now, but if I did, I would just tell him to piss off. I really did think he was a nice kind of guy. Maybe he is deep down, maybe last night, and all that he said, what he did was just a reaction to the situation he finds himself in. Mind you, that could just be a lie too, maybe he's a serial con artist; maybe the fifteen grand was just the start of it. That's how they start isn't it? You hear about these guys, who start with a small amount, and then before you know it, they've scammed you out of every penny you have. He probably is one of those guys. I mean, fifteen grand is not a million pounds, is it? He'll probably already have his next victim in his sights, maybe in another area of Manchester, maybe further away. I doubt I'll see or hear from him again, the bastard. I doze off.

I wake up as we approach Penrith and am a little annoyed that I'd missed the breathtaking views in between Kendal and here. There really is nowhere like it. No one gets on in my carriage, and as I look around, there are no more than ten people sat either sleeping, looking out of the window, or on their phones. I take in the scenery as we head off to Carlisle. It's still breathtaking, and I am reminded that I do miss it up here. The greenness and scenery are awesome. I cannot take my eyes off it. I recognise a few landmarks and realise we are only a few minutes from Carlisle. I get my bag from under my seat and get my suitcase from overhead.

A few faces look up automatically, and I exchange a few smiles. I then hear the announcer tell us that we are approaching Carlisle station. I now have butterflies in my stomach. All of a sudden, I feel as though I am vulnerable as if I am being watched. I know I can't be as no one knows I am here, but as I step off the train onto the station platform, I have a multitude of feelings come over me. The last time I was here was when I was fleeing Jonathan and my other life.

I feel scared and worried like I used to feel all the time when I was here. I take a deep breath and sit down on a bench. I look around. It all looks just as it did the day I left. The place looks the same, as do my feelings, feelings of trepidation, of worry, of being scared, all of the feelings I used to feel. I tell myself that they are just feelings by association. I only ever felt like this when I was here, and I was only ever here when I had these feelings, so I tell myself that it is a normal reaction to me coming back here. I know no different other than to feel scared and anxious whenever I am in Carlisle, as that's all I used to feel. I recall how I told myself on that day I left that the further away I got, the more confident I felt, so it must just be that I associate here with the feelings I now have inside me. I need to be strong; I need to beat these feelings; I need to replace them with nice feelings.

I think about seeing Sally, that makes me excited, I think about hopefully seeing Rose and Mrs Simpson, that makes me feel excited. I now feel a little better, although my breathing is still quite heavy. *'Come on,'* I say to myself under my breath, *'you can do this.'* I really did not expect this. I really thought I would be fine once I got here, but I do feel vulnerable. I just cannot shake that feeling, but I take another deep breath and walk over the bridge to the other side and walk out into the street.

The sun is shining, and as I look around at the people milling about, I realise that no one is taking any notice of me. I'm invisible, totally inconspicuous, so I nod to a black cab driver who pulls over towards me. I get in just as he gets out to help me with my suitcase.

'Where to?' he asks as he gets back in.

'Brampton, please.'

'Whereabouts, what street?'

'Just in the middle, near Moot Hall, will do,' I say. I had not considered the fact that if I pull up in a taxi outside Sally's house and get out with my suitcase, it will look very odd to Jonathan if he is in the house. I decide to just get dropped off near the Moot Hall, and then I will walk the few minutes walk to her house and just pray that he doesn't pass me on the way. My breathing is heavy again. I feel vulnerable, I feel scared, just like I used to feel all the time. I suddenly wish I were back in Manchester.

As I travel through Carlisle, I see all the familiar sites. Even though it's still only been a few weeks, not months since I left, I'm still, for some reason, surprised how it just looks as it always did, I suppose when you are away from somewhere, even for a short space of time, you just expect it to have changed, but of course, nothing has, not even the feelings I always felt when I was here. I just got used to those feelings, I suppose, and it just became normal for me. It wasn't until I was nearing Manchester, and then once I was there, did the feelings start to go. I cannot believe I used to feel like I do right now all of the time. I cannot believe how I had become used to feeling like this. I wish I could get rid of them now.

I do not like the fact that I feel vulnerable and anxious as we drive down Warwick Road towards the M6 motorway. I like it up here, and I just know that one day I will be back, so I do not want to have these feelings associated with Carlisle and Brampton. As we head over the motorway roundabout, and head towards Warwick on Eden, I feel my nervousness getting worse. I feel like I am going to have palpitations of some sort. I try and calm my breathing by breathing long and slow. *'Come on, Anna,'* I say to myself, *'you decided to come here, so get your big girl's pants on and stop being so ridiculous.' What the hell do you think is going to happen?* I tell myself that Jonathan cannot do anything to me. I'm a grown woman who has the right to do whatever I want and to go wherever I want to go.

I feel a little better, my breathing has calmed down, and as we head over the roundabout of the A69 and the A689, I am calming down. I can see Brampton now, and all of a sudden, I feel excited, not anxious, or nervous, but excited all of a sudden. Maybe that little talking to has worked. I take a deep breath and ready myself to get out of the taxi right in the middle of the little square, in full view of anyone there. I instinctively check my wig, I don't know why, but I check that it's still on my head. It is, of course. I take my glasses off and breathe on both sides of the lenses and clean them with the bottom of my top. I feel ready. I take another deep breath as the cab pulls up.

'That's £10.20, please.'

I pay the driver and get out, with my suitcase and handbag. I look around. It's not overly busy, just a few people milling about. I look over at the butchers, oh how I'd love to walk in there as bold as brass. They'd be surprised to see me as I understand Jonathan has just been telling them that I'm not too well at the moment. Yes, they'd be surprised but not gobsmacked. I so want to walk in, but I have my disguise on. I smile to myself as I tell myself that if I get the chance just before I leave to return to Manchester, I will go in, with no disguise, just because I know it will get back to Jonathan.

I blow my cheeks out as I exhale strongly as I realise what that would do to him. Bloody hell, I feel good as I think of how I can play with him like this; boy does it feel good to be giving him a little bit of payback finally. I look around again and see that no one is taking any notice of me. I pick up my suitcase and start to walk down the main street, past all of the little shops that I never had time to even browse in. I still don't today. Well, I do, I could if I wanted to, but I want to get to Sally's as quickly as I can. My anxiousness has subsided, but I know it's still there rumbling around, and I do not want anything to happen to bring it back to the surface.

I turn into our street. The houses are all neatly set back off the road, and the trees line each side. It's a nice street, all with very neatly trimmed gardens, but as I start to walk down it, I realise that I know very few people in it. I know Mr Spencer at No.9 and old George at No. 8 over the road. Everyone knows old George. He's lived here since he was born, and he must be in his mid-eighties now. He's getting frail now but is still very independent, and then I know Mr and Mrs Grayson at No. 18 and Mrs Brown at No. 21, but that's it, I do not know anyone else. Everything looks the same, but as usual, no one is around. I can see my house along the road, just past the middle, about 50 yards after the post box. Sally's is the next one, which means I have to walk past mine.

I am walking slowly, I wasn't, but I am now. I know why; it's because I want to see cautiously if Jonathan's car is in the driveway. It's 3:40pm. He should still be at work unless he's changed his routine, which is very doubtful. I reach the post box. I then decide to cross the road. I want to be a little further away. I just feel safer that way. I can see better from this side as it widens my angle and widens my view. I cannot see his car. I walk forward quite briskly now, and as I get level with it, I tentatively glance to my left and see that his car is not in the driveway, but mine is. It's still there, just like it used to be, adding to the pretence.

I wonder what he thought when he found it abandoned that day along the road. It seems so long ago. I stop and turn to face my house, the house where I suffered so much abuse. It stands nice, just as it always did. The driveway, as always, is weed-free, and the front garden is still well presented. Jonathan has obviously still been looking after it well, even though all of those chores used to be mine. I wonder if he will have a gardener doing it, but I doubt it as that would raise questions unless he got someone from outside of Brampton.

I walk over the road and stand at the end of the

drive. I stand there for a few minutes just looking, just thinking, just recalling the events of that house, the beatings, the sexual abuse, the manipulation, the degradation, all of it, but I still have this overwhelming feeling that I will, one day be back, in that house and that I will be happy. That, of course, means that Jonathan can't be. I could only ever be happy in this house if he were not in it too.

I leave my case at the end of the drive and walk up to look through the living room window. I just cannot help it. It is my house, after all. The room has not changed. The furniture is still the same; the bi-fold doors at the back allow me to see out into the garden. I cannot see very well as it's a large lounge, but I can see our back garden. I feel homesick all of a sudden as if I want to open the door and put the kettle on. I have a real draw to this house even though it harbours such bad memories. I step back and tilt my head backwards and look up and then turn around and walk away. I grab my suitcase, and I glance back as I step onto the pavement but then take the few steps to Sally's and excitedly knock on her door. She must have been stood right behind it as she opens it on the second knock.

'About bloody time,' she says as she pulls me inside.

'Hello to you too,' I say as she flings her arms around me, and I struggle to get in along with my suitcase in one sweeping movement.

'Come on, get inside. You never know who's watching. Ooh, I've missed you, Anna Fox, bloody hell I've missed you,' she tells me as she hugs me so tight, I feel like I'm being squeezed to death.

I still have one hand on my suitcase but have my other arm, along with my handbag around her. I let go of it once I've steadied it so that it does not fall over and hug her tightly back.

'Missed you too, so much,' I say. We hug for what seems like ages, but it is probably no more than 15 seconds, and then Sally breaks from the embrace and takes my suitcase.

'Come on, I'll put the kettle on,' she says as she walks through to the kitchen. She places my case at the bottom of her stairs. 'I'll leave that there for you. Your bedroom is the first door on the right at the top of the stairs. It's ensuite,' she says. I've never been upstairs in Sally's house. I hadn't realised before.

'I had a look through the lounge window,' I tell her.

'What next door? Thought you would,' she replies.

'Have you seen much of him?' I ask. Sally is putting the tea bags in the mugs.

'He's been round three times. Knocked on my door three times, he has. The first time was just to offer his condolences, you know, telling me how sorry he was and all that, which was fair enough I suppose, but he's been back round twice since, twice in three days, saying that he just wants to make sure I'm ok. I told him I was fine and that there was no need for him to worry about me, but he said he'll keep popping round now and again to make sure. He was all nicey-nicey, you know how they are, but I know he's just fishing or that he's just letting me know that he's still around; either way, I don't bloody like it. He might even pop round whilst you are here. I just don't know. I haven't let him in, though. He tried to put his foot in the door the second time, but I just pulled the door to so that he had to take it back out again. I think he got the message.'

I had considered the fact that he might be popping

round and have thought about what I would do or how I would feel. I know I will feel anxious, scared even, but at least now I know it is a distinct possibility so I can prepare myself.

'Anyway, take off that bloody wig and those glasses. You just remind me of when we were doing that camming stuff. I can't look at you seriously.'

I smile and take them off. I'd forgotten I had them on. It's surprising how comfortable they feel and it's easy to just forget they are on your face. I put them on top of my case at the foot of the stairs. We sit down at Sally's table and drink our tea. We stare at each other, and then both burst out laughing at the same time.

'It's just like old times, me and you sat here, a bit later than usual,' I say as I look at my watch, 'but just like old times, sat here having a cup of tea, but now we can take as long as we like and neither of us have to worry about anything, not what time we have to leave, about our chores or anything. Here's to freedom.' We clink our mugs, and Sally winks at me.

'Anyway, seriously, how are you feeling? You know about Terry and everything?' I ask, knowing that even though Terry was Sally's Jonathan, she will still be feeling a sense of loss and sorrow.

'Bloody great mate, bloody great. I was shocked at first, you know as anyone would, but once I'd spoken to you on the phone, I put the receiver down and felt bloody great, and I still do. I don't miss him one bit Anna. At first, I was feeling sad. I was crying and I was wondering what I was going to do. I was missing him but I think I was just on auto-pilot, you know, just reacting as I was expected to react and I think, just being instinctive. Mind you, me acting like that certainly looked good to all of his copper friends, because it was genuine. Although, as I say just an auto-pilot kind of genuine, but now, I'm glad the bastard's gone and only now do I realise how shit I used to feel. That constant feeling of dread, of being scared, of being anxious all of the time has gone. It went in an instant after speaking to you, and only now do I realise that this is how life should feel, no feeling of dread, no brick in your stomach, you know all of the feelings that just became normal, you must know what I mean?'

I do; I know I do. I had the same experience although mine all went a little more gradually but only in the space of around two hours on the train to Manchester. I know exactly what she means.

'I do Sal. I know exactly what you mean. I never realised how I felt all of the time either until I was no longer living next door. It's amazing how quickly those feelings go once you take yourself out of the situation, or in your case once the situation is taken away from you.'

'Well, never again, not for either of us. Fancy a glass of wine?' Sally says as she gets up, assuming that I will say yes. She's more or less got the bottle in her hand from the fridge before I say, 'Yes, lovely.'

'Thought so, anyway, how's that boyfriend of yours, Tony, still moonlight and roses?' she asks as she gets the wine glasses from her cupboard.

'Not good,' I say.

'What? Why?... I thought things were good. Don't tell me it's all off already.'

'Pour the wine, and I'll tell you all about it.'

Sally puffs out her cheeks. 'Sounds serious,' she says. I tell her the whole story.

'Wow, that was not what I expected you to say, what a

bastard. Why are there so many arseholes around? I just don't get it. Why do we attract them?' Sally says, shaking her head in disbelief at what I have just told her. I told her the lot, the good first few weeks, the fake music shop, the fake second shop, and then the incident at his flat once he'd found out I'd not got the money.

'I asked myself the same question. I don't know either. Maybe it's the vibes we give off or something. I don't know,' I reply.

'Is it hell as like, it's them. They're the ones with the problem, not us. Bastards, the lot of 'em.' Sally says as she takes a swig of her wine.

'Well, he's out of my life now anyway, I won't be seeing him again, and if I do, I'll just totally blank him.'

'Too right, good on you. I'm so glad you kneed him in the bollocks. I bet you wished you'd have done that to Jonathan years ago. I wish I had to Terry. They might have got the message early doors then, eh?'

'Yeah, maybe, trouble was with me. I got so used to just obeying him that I don't think I ever would have. I don't think I'd have ever had the strength or the nerve. With Tony, it was different. I went into that relationship, well, if you can call it a relationship, with my eyes wide open. I was sort of ready for it in a way, you know. I just sort of always knew that if he ever tried anything like that sort of thing, that I'd not just sit there and take it. I suppose I went into that one on different terms, right from the start. With Jonathan, it was just so subtle, over time, that once I realised what was happening, I was in too deep. I was too scared of him to do anything. You know what I mean?' Sally looks at me with really sad eyes. She has filled up but is not crying. I can see the glistening of the tears in her eyes.

'I know exactly what you mean,' she says. She opens up her arms, and I lean in for a cuddle. 'We have each other, me and you, Anna. I know I let you down when you went to Manchester, and believe me, I've been beating myself up about it ever since, but I promise you, I'll be there for you always. I won't let you down again,' I hug her tight. I can feel her punishing herself again.

'You didn't let me down, Sal, you are your own person, and you did what was right for you, and that's ok. Honestly, I understood, still do, and I haven't forgiven you 'cos there's nothing to forgive. You are not responsible for me, only for yourself. I love you Sally, and I always will.' Sally wipes tears from her face as we break free. She is crying now.

'Thanks mate,' she says. I take a deep breath and a gulp of my wine.

'Anyway, I'm here to help you out with the funeral arrangements and all that stuff, you know, so shall we make a list of what we need to do, contact the bank, utilities, funeral director, and whoever else you need to get in touch with?'

'Well, the funeral arrangements are all sorted. Terry had a prepayment plan, apparently. Our solicitor told me. I have one too, which I knew nothing about, so when I pop my clogs, you'll know who to contact.'

'Brill, so when is it, the funeral, I mean?'

'A week next Thursday, up at the crematorium on Dalston Road in Carlisle. There will be a lot there. I'll have to put on my best act, the grieving widow and all that,' she says, smiling at the very prospect.

'I won't be able to make it, Sal, you know that, don't you? He'll be there, I'm sure,' I say as I turn my head sideways, pointing in the direction of my house.

'I know, I'd already thought of that. I'll be fine, honest. Rose and Mrs Simpson will be there, so they have both said they will sit with me and help me put on a show.'

'Great, that makes me feel a lot better. I really would love to be there for you but, I just could not risk it.'

'Don't worry. I'll have my big girl's pants on.'

'When is Rose going to Portugal? She must be itching to get there?'

'She should have been there now, but some snag or other with the place she's going to be renting out while she looks for a place of her own. Between you and me, I think she's really gutted that the place she was going to have originally has been sold. She mentions it quite a bit, not in a way where she's blaming us, but you know, just keeps saying, *I really wish my first place had not been sold...* I can't help but feel bad every time she says it.'

'Oh, dear. Have you told her I'm here?'

'No, you said not to, so I haven't told a soul. Her and Mrs Simpson would just love to see you, though. You're gonna see 'em, yeah?'

'Definitely, I just didn't want to risk anything, nothing at all. I can't risk anything now but come on, let's ring them. I bet they'll both come round tonight,' I look at my watch. 'Bloody hell it's nearly six o clock. I'll ring them both now. I bet Mrs Simpson will be in her nightie already,' I say giggling.

'What about that list we were gonna make?'

'We can make that tomorrow, can't we?'

chapter twenty-two

I rang Rose and Mrs Simpson, and they are both coming round for 7:30pm. I can't wait to see them. I've had a quick shower and freshened up, and I am just coming downstairs when the doorbell rings.

'I'll get it,' I say.

'NO!' Shouts Sally. I stop midway down the stairs and turn to face back towards the top.

'What's up?' I shout. Sally comes to the top of the stairs as she puts her earring in.

'What are you thinking? What if it's Jonathan?' she says softly as she reaches the step just above mine.

'Shit,' I say quietly as I put my hand to my mouth. 'I completely forgot.'

'Stay here; it's only ten past seven, look,' Sally says as she grabs my wrist and shows me my watch face. 'In fact, go upstairs,' she tells me.

The doorbell rings again. I tiptoe upstairs, which I have no need to do as whoever it is cannot hear me, and if they could, well they'll certainly have heard me shout *I'll get it.*

I sit on the landing like a naughty schoolgirl who has been sent to her room and try to listen to what's going on downstairs. I can hear Sally's voice, but I cannot make out what she is saying. I am nervous and excited all at the same time. I try not to laugh, but I can't help it. I suppose it's a nervous laugh. It makes no real sound, but it's like when I was at school, and I was getting told off by the teacher. I could never stop myself from laughing. I tiptoe downstairs and reach the midway point. The point where I was when Sally shouted *NO!* I still can't hear what Sally is saying, but I can hear a second voice. It's a male voice. I get to the bottom of the stairs. Sally has closed the vestibule door. I stand in the doorway into the lounge and strain my hearing.

It's Jonathan. I can tell his voice. He's telling her that he just wanted to check on her again. I feel my heart racing. I cannot believe that I am less than fifteen feet away from him, from the man who ruled my life for so long, the man who made my self-worth so low that I didn't recognise myself. I can hear myself breathing. I am breathing so hard that I think maybe he will hear me too. I hear the door close. I take a step back into the living room and hide behind the door. Sally comes through the vestibule door into the hallway. I can see her through the gap in the door. I take a step out and then walk into the hallway where Sally is breathing hard.

'I thought you were upstairs?' she says. 'Bloody hell, I hope he couldn't see the anxiety on my face. I tried to just be normal.' I burst out laughing, just like I am back at school in the classroom.

'Bloody hell, Sal, I thought my heart was going to jump out of my chest. Just think I was gonna open that bloody door. I'm not safe to be out, well I'm not out, but you know what I mean.'

'I need another glass of wine,' Sally says as she walks to the kitchen.

We sit at the kitchen table and just stare at each other for a few seconds as we both hold our glasses of wine. 'What would you have done?' Sally asks me.

'No idea, honestly, I have no idea. I was just so excited about Rose and Mrs Simpson coming that I just clean forgot that it could be Jonathan. That could have been really serious, Sal. I'm sorry. I know I laughed just then, but it's just a nervous laugh, you know, but honestly, I'm sorry. I won't do that again.'

'Good, 'cos my nerves wouldn't stand another episode like that.' We both laugh again and then clink our glasses. 'What we like, eh?' Sally says, shaking her head.

The doorbell rings again. 'Now stay here,' Sally says, pointing her finger at me. I salute her like I am in the army as if I am saying *yes Cap'n.*

I hear Rose's voice as they come through the door. I get up and stand in the doorway of the kitchen. 'Here she is,' Rose says as she opens her arms and walks towards me. She gives me the biggest hug ever. I then see Mrs Simpson behind her but am unable to say anything as I can hardly breathe, Rose is hugging me so tight. I try and smile. She smiles back. Rose then lets me go, and I hug Mrs Simpson.

'Ooh, I've missed you, dear,' she says. Her hug is far less intense. 'How are you?' she asks as she cups my face in her hands.

'I'm fine, Mrs Simpson, all the better for seeing you guys, that's for sure. It really is great to see you all. I can't believe how much I have missed you.'

We have a great night. Rose tells me of the issue she's had with her rented place in Portugal but tells me she should be out there in a couple of weeks if all goes to plan. She's had an offer on her cottage and has accepted, and it's for five grand more than she had hoped to get, so that makes me and Sally feel better about her losing her first place in Portugal. She also tells me how Jonathan is just acting normal at the school governors' meetings and really wants to tell him in front of everyone what a lying bastard he is but refrains from doing so because that would blow everything out in the open. She hates the fact that he is just pretending that I am sat at home, like the good wife he portrays me to be. After Mrs Simpson tried to call him out a couple of weeks ago, they'd thought he might have come clean then, but no, he's still trying to pretend I am still at home. We all agree that at some point, he needs to come clean about me not being there, but we also all agree that he will probably drag it out as best he can. He will then come up with some bullshit story to make him look like the injured party—the bastard.

I get up the following day a little worse for wear, having consumed a bit too much wine but not feeling as bad as I thought I would. I come downstairs to find Sally already up making scrambled eggs on toast for us both.

'Sore head?' she asks.

'Yeah, a bit, but I feel not too bad actually. You?'

'Fine, I didn't have as much as you, though. Mind you, Mrs Simpson drunk a lot more than I'd have thought. She likes her gin, doesn't she?... I thought she was gonna drink my gin stash dry. I'm just so glad she'd brought some tonic. I'd never have had enough otherwise. Brown or white toast?... I have both.'

'White, please. I'll put the kettle on, eh?' I look out of the window into the garden as I fill the kettle with water, and I can't help but look towards my own back garden. It all seems so familiar being back here as if

I've never been away, and I'd love to be able to go back home next door, on my own, and enjoy my beautiful home.

Sally and I eat our breakfast and then make a list of what Sally needs to do and who she needs to contact. It's surprising how many phone calls you have to make when someone passes away. We work our way through them, and as Sally makes the calls and sends the necessary emails, and makes appointments, all I can do is think of my house next door. I just know I will be back there again, but in all honesty, I didn't think it would affect me like it is now that I am here. I wish that I had the strength to go round there right now and tell Jonathan to piss off out of the house, but then I know he wouldn't, plus we'd have to sell it and halve the proceeds, which would be pretty pointless as I still wouldn't have my house. I have no idea how I will get it back, but I just know I will.

It is now just gone 4pm and Sally and I are sat chatting, as we used to do every day. Talking about nothing really but enjoying it all the same.

'When are you going back?' she asks me. I had thought of staying another two nights, tonight and tomorrow night, and going back Friday, and I probably will, but I hate not being able to go out. I didn't think it would bother me, but knowing that bastard Jonathan is next door, and is still stopping me from going out, is really pissing me off.

'I'll stay tonight and tomorrow night and go back Friday if that's ok,' I tell her.

'Of course it is, stay as long as you like. What do you fancy for tea?' Sally asks me. I sit and ponder for a moment.

'You know what?' I say... 'What?' Sally asks in reply... 'I want to go into Carlisle for a few drinks and a Chicken Korma, that's what I want to do. Shall we?' I ask.

'I don't know. It's a bit risky. You'll have to wear your wig,' Sally says. I hadn't thought of that. I can wear my wig no problem, but that's not what I want to do. I want to be me, Anna Fox, out in Carlisle, fancy-free, having a good time, as me, not as Jenny with my wig on, that's not what I had in mind. I think about it for a few seconds and then say, 'You're right, Sal, it's too risky. We can order a takeaway, though, can't we? There's still a takeaway in Brampton, isn't there?'

'There is, I haven't used it in ages. Terry loved the food there, but it's been a while since we had anything from there. I think I've still got a menu, though, somewhere.' Sally goes into the kitchen and returns a minute or so later, holding a menu. 'Here you go, do you need to look at it, or is it a chicken Korma you want?' she says as she tosses it to me. I have a look and decide on a Chicken Pasanda.

'Shall we have another bottle of wine between us first before we order?' I ask.

'Ooh, I love you being here, Anna, a glass of wine and a curry. I bloody love it.'

chapter twenty-three

I'm all packed and ready to go. I walk downstairs with my suitcase and stand in front of the mirror in the hallway and adjust my wig. It does suit me, and if you didn't know it wasn't my natural colour, you'd be hard-pressed to know otherwise.

'I've just made a pot of tea,' Sally shouts from the kitchen. 'You've got time, haven't you?'

'Yeah, no problem. I've got an open return ticket, so I'm not pushed for which train I catch, to be honest, but I'll get going once I've had my cuppa.' I walk through into the kitchen to find Sally drying her eyes. 'What's up?' I ask.

'Ooh, just ignore me. I don't know when I'll see you again. It's not like you're gonna pop up regularly, is it, not with knobhead next door. I'm just sad you're going, that's all.'

'I know, but hey, you can always come to Manchester. Pam and Denis would love to meet you, they've said so a few times, but anyway, I'm going to hopefully get my own place soon, even if it's just a room in a shared house. HMO's, they call 'em. I think it stands for House of Multiple Occupancy or something like that. I've spoken to a few of the buskers, and they reckon they could get me somewhere, but I'm going to be choosy. A couple of them reckon I could get my own flat, but I'm not so sure given my lack of documentation and the fact I have no bank account of my own. Anyway, I don't know enough about it all, but some of them seem to be well clued up, so we'll see. I probably won't even be able to get a room in a shared house, but who knows, at least I can stay at Pam and Denis's as long as I want. They're a real godsend, you know. I don't know what I'd have done without them.'

'They sound really nice. I will come down soon, I promise. Are you sure that you want to walk into Brampton centre to catch your cab?'

'Yes, I'm sure. It just seems right somehow. It's not far anyway and I can call a cab from there. I just hope I don't bump into Mrs Simpson. I think she was a little put out when I said I wanted to catch a cab rather than her take me.'

'Yeah, I thought so too, but she seemed ok about it in the end. She'll just want to help that's all. I thought it strange too though if I'm honest, but if that's what you want then, well, who are we to argue?'

I drink my tea and then say a very emotional farewell to Sally. She checks that the coast is clear next door and confirms that Jonathan's car is gone. I then walk passed my house and see my car still parked on the drive. It looks as though Jonathan has washed it this weekend. I again stand at the end of the driveway for a few minutes as I survey the house. I just cannot help it. I stick two fingers up and poke my tongue out at an imaginary Jonathan stood in the doorway. I smile inwardly to myself as I realise that had he been stood in the doorway I'd never have done that, but he isn't, he can't see me, so I do as I like. I'm so brave, ha ha.

I walk into Brampton and as I approach the butcher's shop I stop and look around. It's fairly quiet again, with not many people about and certainly no one who is taking any notice of me. I stand by the wall at the side of the shop and quickly take off my wig and stuff it in my handbag. This was why I wanted to come into Brampton to get my cab. I want to go into the butchers, as me, as Anna Fox, for no other reason than I know it will get back to Jonathan. The next time he goes in, as I know he will to get his weekly steak, the ladies behind the counter will say, *ooh, we saw your Anna the other day, she looks really well...* or something like that, and it will bloody well infuriate him.

I only wish I could be here to watch it all unfold as he walks out of the shop. The steam coming from his ears will be visible for hundreds of yards. I know it may seem childish, but I just cannot help myself. The devilment in me is just too much to ignore. I just need to put my suitcase somewhere safe. I can't walk in pulling that with me as I want them to think that I've just come from home and that that is where I am going straight back to. I see an old man on a bench outside of the bank across the road. He looks as though he is just passing time. I walk over to him.

'Excuse me, sorry to bother you, but would you mind just watching my suitcase as I go into the butchers. I just don't want to pull that thing around with me, that's all. It'll just get in people's way.'

'Of course, I will, young lady. Happy to help. It'll give me something to do. Not drugs, is it?' he says, laughing at his own joke. I can tell that he has nothing to fill his time with. He looks so sweet with his shirt and tie on and his tank top, and his flat cap. Just like a proper old grandad. I bet he has some boiled sweets in his pocket.

'No, not drugs, just a load of my clothes that now

need a wash and an iron, but thank you, that's so sweet. Would you like anything from there while I'm in, my treat, a steak or something?'

'Oh no, I couldn't, honestly. I'm just happy to help.'

'Do you like steak?' I ask.

'Ooh yes, I do, but don't you go bothering yourself. Just leave this with me,' he says as he pats the top of my case and then takes the handle and pulls it into him. 'I'll not let it out of my sight.'

I walk over to the butchers knowing that as soon as I walk in, they will cut me two steaks; one exactly twice as much in weight as the other, just as they always did. I'm sure they will, so I will give the larger one which would have been Jonathan's, to the old man on the bench, and I will have the smaller one for tea tonight. I am quite nervous as I head towards the door. I again instinctively look round and see no one who even knows I am here. I take off my glasses just as I enter the shop. There are only two other people in there, and no one is at the meat counter. The lady who would normally serve me looks up, and I can see the surprise on her face.

'Hello, how are you?' she says with a genuine sense of being pleased to see me. 'We've been asking after you every time Jonathan has been in, has he told you, haven't we?' she says as she looks over her right shoulder towards her colleague. 'Haven't we been asking after her? Ooh, you do look well; I'm ever so pleased to see you.' I smile a genuine smile. I know that these ladies have their suspicions about what kind of relationship me and Jonathan have, well, the kind we used to have, but they have never been anything but kind to me and have never judged me, always just been there with a smile, a real warm smile, and for that, I was always grateful.

'I'm fine, thank you,' I say. 'Just been a bit under the weather, that's all.' I decide to just humour Jonathan's pretence as I do not want to make them feel uncomfortable. That's not what this visit to the butchers is all about. It's about making Jonathan feel uncomfortable when they tell him I've been in.

'Yes, your husband said you'd not been too well. Nothing too serious, I hope, usual is it, two steaks, just as always?' She says.

I'm not surprised that it's said with the usual undertone that told me that she knew what was going on. As always, though, it was said with no fuss and not a hint of anything that would suggest anything was untoward to anyone in earshot who did not know me or my situation. For that, I was always grateful.

'Yes, the usual two steaks, please, just as always,' I say with a smile. Her colleague has them cut and weighed before I've finished the sentence; they just knew why I was here. I pay for them, and after a little more small talk, I say my goodbyes, and they again say what a pleasure it was to see me and that they look forward to seeing me again soon. I walk over to the old gentleman on the bench and hand him the larger steak.

'A nice piece of fillet there for you,' I say as he takes it from me. He looks inside, and I see his face light up. He looks at me and mouths, *thank you.* I walk along the street in the opposite direction to the butchers, and once I am at the antique centre, I put my wig and glasses back on. I then call a taxi and wait for it to arrive. As I sit on the wall at the side of the road, I wonder about where I am going in life. I wonder where it will take me and what I will be doing in six months' time, or even a year's time. Will I still be in Manchester? Will I still be on my own or will I have found my Simon.

I really wish I knew who Simon was for me. I know it wasn't Jonathan, and I now know it wasn't Tony. I think again what he will be like, what he will look like and imagine being with him, in a happy relationship, a normal relationship, one where we watch T.V together, one where we go for walks together, one where we make love and not just have sex and one where I can be me, one where I can be happy, without having to try too hard. A happy relationship should not be hard work. A happy marriage should be one where neither person has to try that hard, one where everything just comes naturally and just falls into place. I long for that kind of life, one where I can be happy forever. I am awoken out of my trance by a voice that says, 'Fox?' I look up and see a rather scruffy-looking overweight man sweating profusely in a black cab.

'Yes,' I say, that's me, 'Carlisle railway station, please.'

chapter twenty-four

As the train pulls into Manchester, I go into the toilet and take off my wig and put it in my handbag. I get off the train and walk through the always busy station. Carlisle station always seems busy when I am there but compared to Manchester, it's not busy at all. I walk out onto the street past the stand that sells the local newspaper, and I stop in my tracks. I stop so suddenly that a few people behind me bump into me. They shout expletives at me, but I just ignore them. I am too interested in the headline. *Murder?* It says ... just that, murder?... at the side of the headline is a photo of a man. It's Tony. I quickly open my purse and pay the vendor for a copy. As I walk away in a daze, I read the first couple of paragraphs. I take my glasses off as I read better without them.

It says how a man was found yesterday morning on the pavement outside of the apartment block where Tony lived. It suggests he had either jumped, been pushed, or thrown even from his apartment window. Witnesses are reported to have said that they heard shouting and possibly a fight in the early hours coming from Tony's flat. Two men were seen entering the property on CCTV and leaving 15 minutes later. They show photos of the men from the CCTV, but of course, you cannot see their faces. They are in suits and look how you would expect a real gangster to look. I stop and lean against a wall as I read on. It is suggesting drugs as a possible motive. I look at the photo of Tony and burst into tears. I am so sad that he got himself into something like this and that it ended in his death, and such a horrific one at that, but I am so emotional to think that I could have been mixed up in all of this. I think of what could have happened if I'd have lent him the money. Would that have been the end of it, would he have come back for more, or would that have saved his life? I am also sad that I just assumed he was a con artist. I just assumed that he would have just conned me out of that money and moved onto his next victim. I never considered that when he told me that he needed the money to pay people off that he was telling the truth. I could have saved his life, but then I think of how he lied to me, and I tell myself that I am not responsible for any of this. I did nothing wrong. I have no idea what he was caught up in or who he owed money to, but I am just glad that I got out of it when I did. I have been so lucky.

'Are you ok?' I hear a voice ask me. I look up and am surprised to see it's Samantha. I look down and see Harry looking up at me. I can see he has a new pair of jeans on.

'I thought it was you,' she says with a smile. 'Are you ok?'

I wipe my eyes and sniffle. 'Yes, I am. I'm fine Sam, how are you?'

'Fine, look, Harry's wearing his new jeans and trainers that I bought him with some of the money you gave me. I paid the bills too and guess what?' she asks. I think for a moment.

'Your benefits have come through?'

'Yes, yesterday, they came through yesterday. I can

pay you some of the money back, not a lot mind, but some.' I shake my head.

'Keep it, Sam. I don't want it. It was a gift, remember?'

She smiles. 'When are you busking again?'

'Tomorrow probably, probably tomorrow. I'll look out for you.'

'Great,' she says. We walk together a few yards.

'Fancy a coffee?' she says. 'My treat, at least let me buy you a coffee.'

'Ok, you're on, come on, I could do with a cuppa, a bloody strong one at that.'

After having a coffee with Sam, I get the local train to Cheadle Hulme. I think about Tony for most of the way with mixed emotions. I wish he'd not treated me like he did, as I cannot remember him like I want to. I get off at my stop and slowly walk to Pam and Denis's house. I get in and put my case in my room and immediately make myself a brew. I consider having something stronger but decide to wait for later. What a shock that was. I still cannot believe it. I would go to the shop to see Lesley, but as I never actually met her, I decide that would be pretty pointless, and anyhow that would just put me back into the mix, and I just want to stay out of it. I kick my shoes off and sit down in the lounge. The doorbell rings, and I get up to answer it. I bet it's the neighbour from across the road. She used to look after the house apparently when they were away, but as I'm here, there's no need but as sure as eggs are eggs, she's noticed I've been away, and will no doubt want to know the ins and outs of where I've been. I open the door and drop my mug of tea.

'Hello, darling.' It's Jonathan.

chapter twenty-five

I stand there speechless. I'm frozen to the spot. I feel fear and dread rise up inside me. I cannot move. I then look down to see my mug smashed into lots of pieces and hot tea having already formed what looks like a little puddle. Jonathan pushes his way in and closes the door behind him. I instinctively step back. I still haven't said a word.

'What's the matter, my little angel, cat got your tongue?'

'How did you find me?' I stutter. I can hear the fear in my voice. I know Jonathan can too. He smirks as if to confirm it. He looks at the smashed cup on the floor.

'Clean it up,' he orders. I stare at him. I'm in shock. 'Clean this fucking mess up now,' he shouts.

I turn to do as I'm told. He then watches as I return with a dustpan and brush and stands over me as I crouch down and clear up the mess. I then calmly, without saying a word, brush the crockery into the pedal bin.

'Come back here,' he shouts. I return and stand exactly where I was. 'You were saying?' he asks.

'How did you find me?' I ask, my voice a little calmer.

'Ha,' he says as he walks further into the hallway. I continue to move backwards. I am still in shock. 'You think you are so smart, eh?' he continues, 'I knew

you'd have to come back to see Sally. I just knew it.
I know you so well, Anna, better than you probably
know yourself. I've made you who you are, remember.
All you are today is down to me. I saw you when you
stood looking at our house three days ago, standing
there in your wig and glasses, thinking I wouldn't
recognise you, but you didn't see the cameras, did
you? Eh?... stupid Anna, always the same stupid
fucking Anna. I was watching you on my phone sat
in my office in Carlisle. It was so funny.' He moves
into me and strokes my hair. I'm scared, so scared I
really am rooted to the spot. All of the emotions, the
feelings of the past years, come flooding back as if to
consume me all in one go. He strokes my face with
his finger. 'Stupid little Anna, I knew you were there
when I called round to see Sally. I knew you would
be listening. I knew you would know it was me. I half
expected you to open the door but was secretly hoping
you weren't that stupid; it would have spoilt my little
surprise here today, wouldn't it, my little angel? I then
saw you earlier today watching the house again. I saw
your suitcase, ha, the suitcase, that was a purler, a
real purler, you know sometimes things just fall into
place. It was so easy. Plus, I saw that whore Rose and
old busy body Simpson had popped round. What the
hell they were doing there, I have no idea. She's tried
to rile me has old Simpson, but I'm too smart to bite,
too smart for the likes of her.'

If only he knew. I now know that he still has no idea
about Rose and Mrs Simpson, which is good, but what
did he mean about the suitcase? 'What do you mean
about the suitcase?' I ask. My voice is a little firmer
now. I feel a little calmer.

'Well, I saw you poke your tongue out and put two

fingers up to the house, which I assume was meant for me, nice touch, by the way. I did smile to myself. Then I saw you walk towards the town centre, so I jumped in my car. I was only parked on the A69, by the way. I knew you wouldn't be staying too long, I did park up there yesterday, wasted a whole morning actually, but anyway, not to worry, so I parked up just up from the Moot Hall and saw you walk up the main street. I watched as you took off your wig, I watched you as you spoke to the old man on the bench, then I watched as you went in the butchers, without the wig. I assume you think I'll be as mad as hell when they tell me they've seen you... ha ha... stupid little Anna. Anyway, I then sit next to the old man, and as always, when you speak to someone, they let their guard down. He took his eye off the case, I looked at it, and there it was, this address, as plain as day. I couldn't believe my luck. A nice little baggage tag, clearly showing me exactly where you were heading. Funny, isn't it, when things like that happen?'

I cannot believe it. I think back to a few days ago when Pam and Denis were packing for their cruise, and I mentioned that the zip had broken on the little case that Rose had given me, so they gave me one of their old ones. They didn't even know I was going to Brampton; they didn't even know I would need a case while they were away, but they are so helpful and accommodating they just gave me one of theirs out of the loft, so of course, I used it for my trip. I never even noticed that it had a tag with their name and address on it. I turn to my left and look into my bedroom and see it on the bed. I can see the case and can just see the edge of the little tag. My heart sinks.

'Great, isn't it?' Jonathan says, laughing out loud.

He then grabs my chin and squeezes it tight. 'I then set off straight for Manchester train station. I had to hedge my bets that you were getting the train, but luck just seemed to be on my side. I saw you get off the train, but you didn't see me. I saw that you'd taken off your wig. I saw that you stopped suddenly and bought a newspaper. I watched as you read it. Know him, did you? Fuck him, did you? Maybe you killed him too, but no, that's not you, is it, Anna? I bet you'd like to kill me, wouldn't you? Well, I fucking dare you.' He lets go of my chin. It hurts. He then continues. 'Then I watched as you spoke to that young girl with her pushchair. I even sat on a bench outside of the cafe you went into, and you still didn't see me, stupid little Anna. I then laughed so hard to myself inside as I walked back to my car with you still in the cafe and took a nice little drive out here. What a lovely house, and through it all, you never saw me.' He grabs my chin again. 'And to top it all, there's only you here. I must admit I was ready for whoever lives here to make things difficult, but as I watched you arrive, and you still didn't see me, by the way, I saw how you had to use a key to get in. There was no one else here. I couldn't believe it. I tell you, Anna, today is one hell of a day for me.' He lets go of my chin again but grabs my hair from the back and pulls my head backwards. 'Now then, you fucking bitch, you think you could outsmart me, eh? Do you, get your things packed, everything, every little piece of evidence that you were here, get it packed. Me and you are going on a little trip. You, my little pumpkin, will never, I repeat, never, leave me again.' He then slaps me hard across my face. I feel the pain immediately and the sting of his hand. I feel tears well up in my eyes. I stand there motionless, staring at him. I do not move. 'Did you hear me? Get packing,' he shouts. I remain still. He then punches me hard in the stomach. I drop to my knees in agony, coughing. I feel and see snot coming out of my nose and wipe it away with my hand. I can feel the tears streaming down my face. I get up and walk into my bedroom. I unzip the case with the little tag on it and open it out on the bed. I then start to fill it with my few clothes that I did not take with me to Brampton. Jonathan goes into my ensuite bathroom and has a wee.

I take this opportunity whilst his back is turned to open my knicker draw and pull out the wad of money that I still have stashed away in there and my key for my house in Brampton. The money is what I have left of the bit that I did not bank with Rose and a few quid I've added to it from my busking. I do not know how much is there but a couple of grand at least. I stuff it at the bottom along with the key. I just hope he doesn't see it. I put my bank card, well Rose's bank card, in there too. Again, I hide it as best I can. Jonathan starts to chuck my toiletries onto the bed. He doesn't know which are mine and which are Pam and Denis's that were there earlier, but I cannot be bothered to tell him. I then get my case out with the broken zip and put the toiletries and my two pairs of shoes in there. As I am doing all of this, I cannot believe how stupid I have been. Jonathan's right: I am stupid. I mean, I must be. I never even saw him. Jonathan comes out of the ensuite. 'Anything else of yours that you need to get?... anything else from this shitty little life you thought you were going to have?'

'No, that's it,' I say, realising that my worldly possessions are packed into two little suitcases, two suitcases that you take on an aeroplane in the cabin.

That's all I own in the world, well that's all I have in this life anyway. Jonathan picks up both cases.

'Right, get in the car,' he says as he pushes me with the two cases in his hands out of the bedroom into the hallway. I walk slowly out of the door. Once he is out, I lock it and go to put the key in my pocket. 'Put it through the letterbox. You won't be needing that again,' he says as he nods towards the door. I do as I am told.

'Where are we going?' I ask.

'Just get in,' he says as he loads the cases into his boot. I do as I am told. He gets in and drives out of the estate. I look straight ahead. I cannot believe how I feel right now. Half an hour ago I was feeling happy. Now I just feel so sad. Jonathan stops the car.

'Mobile,' he says as he holds out his hand.

'What?' I ask. 'Mobile, give me your mobile,' he demands. I bend down and pick my handbag up off the footwell floor and do as I am told, and hand it over. He takes the sim card out and tosses it out of the window. He chucks the handset onto the back seat. He then drives on. I look out of the window, still trying to contemplate and digest what has just happened to me. I did not see this coming. I did not, for one second, think that he knew I was up in Cumbria. I had no idea he was watching me, and I certainly had no idea he was following me earlier today. I was not looking, I suppose, but even so, I should have sensed it. I got too confident, didn't I? I curse myself as we drive along the roads. I curse myself that I stood outside of our house... twice, how could I have been so stupid, so brazen, so, well, just so stupid. I feel only sad and annoyed with myself. I do not feel frightened. I'm sure I am going to suffer. I'm sure he will make me pay, and I am sure I

will be back in our house in Brampton sometime soon.
The only question is when and in what state I will be in
when we do. I can feel anxiety welling up inside of me.
I can feel panic coming over me when I think of being
back in that house, with Jonathan, back to living the
same life I have done for all of these years.

'I will never be who I was,' I say without turning my
head from looking out of the side window.

'You will be, whoever I want you to be. You really
thought you were free, didn't you, eh? You honestly
thought you could be free of me. You honestly thought
you were better than me, smarter than me, didn't you,
you stupid, stupid fucking bitch. You will never be free
of me, do you hear me, never. You are mine Anna Fox
and always will be. I'll kill you before I see you escape
from me again.'

I can hear the venom in his voice. He means it. He
will kill me before he lets me escape again. That's up
to you,' I say, 'but I will never be that same Anna Fox,
I am not her. I know who I am, and it's not who you
want me to be.'

He stops the car. Two cars drive past him honking
their horns. I see a hand come out of the first one and
give the wanker sign. He checks his mirror. I look in
the passenger-side mirror. The road behind is clear.
The road ahead is clear. He brings the back of his left
hand across my face. He leans over and squeezes my
chin with his right hand.

'It's up to me, is it? Killing you would be easy. I
want you where you should be, by my side, the
devoted wife, washing, cleaning, ironing, looking after
the house, being the good housewife like women like
you should be. I want you bent over when I want, I
want you sucking my cock when I want, I want you

to orgasm when I want, I want you exactly where I want you to be, and believe me, you will be. You asked where we are going, well I'll tell you.' He takes his hand off my chin and strokes my cheek. He then gently strokes my nose. 'Me and you, my darling, are going to Buttermere, to Fred's holiday cottage, where we can be together for a few days, where we can start to repair the damage, you have done to our marriage. We can take walks around the lake. We can enjoy our meals together. We can make love. We can get our marriage back, and then once you are back to the Anna I know and love, we can go back to Brampton. To our lovely house and be together again, forever, like we told each other in our vows, remember, *till death us do part, for better or worse.* Can you remember Anna, those vows? I do, I meant them, did you, did you mean them, Anna, did you?'

I remain motionless. I cannot bring myself to say yes. I would have done once upon a time, but not now. I am determined I will not be that Anna again. I can't. I won't.

'Why do you make me do these things? I love you, Anna. I only want us to be together like we used to be. I wish you didn't make me react like this. I wish you didn't make me hurt you. You can see what you are like, can't you? You've always been the same, always looking to make me angry. All you have to do is obey me. Can you remember Anna when we took our marriage vows, and you wouldn't include obeying in our vows? Can you remember how you specifically asked for that line to be removed, to the vicar, in front of me, your husband to be? Can you remember? How do you think that made me feel, eh? You made me look a fool, Anna, you made me look weak in front of the vicar, all you had to do was obey me, was that too much to ask, eh? To leave the marriage vows as they had been for hundreds of years, but no, you had to change them, you had to make me look a fool, you had to embarrass me in front of everyone, you had to make me do these things to you. It's all your fault, Anna. All you had to do was obey.'

For the first time in our lives together, I can see the emotion in Jonathan's voice. I can hear it, the weakness in his voice as he told that story. For the first time in my life, I hear the vulnerability in him. He just wants to be obeyed. It starts to make sense. He starts the car and continues to drive. I expected another strike off him, but he hasn't. I glance over and can see the anger in his face, the emotion. I can see the redness in his eyes, but it's a mixture of anger, frustration, and sorrow.

All of these years have been about that, about me not wanting to include the words to obey him in my vows, but I didn't want to. I thought that they were old-fashioned. I still do, but the funny thing is that I have ended up obeying him all of our married life by not including that in our vows. It's just been through fear, rather than respect, or from some old-fashioned value of years gone by. Had I never mentioned it would he be different? Would our marriage have been different? I can't answer that. I will never know, but all I do know is that it is no justification for the way I have been used and abused, physically, sexually, and mentally all of these years. I did not deserve that; I do not deserve it now, and I refuse to be abused any longer. I know where we are going. We have been before. Fred is another colleague from the school who has a cottage just outside Buttermere in the lakes. I like it at

Buttermere, it's beautiful, but I just wish I were going in better circumstances.

'It's nice of Fred to let you have it,' I say, trying to make some sort of normal conversation. I need to play the game, to give me time. What for I don't know, but time is what I need.

'He's gone to Europe for a month so gave me the keys at last week's meeting and said I could use it whenever I wanted. He said it might make you feel better if I took you for a few days. I told him I would. They all think you are just at home,' he says, laughing. 'Why is the world so full of stupid people? Are you related to him?' he says, laughing even louder. 'Everything just fell into place, even having somewhere to go today, for a month if needs be. I couldn't have planned it better myself.'

As we drive up the M6 towards the Keswick, turn off, I try to think what I can do to escape. I know it will be hard, but even if he does kill me, there is no way I am going back to that life, no way, I would rather die and tell myself that if I have to, then I will. I cannot see what I can do, though, other than scream at the top of my voice that I've been kidnapped, but who would believe me? Being kidnapped by your own husband, I mean, is that possible? Is that a crime? Can a wife be kidnapped by her own husband? He would squirm his way out of it anyway, he's a solicitor at the end of the day, so I would be no match for him trying to convince the authorities. He'd wipe the floor with me. He spends his life helping women like me, that's the ironic thing about it all, so he will know all of the tricks, and I'd just end up not being believed and probably certified insane or something. I just need something to happen, something to present itself out of the blue, a bit like it has for Jonathan in all of this. I still cannot believe it all.

We reach the cottage. As we walk in, Jonathan shouts.

'I'll get the cases from the car and the few groceries I bought. I've bought some tea, some milk, and some bread and a few bits for sandwiches. That'll do us for tonight until we go shopping tomorrow in Keswick.'

I stand alone in the kitchen, realising that I am in the middle of nowhere. Buttermere is over a mile away, and anyway, there are only a couple of pubs and a tearoom and shop, and Keswick s about 10 miles away. I'd forgotten how remote this cottage was. I am all alone here. I have no phone; there is no internet, nothing. No one knows I am here, no one. I suddenly feel so isolated and scared. How the fuck am I going to get out of here? Jonathan comes back in and puts my two cases on the floor.

'You can unpack later, but first make some sandwiches and a pot of tea; I'm famished.'

I do as I am told. We eat in more or less total silence. I cannot be bothered to play the game. I feel so dejected. I can sense Jonathan getting annoyed. He finishes his mug of tea. 'Look, it's up to you how long we are here. I can easily do the month, well, three and a half weeks now as Fred went a few days ago, and it's entirely up to you how enjoyable it is for you. If you continue to play hardball with me, sitting there in silence, trying to wind me up, you will just make me angry, and you will make me hurt you again. That's not what I want, but it really is up to you. Now, do the pots and then run me a shower. The hot water should be fine now. It's the least I deserve after chasing you around all day.'

I get up to do as I am asked. I really do not want

another backhander or worse. I do not believe that he could do a full month here as he'll have a few cases on the go at work. He must have, he always does, unless he's handed them all over, but I reckon he's just trying to frighten me. Jonathan goes out to the car. He comes in a few minutes later, just as I come out of running the shower for him. He places the car keys on the table and comes over to me. He cuddles me. I do not want to cuddle him back but feel as though I have no choice. I put my arms around him and squeeze his as lightly as I feel I can get away with.

'Whilst I am in the shower, I want you to unpack your cases and then put the toothbrush and toothpaste I brought myself in the bathroom cupboard. I also bought myself a tee shirt to sleep in. I want you to lay that on the bed for me like you used to, and then I want you to come in the shower with me. It's so long since I saw you naked. I want to fuck you from behind.'

He kisses the top of my head and then lets me go. He then walks through into the bathroom and closes the door. I wait for a few seconds and then look at the car keys. I cannot believe he has left them on the table. I wait some more. I walk towards the bathroom door and listen. I hear the shower still running. He must be in it now. I turn and grab the car keys off the table and walk towards the door. I turn and look towards the bathroom. The door is still closed. I walk outside and close the front door quietly. I run to the car. I press the key fob but find the doors are unlocked when I get there. I try the driver's door. It opens. I cannot believe it. I get in the car. My heart is racing. I am breathing heavy; I press the start button. Nothing. I press it again. Nothing. I press it again. Nothing. I hear laughter. I look round and see Jonathan standing in the doorway of the cottage. He is laughing uncontrollably. I press the start button again. Nothing. I then realise that no dashboard lights come on. The car is dead. I lean forward on the steering wheel. I hear Jonathan's footsteps. He has stopped laughing. He opens the door.

'Get out,' he shouts. He then grabs my hair and drags me out of the car. I fall onto the floor. He stands on my face, pressing his shoe into my cheek. 'Stupid little Anna,' he shouts. 'Do you really think I would leave my car keys on the table while I had a shower if I'd not disconnected the battery, you stupid girl? Did you not realise that the doors didn't make a sound when you pressed the key fob? You really are stupid Anna, you really are. I left the car unlocked 'cos I just knew you'd do this, and I wanted to be able to stand there laughing at you as you tried to start the car. You are so predictable but funny, really funny.' He takes his foot off my face and bends down so that his face is nearly on the ground next to mine. 'You've just failed your first test, my sweet. Tut-tut, when will you ever learn? Now get up and get in that shower and wash your face. I know I won't see it when I'm shagging you from behind, but I do have some standards.'

chapter twenty–six

Jonathan made me sleep with him twice tonight, once in the shower and then once an hour or so later in bed. I can't believe how easy it was to disconnect from what was happening whilst we were, in Jonathans eyes, making love. As I lie here next to him I feel nothing, well nothing for him, only anger, resentment and hatred for the man who does this to me. I have to sleep next to him. I have not slept, of course. I cannot. Jonathan is asleep, but my face is sore from his shoe. He pressed it so hard into my cheek. I am soon back into this life. This is how things used to be, but I have not lost any of my determination to break free again. I am prepared to die. I do not want to, but I am prepared for it. I let him sleep with me as I have not got the strength to fight him off, and I know that I am being submissive, and I am letting him control me and abuse me all over again, but this time I am determined that it will be short-lived.

I ask myself if I am prepared to kill him, could I kill him. Am I a killer? I may be able to, but not in a violent way. I could not stab him or shoot him or anything like that. I just don't have it in me. I tell myself that I could go into the kitchen right now and get a knife and stab him to death, but it's not who I am, and Jonathan knows that. He knows I couldn't do it. He said so earlier when he first tracked me down, and whilst he knows that he can sleep soundly in his bed. I could have done it so many times over the years, but people say that in life, you have to figure out who you are, but it's just as important to know who you are not too, and I am not a killer. I may have to be, I know that, but in a different way.

I could poison him, I think, but I have no poison. I could suffocate him, I suppose, but he is too strong for me to do that and would fight me off. I could give him an overdose of drugs, but then again, I have no drugs, not even headache tablets, so that's a non-starter. Then I remember. I sit bolt upright in bed. I look over, and he is fast asleep. I know he is because of his breathing. He can't hide it. I think hard, and I remember when I was with Tony at his flat that first time, and he told me he was on penicillin. I took two off his strip and placed them in my handbag that night at his flat. I have no idea why I did it, I just did, but I remember saying to myself *I might need these one day.* Something inside me, a sixth sense, or female intuition told me to do it. It was like I was on auto pilot at the time. I remember.

Jonathan always told me how severely allergic he was to them, far more than I am. I just come out in a rash, my mum told me, but for Jonathan, he always said it could kill him. I was never convinced. I'm not sure if a penicillin allergy can actually kill you, no matter how severe the allergy is but was I prepared to find out? If it worked, I'd be a killer, but no one knows I'm here. If it didn't work and he had a less severe reaction to it, he would know what I'd done, and at the very least, I'd suffer terribly for it.

I lie back down. My breathing is heavy again. It must be the adrenalin. I try hard to recall if I had seen them in my handbag since that night. I can't recall seeing them again, but they must still be in there. Like most women, my handbag is full of crap I don't need. I need to find them. They could be my way out of here. I tell myself that tomorrow, I need to put my big girl pants on. I've never needed them as much as I do now. I decide I cannot go to my handbag right this moment, as it will raise too much suspicion if Jonathan wakes up. I must look tomorrow when I have chance.

chapter twenty-seven

I am making a pot of tea. It's 7:35am. Jonathan is still in bed. He wants a cup taken through to him. I want to check my handbag, but I'm scared to in case he comes through. I may only have one chance, and I need to know I have time to rummage through. I have no idea where they in there, or even if they are still in there at all. I take his tea through, and I ask him if he wants any toast making for breakfast. He does. I walk back through and put three slices of toast in the toaster. I did it without thinking. Two slices for him and one for me. If he had four slices, I could have two, but if he only has two, I can only have one.

It's surprising how things come back to me so quickly and instinctively. I hear him come through. He walks into the bathroom and closes the door, locking it behind him. He must be going to use the toilet. This is my chance. I open my bag and frantically look through it. I can't see them. I start to empty things out onto the table, but I am under pressure. If he comes out and sees things all over the table from my handbag, he will probably take it off me. *Come on, where are you?* I ask myself. I cannot see them. They mustn't be here. I want to scream. Then I see the zip to a small inside pocket. I unzip it. There they are. Two penicillin tablets still in their strip. I want to shout *yes,* but again I can't.

I quickly put everything back and put my handbag

where it was. I look at the bathroom door. It is still locked. I take the tablets out of the strip and wonder whether to put them in his mug of tea on the bedside table in the bedroom or to wait for his next one. I decide to wait. He may not drink the one he has if he's in the bathroom too long. I need to know he is going to drink it. I then smell burning. *Shit,* I say to myself, as I realise I have burnt the toast. I did not check the settings. Jonathan then comes out of the bathroom. I quickly put the empty strip back into my handbag and put the tablets in my nightie pocket.

'What the fuck's going on?' he shouts as he takes the toast out of the toaster and throws it at the wall. 'Can't you even make toast these days? Are you that stupid? Get some more toast back in the toaster and fuckin' watch it this time.'

He then storms into the bedroom. I pick up the burnt toast and place it in the bin. I'm just about to put some more toast in the toaster as he comes back out of the bedroom and throws his tea down the sink, 'and make me another mug of tea, that one's lukewarm. I want it piping hot, for fuck's sake.'

I watch as the tea disappears down the sink and thank my lucky stars that I didn't use the tablets on that one. I look up to the heavens and mouth, *thank you.* I decide there and then that I will use them on this next piping hot mug I am about to make. Somehow, I need to get the contents of these tablet capsules into his mug. I feel my knickers through my nightie. *'Yep, they're big enough,'* I say to myself.

I boil the kettle and wash the mugs. I decide to make two mugs of tea, one for both of us. I am surprised how, all of a sudden, I feel calm. I know exactly what I am going to do. I just hope and pray with everything I have that it works, that the allergic reaction is enough to kill him. I have no idea what I will do if it works, no idea whatsoever, but if it does work, at least I will never have to feel his hand across my face or his knob inside of me ever again, and right at this moment, that is worth taking the risk. If it doesn't work, well, I just cannot even bring myself to think about that.

I can recall reading about a penicillin allergy. It was a few years ago, but I seem to recall that for someone like Jonathan, who is severely allergic to it, it can result in death. I only have his word for it that a reaction can kill him, but when I think of how paranoid he would get if anyone were taking it, then I can only hope and assume that he was not exaggerating. From memory, any reaction should happen fairly quickly. I seem to remember it should be within the hour or thereabouts. If my memory serves me correct then he should have trouble breathing, his airways should start to close, and he should become weak and hopefully bloody well die.

I get the two capsules out of my nightie pocket and wonder whether to use both now or just use one and see how it goes; that way, I will have another one for later if needs be. I think *no fuck it,* all or nothing, that bastard has abused me long enough. I empty the contents of both capsules into his mug and stir well. I put the empty capsules back in my pocket. I look into the mug. I cannot see any evidence of the tablets being in there. I wonder about the taste. I'd not thought of that. I think about tasting it, but I can't; I'm allergic too. Shit, I feel anxious all of a sudden. What if he can tell somethings wrong with his tea? I can feel myself starting to panic. If he suspects anything, anything at all, then it's all over. My chance has gone. I can't see a small sip killing him. I think about tasting it again, as I say, one small sip on the lips surely can't be enough to have much of an impact. I think for a moment. I don't have long. I take a very small sip, so it barely touches my lips. It tastes fine, just like tea should. I sigh with relief.

'Well, this is it girl,' I tell myself as I place his mug on the table. I keep mine in my hand. I don't want him to start drinking the wrong one. I'm nervous. I was on autopilot a moment ago when I first started to make the tea, but now, I'm nervous. He could be dead in an hour. What will I do? I can't think, I'll have to consider that if and when it happens. I don't want to get caught. I don't want to spend 20 years in prison for murder. I look at the mug. What have I done? Shit, what have I done? What if it kills him? I go to pick the mug up to throw it away, but Jonathan walks in. I stand there and must look like a rabbit caught in some headlights.

'This better be hot,' he says as he sits at the table. 'Toast?' he says as if to say, where's my fucking toast?' Shit, the toast. I look towards the toaster. I put the bread in, but I forgot to press it down.

'I wanted to make sure it was perfect for you, so I thought I'd wait until I'd made your tea so as not to ruin it again.' I say, hoping that will pacify him.

'Mmm,' he says but then picks up his tea. I press the toaster down whilst keeping one eye on Jonathan. He sips his tea. 'Ah, that's better, lovely cuppa,' he says, 'Wasn't that hard, was it? I can see you will need some time to get back into our little swing of things, but don't worry, I'll try and be patient,' he says as he gets up and walks over to me. He then whispers in my ear. 'But, don't take the piss, will you?'

I shake my head. I can only stare at his mug of tea. I pick mine up. I cannot risk him mixing them up. He sits back down. I watch the toast. I can see him sipping his tea. My adrenalin is pumping through my body, and I am having to really concentrate on not altering my breathing. I am taking slow breaths. I just hope Jonathan doesn't notice. I butter the toast and check the cupboards for any jam. I find a pot that's unopened.

'Would you like any jam on your toast?' I ask him, 'Mmm, yes, I think I will, not too much mind, and don't you have any? You look like you've put a couple of pounds on to me. We will have to weigh you as soon as we get back. I can't have you getting fat, can I?'

I don't think I have put on any weight at all. He's just saying that to play mind games with me. I tell myself that I won't have to worry about that in an hour or so. I try to eat my toast, but I'm too nervous. I can't sit down. I just have to keep moving. I sweep the floor; I wash the breakfast pots. Jonathan has drunk every last drop of his tea. I wipe the benches down.

It's been 35 minutes now, and nothing is happening. Maybe he's no longer allergic to it. I'm sure I read that things like that can happen, or am I just imagining it? I don't know. All I do know is that I can't do this for much longer. I tell Jonathan that I'm going to get ready.

I pick up my handbag and take it with me. I can't just stay in the kitchen watching him, waiting for something to happen. I walk into the bedroom and put the two empty capsules back into the zipper part of my bag. I check under the bed. My two cases are still here. Luckily, Jonathan didn't touch them again as I unpacked them. I just slid them under the bed with my cash and bank card still in there. He hasn't mentioned them, so he can't have checked inside them at any point. I hear him cough; I hear him cough again. I stand still, listening. Could that be the start of it? Is that a symptom? I bite my lip. If it is then I could be at the point of no return. I listen some more, nothing. Maybe it was just a cough, nothing else.

I quickly get dressed in the same clothes I had on yesterday. I then walk out to go to the bathroom. I hear him cough once more. Then he tries to clear his throat. He coughs again. 'Are you ok?' I ask him as I stand with the bathroom door open.

'Yes fine, just feel a bit light-headed, that's all. I'm fine, just get dressed as we need to go to Keswick for some food and bits. I'll go and sort the car out; just hurry up,' he says in his usual aggressive tone. I shut the bathroom door and stare at myself in the mirror.

'You bloody well need some big girls' pants on today, lady,' I tell myself. I am unsure if the penicillin is working or not, well not so much working but causing an allergic reaction. He's not coughed at any time since yesterday except for just now, so maybe it will work. I am still looking at myself in the mirror. *'What will you do if you walk out of here and find him dead on the floor?'* I ask myself. I still have absolutely no idea.

chapter twenty-eight

I have just finished brushing my teeth and have washed my face. I wipe my mouth with the towel and blow out my cheeks. I am unsure what I will find as I open the door and walk out into the kitchen. Jonathan is not there. He must still be outside sorting out the car. I walk towards the door and see the car bonnet is still up. I cannot see Jonathan. I can hear a faint voice. I strain my ears and turn my head sideways. I can hear a voice, a very faint voice. I walk out onto the gravel path, take a few steps towards the car, and then stop. The noise of the gravel is too loud. I can hear it clearly.

'Help, Anna, help me,' the voice says. It's Jonathan. I rush around the other side of the car. Jonathan is on the ground. He's clutching his throat. He can hardly breathe. He looks up at me and puts one arm out towards me. 'Help me, Anna, I can't breathe,' he says very quietly. It's as though he is whispering, but I can tell it's strained and that he cannot speak any louder. I stand there and stare. He asks me again. He then coughs. 'I can't breathe,' he says. 'My throat, it's my throat. I can't breathe. Help me?' I watch him for what must be a whole minute, saying nothing. I then turn on my heels and walk back inside the cottage. I need to think. I need to think hard.

I sit down at the kitchen table. It's happening. Jonathan could be dying. I stand up, then sit down again. I bite my lip. What am I to do? Come on, Anna, think. Think, girl. What do you do now? I need to get away from here, but how? I could walk into Buttermere, but people may see me. I can't afford anyone to see me. How do I make it back to Brampton with my two suitcases without being seen? Shit, what have I done? Maybe he won't die. Maybe he'll survive and report me for attempted murder. He's a solicitor. I'd never win. I'll be locked up for years. Shit, come on, think.

I stand up and pace around the room, thinking hard. How can I get back home unseen, but more importantly, how can I ensure he dies? He has to die now. I have to see it through, fuck me, I have to see it through. There's no going back. No one knows I'm here. I have to figure out a way of getting back to Brampton without being seen. I need to check on him, need to see if he's dead. I walk out to the car. He's still alive but is taking short breaths. He looks at me; he looks helpless. I have no emotion. I want him to die. As I look at him lying there, trying hard to breathe, looking up at me for help, I feel nothing. I touch my face as I recall the previous day's events, the slaps, the shoe on my cheek.

'You deserve this, you selfish bastard,' I say to him. 'Who's the clever one now?' I bend down and put my face next to his. 'Stupid little Jonathan, didn't see that coming did you, eh?' I whisper in his ear. He tries to speak. I can just about make out what he is trying to say.

'What have you done to me? What have you done?' he says softly.

Even though my head is next to his, I can only just make it out. I stroke his face, then I stroke his nose.

'Penicillin, my sweet,' I say. I hear him groan as I get

up. He tries to grab my foot but only manages to stroke it, given his weakness. I stand over him and again feel no emotion. I want him to die right there in front of me. I have no idea if he will. I have no idea how long it will take, or even if he will die at all. This is my dilemma, what if it doesn't kill him? If this does not kill him, then I do not know what I am going to do. I try not to think about that as I decide I need a cuppa. As I walk towards the front door, I hear a voice, a woman's voice.

'This is it, there's his car,' I hear the voice say. I know the voice, and as I turn around, I see Mrs Simpson pointing up the path, followed by Sally and Rose. I walk quickly back towards the car. They see me. 'Oh, thank God, you are safe.' Mrs Simpson says. She looks behind her. 'She's safe, she's here, look.' She tells Sally and Rose, who are a few feet behind. I run past the car, past Jonathan, and give Mrs Simpson a big cuddle.

'What the hell are you lot doing here?' I ask. We are now having a group hug.

'Coming to save you,' Sally says.

'But ... but how did you know where I was? No one knows I'm here.' I stutter.

Rose interjects, 'We'll tell you that in a minute but...' She points up the driveway towards the house. The others look. Sally puts her hand to her mouth. Rose continues, 'I take it that's who I think it is?' I nod and then blurt out, 'I think I've killed him.'

'About bloody time,' Rose says.

'Is he dead then?' Sally asks, 'Really dead, you know, really dead?'

'There's only one kind.' Mrs Simpson says as she hugs me for a second time.

'I don't think so, not yet,' I say. Rose takes a deep breath and blows out her cheeks. She then checks her watch. 'Nine-thirty am, is it too early for something strong, 'cos I need a bloody drink, and a large one at that,' she says.

'I've only got tea,' I reply.

'Make it strong,' she says, and she ushers us up the gravel path past the car and past Jonathan, who is still taking slow breaths. He's still alive. We all stop momentarily, as we reach him, but only for a brief moment as Rose says, 'Come on, let's get inside, we need to talk, all of us.'

I make the tea as I tell them all about the penicillin, how I put it in my handbag at Tony's, how Jonathan tracked me down. The cameras he told me about, the butchers, the suitcase, the lot, right up until I opened Pam and Denis's door to him in Manchester.

'What did you do?' Sally asks.

'I dropped my mug of tea, in fact, it smashed into many pieces. He made me clean it up, though. Stood and watched me, he did. Just like he always used to,' I say, feeling momentarily ashamed that I reverted back to submissive Anna so quickly. There's a pause whilst they all, I assume, picture the moment.

'So, what happened then?' Sally continues.

'He knocked me about a bit, made me pack, and drove me up here last night. He took the sim card out of my phone.'

'I knew it, didn't I say that?' Sally says, looking around for confirmation. The other two nod to confirm. Sally sits shaking her head.

'I thought I was going to escape last night. He left the keys to the car on the side over there and went for a shower. I took the keys and thought I could make a dash for it, but he'd disconnected the battery. He was stood in the doorway laughing his head off, watching me try and start the car. I never even realised the key fob didn't work, even when I saw the car was left unlocked, the bastard.' I say as I point to the doorway. 'That's when he stood on my face, and I realised I had to do something, but I had no idea what, and then last night in bed, I remembered the penicillin I'd taken from Tony on our first date. I'd forgotten all about them. I still do not know why I put them in my handbag that night other than I remember saying to myself that I might need them one day. I wasn't sure if I still had them, but this morning when he went to the loo, I searched my bag, and they were there, in a small zip pocket. So, I put both capsules in his tea this morning, about an hour and a half ago. I didn't know if it was going to kill him, but I'd read somewhere once that it can do for people who have a severe allergy. I was just praying that it would, but as you can see, he's still alive. What am I going to do? I'll go down for this. I'll be in my fifties before I get out. I'm scared. I don't know what to do?' They all sit there in silence. I was hoping for some help, but they all look like they wished they'd stayed at home today. 'Anyway, how did you know I was here?' Rose nods towards Mrs Simpson.

'Old sleuth of the year over there, I tell you, she bloody amazes me.'

'How did you know?' I ask.

'Well, I knew that once you'd been back to visit, that I needed to keep a very close eye on Jonathan. He's been very calm and well, normal really since you ran off, and that's not normal. Even when I tried to get a reaction off him the other week when I told him I'd seen you in town, he managed to keep his anger intact, so I thought that maybe he was a lot cuter than I'd given him credit for. After you went yesterday, I watched his house. Nothing. He didn't come home last night, which he's never done before, so that was strange. Around 8:00 last night, he was still not home, and you were not answering your phone. In fact, you'd not rang or sent a text or anything to any of us, not even to Sally to say you'd got home safe or anything, so that was very strange.

I took a close look at the house. I walked around the front, the back, looked through every window I could to see if anything jumped out at me, and then saw the cameras. Two of them were hidden by the hanging baskets on the front. You wouldn't see them unless you were really close. They were well-positioned. That's when I started to figure it out. He must have seen you when you were here. You told us that you had stood and looked at the house when you arrived, so I assumed you'd struggle to leave without doing the same. I knew he'd had to have come after you.

It was the only explanation to explain why you hadn't rung and why no one could get in touch with you. Trouble was, no one knew Pam and Denis's address. Sally knew it was in Cheadle Hulme, but that was it. Anyway, to cut a long story short, I remembered old Fred giving Jonathan the keys to this place. I just hoped that two and two were making four and that this is where he would bring you. I know his type, as you know I've lived through it, and I knew he would want somewhere remote in which to beat you into submission before he brought you back and pretended that nothing had changed. I've stayed here before, a good few years ago, but I could remember roughly where it was. Anyway, I told Sally and Rose my theory last night, and well, here we are. We didn't expect to see Jonathan dead, though, when we got here. That has given us a quandary.'

'Is he dead?' Sally asks.

'Don't know, maybe he will be by now,' I say.

'I doubt it,' Rose says. 'A death from a penicillin allergy is very rare. Very rare, so I doubt it will kill him.'

'I need to check,' I say as I stand up and walk towards the door. They all follow me. We see Jonathan still lay on the gravel. I cannot tell if he is breathing or not until I am only a couple of feet away. I can hear him gasping for breath. 'Help me,' he says very slowly.

'He's still alive,' Mrs Simpson confirms.

'What's in there?' Rose asks as she points towards an outbuilding. It's a kind of garage come shed, but not really either but is a decent size. I'd not even noticed it previously.

'I have no idea,' I say.

'Wait here,' Rose tells us, as she walks over to it. She tries the door. It opens. Mrs Simpson, Sally, and I wait, looking at each other and shrugging our shoulders. A minute or so later Rose comes out. 'I've got an idea,' she says. 'Come on, let's go inside.'

As I close the door behind me, I ask Rose, 'What's your idea?'

'I hope we've all got our big girls' pants on 'cos this is serious, but I for one, will be up for it. That bastard needs to go, well for me he does anyway, but we all need to be comfortable with this.' She looks at me and takes my hand. 'We're with you, Anna,' she says. She then continues. 'There's a hosepipe in that garage, a normal hosepipe, and amazingly enough, a box of disposable vinyl gloves.'

Sally interrupts her, 'We're gonna strangle him,

aren't we, bloody hell this is serious.'

Rose shakes her head. 'No, we're not going to strangle him, but we could stage his suicide.'

She stops and pauses, looking around at all three of us, obviously looking for some sort of reaction. No one says a word. Rose continues, 'We could cut a length of hose and run it from the exhaust into the car, with Jonathan in it of course, and just leave him to die. We can all wear some gloves. Then we can clean this place to within an inch of it's life, eradicating any trace of any of us, especially Anna being here.' Again, she pauses, looking for some kind of reaction. I think about what she has said for a moment, trying to process it. It sounds perfect, but can it be that easy? I feel as though I need to say something.

'I'm up for it,' I say, looking at Sally and Mrs Simpson. They look at each other and nod simultaneously. 'What about the car? I don't know if Jonathan connected the battery again before he collapsed?' I say, hoping this will not be an issue.

Rose shakes her head, 'No problem,' she says, 'I can reconnect the battery.'

We all look at each other as if we are waiting for a leader. Sally, Mrs Simpson, and I look to Rose. She is the leader, the one we look to for leadership. She knows it and takes the looks as confirmation to go ahead.

'Right, come on, we need to get Jonathan in the car first. I'll go and get the gloves.'

With that, she gets up and walks towards the door. We all follow. Rose gets the gloves, and we get Jonathan up off the path and into the driver's side. He tries to resist but is so weak he cannot do much about it at all. He tries to swear at us, but to be honest, I still have no emotion and try to blank it out. Once he is in the seat, Rose checks the battery. It is half done, but she manages to reconnect it fully. She then goes to the outbuilding and cuts a piece of hose off the reel. I walk towards her as she comes back to the car.

'Let me do it,' I say. 'I need to be the one to kill him. He's been my problem, and I'm the one who created this mess. Plus, if it all goes tits up, then at least I can say I am the one who killed him. It'll be me they want.'

Rose nods in appreciation for what I just said and also, I think, with a little bit of relief in there too. I place the hose in the exhaust as far as I can and run the pipe through the rear passenger side window. I sit in the passenger seat and press the button to start the car. It starts the first time. I get out and place the keys on the floor a few feet away from the driver's side door as if Jonathan has thrown them out of the car. I stand and watch with Sally for nearly 45 minutes as Jonathan dies. I then walk towards the car, open the driver's side door, and place the two empty penicillin capsules into his trouser pocket. I reckon that they'll do a post-mortem or something at some point, and I bank on the idea that the authorities will assume he tried to kill himself with penicillin first. Hopefully, that will explain the reason for the drug being in his system. The only thing I know will look suspicious is why he didn't just swallow the capsules. I pray that won't be my Achilles' heel.

I have no idea if he died within that time or not, but for some reason, after around three-quarters of an hour, I walk inside the cottage to pack my suitcases. Rose and Mrs Simpson have been cleaning away, wiping every surface down. I am on autopilot again. I now know that I will have to take what comes, whatever that is, but I know once and for all that he can never hurt me again. I come out of the bedroom with my cases. The three of them are sat at the table waiting for me.

'Sit down,' Rose says. 'We need to agree on what you do from here. We're all part of this at the end of the day.' I sit down, and we come up with a story, a plan that we all recite and that we are all happy with. I will report him missing. I will say that he does this from time to time, that he goes off for a day or so to have some time on his own, to think about the cases he has on the go but that he's usually back home by now.

I will ring his mobile multiple times when I get back home and leave him messages saying how worried I am, how he needs to ring me to let me know he is safe and all that shit, and when they find him, I will act the grieving widow. I will play a blinder. I have to. It's all I can do now to keep any suspicion off me. Sally, Rose, and Mrs Simpson will, if needed, back up my story of how he tends to go off on his own from time to time and how I have been home all the time over the last couple of months, plus the ladies at the butchers can confirm I was there only a few days ago. They can testify how Jonathan has told them all along how I was at home resting. Now, why would any husband lie about that?'

As we close the door to the cottage, the car engine is still running. Thankfully, Rose's car is parked a couple of hundred yards down the lane, so no tyre tracks from another car to worry about. I stop at Jonathan's car. I cannot see him. The car is full of fumes. I wonder if he will be found before the engine stops, then I realise I couldn't give a flying fuck.

chapter twenty-nine

Two months later – Brampton, near Carlisle, Cumbria.

I am sat in the garden of my lovely home. The sun is shining. I am sat with Rose, Mrs Simpson, Sally, Pam, and Denis, who are up for a couple of days staying with me. Rose has postponed her move to Portugal and is staying with me for a while. Her house sale went through ok, so she is sitting pretty but reckons things are far more interesting here. She still has plans to move over there but is just chilling out with me for a while. She likes the little set-up that me, her, and Sally have now. We love it.

Jonathan was found the day after we left him, not by the police but by a dog walker. Unbeknown to any of us, there was a public footpath that ran right through the garden of the cottage. I had reported him missing by then, of course, and was frantic, as you would expect a worried wife to be. The police got involved, they had suspicions as the post-mortem found traces of penicillin in his system, but as they found two empty capsules in the pockets of his trousers, it was never expanded on.

They looked into my medical record and know I am allergic to it too, but it's something that can easily be explained away. I have played my blinder. So well, in fact, that I know my mum was right. I should have been an actress.

I rub my stomach. I had my scan yesterday. I'm 10 weeks' pregnant. I could not believe it. A child is all I've ever wanted, and even though Tony turned out to be a wrong 'un, he gave me my child, and for that, I will always be grateful to him. I will love my baby more than anything in the world and will not let anyone ever hurt it, ever.

I hear the doorbell ring and go to answer it. I open the door to be greeted by the Detective Inspector who investigated the case, the man who has been in charge of it all. He's a nice enough bloke, although I know he suspects me. He can't really hide it, but I also kind of get the impression that although he'd love to find a way of pinning some of this on me, I think he knows deep down what Jonathan was like. He's a copper at the end of the day.

'Afternoon, Mrs Fox,' he says, in his usual slightly aloof manner.

'Afternoon, Inspector, would you like to come in?'

'No, it's ok, this won't take long. I just thought I would tell you that the case into your husband's death is closed. We accept the coroner's verdict of suicide and can see no reason to continue our investigations. We are not looking for anyone in connection with your husband's death.'

I try and look a little sad and disappointed. 'So, you think he committed suicide after all then?' I say, sounding a little distressed, just to add to the drama.

'As I say. We are not pursuing it any further. Case closed.'

I can sense his tone is a little firm. I can sense the disappointment in his delivery.

'Right well, I suppose that's it then. I don't suppose I'll see you again?' I say, trying to work out what he's really thinking.

'Probably not Mrs Fox.' He stands there just a little too long, and for a moment, there is an uncomfortable silence between us.

'I don't suppose we'll ever know where the penicillin come from. Just one of those little mysteries that will never get proven, no doubt. I mean, why would he have two capsules of penicillin with him? It's as though someone put them there afterwards to try and make us think that he'd attempted suicide by taking them. Surely, he'd have swallowed the whole tablet if he were planning that. Wouldn't you think?' he said as he continued to study my body language. I say nothing.

He then continues, 'Then there's that old mobile phone on the back seat of the car too, we never did find the sim card.' He continues to study me. He then looks down at my side before bringing his gaze back up. 'I could never work out why such a devoted wife like you, who is obviously so distraught at having lost her husband, doesn't wear a wedding ring, but as I say, I've got other cases to investigate, so I'm sorry to tell you that if there was any foul play in your husband's death, it looks as though the person or persons involved may have gotten away with it.'

'Do you think there was any foul play, Inspector?' I ask.

'The thing is, Mrs Fox,' he says abruptly, 'the penicillin capsules, given that he's allergic, suggests he tried to commit suicide that way first, but after that didn't work, he must have decided to try it another way. So, he was determined it would seem, so as I say case closed.'

He holds my gaze. I hold his. He's never mentioned my wedding ring before. I try not to show any reaction on my face.

'Well thank you for all you have done Inspector, I'm sure you did your best.'

He smiles a wry smile. 'And, I'm sure you did too Mrs Fox,' he says as he turns to walk away. He then stops and turns to look at me again. 'Sorry, I meant to ask you last time, is it a boy or a girl?' He points to my stomach. 'A boy,' I say, 'I had my scan yesterday.'

'Picked any names yet?' he asks.

I smile and nod, 'Simon,' I say. 'He's going to be called, Simon.'

-the end-

Acknowledgements

There's a few people I'd like to thank for their support and belief in me, whilst I was writing not only this book, but in my desire to become an author and of course those who read A Bitter Pill whilst I was writing it and who gave me some really valuable feedback.

Firstly, my wife Debbie, who unconditionally continues to be my wingman. Thank you, I love you more than you will ever know.

My mum for reading this as I was writing it but had to read my watered-down version called "Mum's copy," ... you'll see why when you read it!

My mum-in-law Jean, who managed to read the full-fat version and, to my surprise, found it all a breeze!

My very good friends John, Elaine, Mike & Anne, for playing their parts in this. Fabulous people who me and Debbie love to bits and who will know what I mean by the above.

Bob Hart, a great man and friend, who again read it as I was writing it and who, as always, gave me very constructive and helpful feedback.

Andrea Colbert who read it for me and loved it in equal measure to 'The Wrong Man,' my debut novel.

Nick and Mandy, our drinking buddies, and neighbours,

for their support and feedback.

Andy Shaw, who read this one after he'd read The Wrong Man and liked it just as much. Great feedback as ever Andy.

Heather Brown, a very lovely lady and friend who always gives me great encouragement.

Maria & Terry, friends of ours from Australia, who always give me some wonderful words of encouragement and who read the book as I was writing it.

About The Author

For many years I worked in 9-5 jobs, leaving the house early in the morning and not getting home until ten or eleven hours later, and like many people, I just thought that was how life had to be. I'd seen from a very young age my father working hard in a factory to provide for his family and, like most other young people, just assumed there was no other way, but my wife would often tell me that it didn't have to be that way. In 2019 I decided to do something different with my life and decided to leave a well-paid position in a company that I had shares in and do what I wanted to do. Initially, I had planned to go into buying and selling property or to become a landlord, but of course the pandemic hit us, and lockdown came, so I put the property dream on hold.

I then decided to become a Funeral Celebrant, providing services for non-religious funerals. I do this on a part-time basis, meeting some wonderfully interesting people. I find it very rewarding. The families I meet are so appreciative of what I do in helping them in this emotional time. But I still had one other dream. I'd always wanted to write a novel. I have always been a fan of crime fiction, and psychological thrillers. My debut novel was a crime thriller called The Wrong Man, but I also wanted to write a psychological thriller, so after I'd published The Wrong Man, I set about publishing this, my second novel called A Bitter Pill. My wife Debbie has always believed in me and knew if I put my mind to it, I could do it.

I wished I'd done it years ago. I remember sitting in my garden, with the sun shining, writing away, listening to the water trickling down the water feature in the corner of our garden thinking, *this is how life should be. This is not work!* So, between delivering funeral services and writing, I feel very fulfilled and content.

I have been married to my wife Debbie for nearly twenty-seven years. We have two daughters, Heather, and Georgina, and three grandchildren. I am fifty years old and live in Mansfield in the heart of Nottinghamshire, a short drive from Sherwood Forest, and I hope that I can make a career from writing novels to sit alongside the funeral services I do.

M J Elliott

Other books by M J Elliott

Frank is at the top of his game. He has grown through the ranks of the criminal underworld and is now at the top table. Born into violence, for twins Daniel and Richie, there are certain expectations. There can only be one heir to the Pearson kingdom – Frank doesn't see any of it coming. He has to face his demons and look at himself for once, and just maybe, Frank is the one who is ultimately responsible – responsible for it being the wrong man.

Available on Amazon as a paperback and Kindle and of course on my website www.mjelliottauthor.co.uk

Contact Me

Email: info@mjelliottauthor.co.uk

Facebook: mjelliottauthor

Instagram: @mjelliottauthor

LinkedIn – Michael Elliott

Website: www.mjellliottauthor.co.uk